# PRIVATE LIES

# ALSO BY CYNTHIA ST. AUBIN

The Case Files of Dr. Matilda Schmidt,
Paranormal Psychologist

*Unlovable*

*Unlucky*

*Unhoppy*

*Unbearable*

*Unassailable*

*Undeadly*

*Unexpecting*

*From Hell to Breakfast*

The New Adventures of Dr. Matilda Schmidt,
Paranormal Psychologist

*Unraveled*

# PRIVATE LIES

## A JANE AVERY MYSTERY

## CYNTHIA ST. AUBIN

THOMAS & MERCER

Text copyright © 2018 by Cynthia Olsen
All rights reserved.

Published by Thomas & Mercer, Seattle

www.apub.com

Amazon, the Amazon logo, and Thomas & Mercer are trademarks of Amazon.com, Inc., or its affiliates.

ISBN-13: 9781542045506
ISBN-10: 1542045509

Cover design by David Drummond

Printed in the United States of America

*For my oma, Marion Elizabeth Matilda.*
*You are all things brave and beautiful.*

# Chapter One

I can tell you the exact minute my mother disappeared.

Right after my full name was read but before I stuck my hand in Dean Koontz's crotch. No, not Dean Koontz of gripping-horror-novel fame. Dean *David* Koontz of Denver's Sturm College of Law.

Mind you, the dean and I were on a first-name basis, but this wasn't our standard handshake, nor a last-minute bid on my part to finagle the three-tenths of a GPA point that would have launched me into the padded valedictory chair of Melanie Beidermeyer, my nemesis.

This was about me—Jane Marple Avery—striding across the stage to claim the certificate proclaiming me a doctor of jurisprudence while repeating my mantra of *I will not fall. I will not fall. Please, dear God, don't let me fall.*

I stopped on the cue, aligning myself with a spray of mums at the edge of the stage, the photographer just beyond it. My eyes sifted through myriad faces, returning to the area where I had spotted my mother earlier among the other graduates' restless relatives trapped in the standing-room-only section at the back of the auditorium. Searching, searching, and finding . . . nothing. A space where my mother's face had been, but no longer was. I hesitated, scanning the crowd past the purple tassel swinging in one corner of my vision.

A flat leather folder pushed its way into my clammy palm. My right hand swung up instinctively to shake the dean's hand, as we'd practiced at the rehearsals. Only, with my eyes glued to the space that did not hold my mother, I miscalculated.

By at least five inches.

My mind did not process this information in time to keep my fingers from squeezing. Only when I heard the grunt and a sudden exhalation of air and turned to look into Dean Koontz's reddening face did I realize what I had done.

Somewhere in my desk's overcrowded junk drawer, there exists the photo taken at the exact moment when I released the dean's man tackle with a horrified gasp and covered my mouth with the leather diploma case.

"I'm so sorry," I whispered, blood boiling up to vent an instant sheen of sweat on my upper lip.

"Please go, Jane," the dean said, a phrase oft uttered on my visits to his office after many, many spirited debates with my professors.

And I did. Looping around in the prescribed manner back toward my seat to make way for the next graduate, and the next.

As I sat there, looking out on the indistinct sea beyond the overhead lights, watching the lazy flutter of hundreds of programs used as makeshift fans, I searched the crowd once more. I could almost hear my brain's engine milling through and rejecting image after image, looking for the familiar bone structure that had been imprinted on my retinas since birth.

My mother's face was nowhere to be seen.

And what about my mother's voice? Why hadn't I followed the sound of her screams of jubilation when I walked across the stage?

Because she hadn't cheered.

The realization filled me with a cold and settling dread.

In twenty-eight years of school plays, ballet recitals, high school debates, and college award ceremonies, my mother had never—not once—been absent.

Her world turned on cogs of perfectionism long worn smooth by habit. A stark contrast to my world, fueled mostly by last-minute panic and lies.

Lots of lies.

My eyes remained fixed on the doors at either side of the auditorium, which were propped open to encourage air circulation on the unseasonably warm spring afternoon. My mind manufactured my mother's shape in the light box of those glowing rectangles at least a dozen times. It was the only reasonable ending to the current situation.

Any minute, any second, she would appear backlit in the doorway, sending me a little finger wave and an apologetic smile. Later, over our postgraduation dinner of sushi, warm ceramic shot glasses of sake cradled between thumb and forefinger, she'd explain how she'd had to nervous pee on my behalf and had fought it until her eyes turned yellow, then darted to the bathroom at the last second. The story of How Mom Missed My Graduation would weave itself into the tapestry of our small family's history, and that would be that.

It *had* to be.

Time takes on an odd, slippery quality in the minutes after your world begins to slide from its moorings. I sat through endless protracted silences interrupted by the occasional rise of applause as my fellow graduates made their way across the stage. A roller coaster of sound carrying me further into my growing worry.

"And the university wishes to express its *fervent* thanks to the following for their generous contributions . . ." Dean Koontz had taken the podium again, droning on in a register perhaps slightly higher than the one he'd used at the beginning of the ceremony. "Archard Everett Valentine and Associates, Grace and Garland Beidermeyer, the Swedish Hospital of Denver, B-Tech Incorporated, Front Range Contractors . . ."

I might have been in my seat for five minutes or five years when a strange shadow passed over my lap, and I looked up just in time to catch a leather folder in the eye.

My hands flew to my face, where tears started to leak from the offended ocular cavity.

"Oh, honey, are you okay?" I recognized the pecan-praline, syrupy Texas drawl of Melanie Beidermeyer approaching from the direction of my newly minted blind spot. She continued, "I'm so sorry. I just got so excited that I threw the first thing I could grab."

"I'm fine," I said, unsuccessfully trying to blink away the tears. Not only was I *not* fine, but I was wishing I had a spoon to dig out my own eye.

"Well, if you decide to seek damages against the university, I know a good lawyer." She winked her artificial beauty queen eyelashes at me. "I think you have a case."

The sound that came from me wasn't so much a laugh as the unholy offspring of a hyena and a buzz saw.

"Of course, you might want to lie low. Just in case Dean Koontz decides to file a countersuit."

We both looked in the direction of the faculty seats, where the dean stood a few degrees south of plumb as he spoke to the broad shoulders of Brioni-suit-wearing architect and entrepreneur Archard Everett Valentine. Apparently the man was rich enough to buy himself the honor of a commencement address a hundred times over despite his recent tango with allegations of nose candy and whores in the tabloid press.

"Might want to stop by a restroom, darlin'," Melanie said, leaning into me, her shampoo-scented corn silk hair brushing across my cheek like a kiss. "Your mascara is running, and you look a mess."

I entertained a brief but vivid fantasy of yanking the purple doctor of jurisprudence hood against the slim column of Melanie's neck and riding her to the ground with my knee lodged between her shoulder blades.

Instead, I swiped my fingertips below my burning eye and came back with a grayish sludge. Lovely.

"Yoo-hoo!" Melanie waved over my shoulder. "Well, those are my people. Gotta go."

I didn't turn to look, but I imagined a tribe composed of blond-haired, blue-eyed, waspy types. Lots of blazers and diamonds and whitened teeth.

*My people.* Why did the phrase induce within me such instant, teeth-grinding, orphan-kicking irritation?

Because I had only one person.

And she was missing.

———

I stood below the Frank H. Ricketson Jr. law building's clock tower, a meeting spot my mother and I had arranged over her famous home-made maple bacon cinnamon rolls that morning. I'd sat there watching her back from the vintage '50s table we'd scored during one of our weekend trips to the flea market.

It was my habit in the mundane moments to commit every possible detail to memory. *You never know what might be important, Janey.*

Today it had been the threads of silver winding their way through the neat coffee-colored braid my mother had tamed her hair into before shuffling downstairs to start the coffee. She stood at the ironing board in her black silk bathrobe, scratching the back of one shapely calf with the toe of her opposite foot.

Curls of steam sighed in time with the practiced sweep of the iron up and down my graduation gown at the end of her arm.

"You're stopping by your apartment?"

I licked maple glaze from my finger after picking at the rubble of crispy bacon on the top of my roll. "Mmhmm. I forgot my cap."

"Well, don't forget the bobby pins. It's a real bitch keeping those things on. Especially with hair like yours."

"I won't," I said, pushing myself up from my chair to offer her the badly used hanger the robe had come with.

We both stood back to admire her handiwork.

Perfect, as usual.

Her arm slid around my waist and hugged me into her side, into the familiar softness of her scent—a mix of Dove soap and the cream she slathered on nightly as part of her elaborate bedtime ritual.

"On a scale of one to ten, how sick are you of hearing how proud I am?"

I pretended to consider for a moment. "A solid three. You've got wiggle room."

She planted a kiss on my temple. "Baby, I couldn't be prouder of you if you got away with murder."

"I understand getting away with murder is the next step after making partner."

I felt her laugh in my ribs. The short, unrestrained bark she made when something really tickled her. It was one of my very favorite sounds on all the earth.

Not so for the pealing of the old clock tower's bell tolling out over the University of Denver campus. Especially now, when it reminded me I had been there for half an hour, watching the crowd streaming from the Magness Arena thin to a dribble, then to a drool. Occasional puffs of marigold-scented air from the mound of landscaped flowers opposite the building's main entrance lifted strands of dark hair across my vision.

My mother failed to materialize beyond them. I reached into my gown to pluck my phone from my bra in the off chance that I might have a text.

"I found her!"

I looked up to see a handful of classmates I recognized from occasional study groups making their way toward me. At the head of the pack was Lauren Hayes—short, curvy, and with enough black hair and scarlet lipstick to give a '40s pinup a run for her money—our class's self-appointed social coordinator who had, for the last three years, attempted to pry me from my monk's cell of study.

Of all my classmates, I easily disliked her the least.

Lauren sidled up next to me and squeezed my elbow, her friends—my acquaintances—filling the space around us.

"We've been looking for you everywhere," she said. "A bunch of us are going to head over to the Tilted Tiger for a quick drink to celebrate. *Please* tell me you'll come."

She was so damned jubilant, so rosy cheeked and bright eyed, that a celebratory thrill almost shifted the thunderhead of worry gathering in my chest.

"I wish I could," I said. "But—"

She pooched out her painted lips in a mock pout.

"Oh, come on, Jane. For three years I've been inviting you out, and for three years you've turned me down. It's graduation day! What possible reason can you have for turning us down today of all days?"

The same reason I'd always had.

My mother.

Today, because she was missing. For the three years before that, because I couldn't help but hear her constant refrain in my head.

*Be careful whom you get close to, Janey. Everyone wants something from you, and sooner or later, they'll show you what it is.*

"Look, Lauren, I really appreciate it, but I'm waiting for my mom."

Her penciled brows drew together, creating a crease in the otherwise smooth porcelain of her forehead. "Do you want me to wait with you?"

I bit my lip hard. Of all the tendencies about myself I resent—and they are many—my propensity to burst into tears at the smallest offer of kindness has got to be in the top five.

"Oh, no. You don't have to do that," I said. "Really, I'll be okay. She should be here any minute."

*Lie.*

Lauren held up a hand, her abbreviated fingers decked out with all manner of chunky vintage rings. "Say no more. But if you change your mind, you know where to find us."

She gave my elbow one last squeeze before departing. The simple warmth of that gesture tingled all the way into my shoulder.

And so I stood.

And I waited.

"Excuse me?"

The voice had already spoken once, but my mind had made no record of what it had said previously. Sudden hope fluttered tremulously in my heart.

"Yes?"

"I said, would you mind moving? You're in our shot."

"Oh." The pinpoint of my awareness expanded to register one of my three hundred fellow graduates flanked by Mom and Dad and both sets of grandparents, smiles growing overly toothy from being held too long. "Sure."

I descended the wide cement steps, my hand already mining my pocket for the cell phone I'd checked about every thirty seconds over the last half hour.

No messages. No missed calls.

Calls placed to my mother had gone straight to her voice mail.

Still, I listened again, wanting this connection with her to thicken from an invisible thread to a tangible lifeline.

"You've reached Alexis Avery, private eye. Spring is cheating season. Do you know where your husband *really* is? Leave me a message."

I waited through a few beats of silence, knowing that somewhere in the world, a repository caught the absence of words I couldn't bring myself to speak. My throat tightened as I thought of the slim, nondescript gray phone warm against my mother's chest, tucked in her bra. She never carried a purse, and neither did I. Phone in one cup, slim wallet in the other.

*Never carry more than you can conceal on your body, baby girl.* My mind recalled her voice so easily. Warm, sleepy, smoky enough that people assumed she had a lifelong cold.

I saw her wink then, her iris disappearing beneath dark lashes for a split second as she adjusted her bra. Anyone looking at me at that moment would have seen eyes the same odd color. Not quite blue, not quite gray, pale enough to look eerie by moonlight.

Someone cleared his throat, and I looked up to find the same photographer with one hand holding his expensive-looking camera aloft, the other propped on his hip.

"Again?" I asked. "Why don't I just crawl into a dumpster and be done with it?"

"We want to get one in front of the flowers," he said by way of an apology.

"Good for you," I said. "Am I okay to go to the parking lot, or is there a sedan the family wants to get a picture with?"

His affected smile dissolved quicker than toilet paper in the rain.

I didn't wait for an answer, jamming my phone back in my pocket and threading my way through the startled family without further comment.

The parking lot was already clearing of cars by the time I started walking its perimeter. I had taken the light-rail from my small off-campus apartment to the arena, having had to arrive an hour before the ceremony started, but I'd recommended the north parking lot to my mother for its convenience to the law building where we had planned to meet.

I often had trouble finding my mother's car—a gray Honda Civic, not too old, not too new—even in smallish supermarket parking lots. Add to that the vehicles of three hundred graduates, plus faculty and staff, and you have a task about as fun as looking for a needle in a turd pile.

*Flashy cars get made early. Never get made in the first hour, Janey.* My mother had spoken these words with the same significance she reserved for explaining why I had to brush my teeth before bed or take a bath after playing in the rain.

I stood at the curb, hearing her voice as I scanned the endless rows of cars bathed in the afternoon sun. I might have jumped a full foot in the air when my phone buzzed in my pocket, great rivers of relief rushing over me. I fumbled it, dropped it, picked it up, and sank into disappointment when I didn't recognize the number.

"Hello?"

"Hello, this is Sushi Den. You had a reservation at five thirty?"

"Oh, yes. Hi. Sorry." In my worry, I had forgotten I even had a stomach much less that it was very empty and actively aching with hunger.

"Are you close? We can't hold your table much longer."

I pictured our usual table just beyond the door, next to the bubbling blue expanse of the tropical fish tank, chairs empty, awaiting our arrival. It felt as far away as a parallel universe, one in which this day had gone exactly as I had planned it.

"No. Go ahead and cancel our reservation."

"Okay. Bye now."

"Bye."

One by one, the explanations I had given to myself were peeling away like layers of skin, leaving raw, unexposed fear open to sting in the sun.

Salt sprinkled down upon the wound in the form of a familiar, feminine giggle.

Melanie Beidermeyer, accompanied by the whole towheaded Beidermeyer clan, was sashaying down the sidewalk in my direction.

I spun on my heel and walked as if I were leaving the scene of a crime.

"Jane!"

"Kill me now," I grumbled, knowing there was no use pretending I hadn't heard. With her thirty-six inches of legs, Melanie would make quick work of catching up to me.

"Jane! I want you to meet my parents."

I took a deep breath and turned, plastering a smile on my face.

"My God," the Beidermeyer matron gasped. "What happened to your eye?"

"Is it bad?" I asked, fighting an instinctive need to cover it with my hand.

Melanie dug through her oversize Prada purse and withdrew a compact, which she handed over.

*Bad* was an order of magnitude too mild to describe what was happening beneath my right eyebrow. The eye was swollen and puffed, the area around my iris an angry red. What remained of my makeup had migrated down my cheek like spring runoff.

"You want to borrow some mascara?" Melanie offered, already up to her shoulder in her bag.

"Unless you have a fairy godmother or a priest hidden in there, I think I'm SOL," I said, clipping the compact closed and handing it back.

"Jane Avery, this is my mother, Grace, and my father, Garland."

Grace and Garland. Of course they were.

"Mother, Father, this is Jane."

"Shame about those three points," Garland said, offering me a large spray-tanned paw and a car salesman's oily grin. "Hope there're no hard feelings."

"Three-tenths of a point," I said, enduring his cool, moisturized grasp.

Melanie's platinum-haired mother clasped the leather strap of her equally cavernous bag with one hand and fingered her necklace with the other. She must have had thirty-six-inch biceps hidden under her lilac suit jacket to haul that hand upright. The diamond fastened to her nimble claw was roughly the size of a cat.

"Jane Avery, at last." Grace Beidermeyer squeezed my knuckles and offered me a smile as tight as her grip, which, I had to admit, was pretty impressive for a biochemist.

"Melanie has told us so very much about you."

"Like what?" True, it was a very impolite response to a very polite conversational beach ball, but morbid curiosity got the better of me.

"When you're as bright and as beautiful as our Melanie, it can be exceedingly difficult to make friends." Mrs. Beidermeyer reached out an affectionate hand and stroked her daughter's hair. "Real friends, like you."

*Friends?* Is that what Melanie thought we were? Or was Momma Beidermeyer subtly guilting me for all the not-so-subtle snark I'd served up to her offspring over the years?

"Speaking of friends." Melanie's mother scanned the area in our immediate vicinity with eyes the same shade of sapphire blue as her daughter's. "What are you doing all alone in the parking lot?"

"My mother just stepped away to summon our driver." The lie spilled from my lips without effort.

It was often like that for me. I could be having a conversation about something as mundane as the methodologies of proper sock folding, and *boom*.

*Lie.*

They didn't even surprise me anymore. I'd come to think of them more as overprotective relatives who showed up uninvited to rescue me from the frequent discomfort of social situations. It was a wonder a whole herd of fibs hadn't shown up for a meet and greet with *the* Melanie Beidermeyer.

"Ugh." Melanie's pretty face creased with affected commiseration. "I *hate* it when our driver goes missing."

That was the moment when I noticed that given the angle and slope of Melanie's upturned nose, it would take less than a pound of pressure to fold it back into her brain.

*My* mother had shown me how.

Just then, a long black Rolls pulled up to the curb, and a man in a dark suit unfolded himself from the driver's seat. He walked around the front of the car and opened the door.

"After you, darling." Garland Beidermeyer swept an arm toward the open door in an overly theatrical manner.

"Shouldn't we wait here with Jane?" Mrs. Beidermeyer turned back to me wearing a carefully calibrated frown. "At least until her mother turns up?"

She hadn't bought my story about the driver. Not for a minute.

"That won't be necessary," I insisted. "I'm sure she'll be along any minute."

"I'm sure she's right," Mr. Beidermeyer agreed. "And if we don't get going, we'll be late for our cocktail hour. We don't want to keep the dean waiting, now do we?"

"The dean? You're meeting Dean Koontz for cocktails?" A pang of jealousy rattled through my brain. I couldn't even get the man to let me snitch one of the candies from the giant apothecary jar he kept on his desk. And here he was having *cocktails* with Melanie and her family? "Did he not get enough of a chance to heap praise on you at the graduation for your *slim* victory?" I asked.

Bitter? Who, me?

Grace Beidermeyer's wooden smile slipped from its moorings. Not that my own mother would have been pleased, had someone minimized my scholastic accomplishments.

"Heavens, no." A vivid blush drew rose petals to the surface of Melanie's cheeks. "Dean Koontz is a family friend. He and Father have been golfing together for years."

"How very fortunate for him," I said. "It's a good thing he has friends like your parents to lean on. I'm sure Mrs. Koontz's recent passing has been very hard on him."

"Yes," Mrs. Beidermeyer agreed. "It has. Prolonged illness is a misery unto itself."

"Which is all the more reason why we shouldn't keep him waiting," Mr. Beidermeyer said, nudging his whippet-thin wife into the car. "Pleasure meeting you, Jane."

"Likewise," I said.

*Lie.*

Melanie hung back on the curb, glancing from me to the waiting car. "Will I be seeing you at Dawes on Monday?"

*Dawes* was short for Dawes, Shook, and Flickner, Denver's most prestigious law firm. Melanie and I had both worked summer internships there last year and been offered jobs upon our graduation.

"You sure will," I said.

"Here's hoping your eye is looking better by then," she said.

"And your face," I muttered.

"Thanks, sugar." She blew me a kiss before disappearing into the back seat of the limo with her parents.

The car pulled away, leaving me in a wake of exhaust as expensive and pungent as caviar farts.

In the sudden gap the limo left behind, I saw through a newly empty parking space to a gray Honda Civic, neither too new, nor too old, with no distinguishing features save one.

The driver's side window had been shattered.

# Chapter Two

"Jesus. What happened to your eye?"

Officer Bixby was younger than me, and by the looks of it, a first-class bro in his time off. Hair that had been artfully sculpted with product, the gun in his belt no match for those straining the sleeves of his blue uniform, a goatee that required at least three different electric razor attachments to shape. Probably had a fridge full of Denver's finest microbrewery beers and precooked egg whites for extra protein.

"Pink eye," I said. "My doctor tells me it's wildly contagious. We might want to hurry this along before I infect you."

*Lie.*

After the third time running through the day's events to the best of my recollection, I was beginning to see exactly why my mother hated cops.

Okay, maybe *hate* was too strong of a word. Detested? Resented? Frequently wished a virulent case of the clap upon?

*Oh, the boys in blue are super helpful,* I heard her say in my head. *Once you're already dead.*

Over the years she'd worked too many cases the police wouldn't touch, one of those being a girl they'd stamped *runaway* but who my mother discovered had really been abducted by an online predator and sold into sex slavery.

Letting a cop paw through her car now felt a little like giving him free access to her panty drawer. She would have hated this.

*Will hate this,* I corrected. She'd grab me by the scruff of my neck and aim me toward the kitchen table and say, *Let's discuss this over pudding,* the way she did whenever we had something serious to talk about.

Like sex.

"Could you back up?" Bixby asked. "You're in the shot."

"Not you too."

"Me too what?" He looked from above the camera with one eye squinted.

My hand flew to my face. "Are you mocking me?"

"No. I was just—the camera. It helps me focus."

"Whatever. Just get on with it so you can get back to your doughnuts and coffee."

"That's a hideous stereotype, you know. I don't even like doughnuts."

"Let me guess. Creatine shakes?" My gown had officially become a personal sauna. I hauled it over my head with one hand and tossed it on the hood of my mother's car, picking up my discarded tam to fan my face.

Bixby's mouth dropped open.

I looked down.

Right. I'd decided to forgo a shirt after the gown kept catching on the collar. I'd asked my mother to bring one for me to change into.

Through the glittering maw of the broken window, I spotted the blouse in the back seat.

"So, this is my bra."

"I see that."

"My shirt's in the back there." I stepped around him and reached for the car door.

His hand closed over my wrist. "I'm afraid I can't let you do that."

"Excuse me?"

"This is a potential crime scene. Everything in this car has to be documented."

I looked behind him and gasped, throwing my arms up in the air. "He's got a gun!"

Bixby pivoted on the heel of his department-issued shoes, hand swinging expertly to the sidearm holstered at his waist.

He turned back around just in time to see me shrugging the shirt over my shoulders. The skin around his lips turned a fascinating shade of white.

"You mad, bro?" I asked.

"Miss Avery—"

"Look, when your chief puts you on suspension for failing to secure the H&M eyelet lace blouse that would have broken this whole case wide open, I'll buy you a beer. Until then, make with the pictures, clicky-click, do what you have to do."

He shook his head, showing the first signs of the long-suffering sigh that eventually every male in my life adopted.

"At least take your robe off the hood of the car so I can get some pictures."

The black cloth was warm in my hands, having sucked in every ray of light the sun overhead could discharge. I folded it into a bundle and tucked it under my arm, not willing to wrinkle what my mother had so carefully ironed.

Hearing Bixby whistle under his breath had me peeking over his shoulder.

"Your mother always keep a police-issued Taser on the dashboard?"

"Clearly you've never waited through a Starbucks drive-through at eight a.m. on a Monday."

"You're right about that," Bixby said. "I make my own coffee." He reached in and depressed the latch for the glove compartment, jumping back a full foot when an arm fell out. "Holy Christ!"

"It's plastic." I picked up the arm and demonstrated, slipping the accompanying sling over my shoulder. The real arm beneath it was then free to manipulate the tiny state-of-the-art video camera peeking out from a daisy drawn on the fake cast.

"Tasers, fake arms. What? Your mother was some kind of spy?"

"*Is* a private detective. And these," I said, patting his mounded shoulder with the fake arm, "are some of the tools of the trade."

He shrugged it off and shuddered. "You are not a normal person," he said.

"Now that just hurts my feelings." I used the fake arm to gesture to the general vicinity of my heart.

I took a moment to admire the payoff of Leg Day as he stalked back to the patrol cruiser blocking my mother's car. He returned with a large paper bag and held it open while I dropped the arm in.

Next he opened the back door of my mother's car and dubiously eyed the duffel bag resting on the seat.

"More body parts?" he asked.

"Snacks and disguises."

He unzipped the bag, and when he opened it, a puff of air worked its way upward, carrying with it the concentrated scent of *Mom*. Thousands of childhood tickle fights, gentle hands braiding my hair before bedtime, and most recently, her scratching my back while I bawled the night before my final exams, convinced I would fail.

"You want a tissue or something?"

I hastily wiped my eyes with the back of my hand. "I'm fine."

"Look, it's okay to be upset. But I gotta tell you, this doesn't look like an abduction to me. It looks like your everyday, run-of-the-mill smash and grab."

"But they didn't grab anything," I said. "The stereo is still there. There's even change in the change cup."

"Could be someone spotted them before they could finish the job."

"Then how come the witness didn't call the police?" I asked.

The officer shrugged. "Lots of times people don't want to get involved. Especially on a day like today. Once they call something in, they have to stick around and wait for the police. Miss their dinner reservations."

"I hate people," I said.

The officer raised a gently manscaped eyebrow.

"Well, I do. Everyone and their greyhound has been in this parking lot today. And not one of them called the police, because they didn't want to be late for their steak dinner?"

"Human nature," he said. "Most people have no idea what's going on around them ninety percent of the time, and the other ten percent of the time, they don't care anyway."

"My mother likes to say something like that." Only her rendition included a buffet of four-letter words.

"Smart lady," Bixby said, plunging a latex-gloved hand into the side pocket of the duffel bag. "And smart ladies have a good chance of turning up once they go missing."

"I hope you're right."

"I am," he said. "I'm also charming and I can cook." A business card came with his hand when it emerged from the pocket. He looked it over and grunted, holding it up for me to see. "This mean anything to you?"

I scanned the creamy linen finish and blinked at the name moving across its face in lurid cursive script.

*Archard Everett Valentine.*

Prickles crawled down the back of my neck like a stampede of tiny insects.

Below the name, my mother had written two things: today's date, and *1:30 p.m.*

My mother—Alex Avery, private eye—had met with uberwealthy architect and scandal lightning rod Archard Everett Valentine exactly one hour before she'd disappeared.

# Chapter Three

"That's disturbing," Bixby said.

"Tell me about it. I didn't know my mother knew Archard Everett Valentine. What's she doing with his business card?"

"I meant your eye. I've never seen anything twitch like that."

"Are you actually trying to make my day worse, or have all the 'roids dissolved your verbal filter?"

"Sorry." He smoothed a quick hand over his dark locks, which, I hated to admit, had taken on the panty-dropping tousled quality I had a particular weakness for. "Who's this Valentine guy?"

"You live under a rock or something?"

"Under a house. A basement, if we're being specific."

"As long as it's not your mother's," I said.

His eyes skated to the side.

"Oh." My imaginary panties rocketed back up so quickly I gave myself a mental atomic wedgie.

"It's temporary. Until we can find in-home care for her."

"Uh-huh."

"You're awfully judgy for a cyclops."

"Judginess is my career path. Law school and all."

"Right," Bixby said. "Tell me about Valentine."

"He and his old lady have been going through a crazy-ugly divorce. You know the drill. Billions of dollars at stake. He alleges she's cheating, she alleges he's the Antichrist, yada yada. Before you know it, she has him followed and gets pictures of him snorting coke off a hooker's boobs, and it's all in the papers."

Bixby blinked rapidly at me.

"Sure, rub it in. You have two working eyelids."

"And you have a combative attitude."

"Thank you," I said, knowing he hadn't meant it as a compliment.

"Have you heard from any of your relatives? Anyone in town for the graduation she might have gone off with?"

"No," I said.

"No you haven't heard from anyone?"

"No, there isn't anyone in town for the graduation."

"Aunts?" he prodded. "Uncles?"

"Don't have any."

"Grandparents?"

"Dead."

"Dad?"

"Sperm bank."

"Friends?"

"In case you haven't picked up on this yet, I'm not especially pleasant."

"Well, yeah. But I thought your mom might at least have a few friends who might come to watch the graduation with her."

"You thought wrong." I picked at imaginary fuzz on the sleeve of my blouse. "Anyway, we moved around too much to keep up with anyone."

"That's sad."

"So is your knowledge of local celebrity gossip. Will Valentine be the first one you question?"

"Question?" Bixby said.

"You know, like, 'Hey, Valentine, why were you meeting with Alexis Avery mere minutes before you were scheduled to give the commencement address at her oddly endearing daughter's graduation from law school?'"

"Well, for starters, it hasn't even been twenty-four hours—"

"No," I said. "No. According to section one, title sixteen dash two-point-seven dash one hundred two, subsection four of the Colorado Revised Statutes, *and I quote*, 'a law enforcement agency shall not refuse to accept a missing person report on the basis that the missing person has not yet been missing for any length of time.'"

"Oh, good. You know the law. Then you'll remember in section one, title sixteen dash two-point-seven dash one hundred three, it states that the law enforcement agency shall then determine the best course of action based on the circumstances. Which is precisely what I am doing now, Miss Avery."

"Don't you 'Miss Avery' me. I've been studying criminal investigation procedures for the last three years, and I know that leads start disappearing after the first forty-eight hours. You have to start today. Now."

"I'm sorry. I understand you're worried. But there's absolutely no evidence that says your mother didn't just take off."

"What about the broken window?"

"Very common occurrence at large events. Thieves often target public parking lots for this very reason. Lots of people, inadequate security."

"The security tapes!" I said. "We could review the parking lot security tapes."

"And *I* probably will. But first I have to fill out the paperwork, then it has to be approved by my supervisor—"

"Fuck your supervisor!"

"I think that requires different paperwork altogether."

"Listen, Bixby. My mother once broke out of the county jail so she wouldn't miss my debut as Left Badger in the third grade production of *Chicken Little*. She would *not* have just walked out of my graduation. Without a text. A call. Something to let me know where she was going."

"You're lying," he said.

A familiar filament of shame woke and warmed my face. I had to scan my previous sentence several times through before responding. "I'm really not."

"There were no badgers in *Chicken Little*. And what was your mother in jail for?"

"Well, there were in my elementary school play. And I'm sure my mother's criminal record is readily available to you. Should you be inclined to do any actual investigating."

"I'm sorry. With the evidence I have here, I can only call this in as a missing person report and a vehicular break-in. I'll have the car towed down to the station. And you should probably ride over with me to make an official statement. It could be, after my supervisors review all the information, they decide to move forward immediately. Either way, I'll call you and keep you updated, if you'd like me to."

"That would require giving you my phone number."

"Which I intend to use only for official correspondence about this case." He held out the pad where he'd been recording notes about my mother's car and offered me a pen.

I reached out as if to scrawl my information but snatched Valentine's business card instead and took off.

"Hey," Bixby shouted. "Come back here."

"Fat chance," I called over my shoulder, willing my legs to remember their brief and unspectacular career in high school track. "You can't detain me. I know the law."

And then I came into contact with a different law entirely. One originated by the powdered-wig-wearing melon of Sir Isaac Newton.

*Objects in motion will stay in motion unless acted upon by an outside force.*

The outside force in this case being the edge of a pedestrian crossing sign I failed to see in my impromptu flight.

I went down hard, relieving my knees and palms of a couple of layers of skin and folding back several fingernails in a disastrously ineffective attempt to catch myself.

As I rolled, groaning, from curb to gutter, I had a little time to think.

*Should I take the D line back to my apartment? Or the E line to Archard Everett Valentine's office? Or the C line to my mother's house?*

Sure, going straight to Valentine's office would have an advantage. Get the jump on him before he had time to hide anything and while the memory of my mother was still fresh. Then again, if I went to my apartment, I could change into more comfortable shoes, wash my face, pick the gravel from my teeth. But if I were to go to my mother's house, I could do all those things in addition to looking for clues as to what she might have been up to these past few days. This was to say nothing of the soothing ointment that leftover maple bacon cinnamon rolls would be to my newly scraped knees, broken fingernails, and probably damaged temporal lobe.

*Done.*

With infinitely less grace than I would have liked, I hoisted myself to a vertical position and staggered toward the approaching train.

I launched myself through the doors just before the automatic sensors drew them closed. Collapsing into an open seat, I plucked a tissue from the small, cleavage-enhancing mound in my bra and pressed it to one weeping palm.

As the train trundled into motion, I felt a pang of sympathy for Officer Bixby, now standing at the curb and literally scratching his head.

I knew just how he felt.

———

My mother's door was already open.

A distinctly unwelcome sight after the two-block limp from the Littleton–Downtown train stop to the modest turn-of-the-century home where I'd breakfasted only just that morning.

I checked for signs of forced entry but found nothing. No broken windows. Doorframe intact. Still, in the twenty-eight years I had been my mother's daughter, I had never known her to forget to lock up.

I paused near the old-fashioned lamppost halfway up the walk and stared at the sliver of shadow bordering the open door, feeling the darkness stare right back. This small detail in a home bearing three years' worth of my mother's cozying influence seemed especially malevolent by comparison.

Orderly ranks of pink-and-green parrot tulips nodded their greeting, the flowerbeds flanking the cobblestone path that led up to the front door painted my mother's favorite Tiffany blue. The same color played peekaboo among the decorative woodwork framing the windows and eaves, a Candy Land aesthetic against shingles the color of clotted cream. I'd often thought it looked as if a pastry chef and not a painter had finished the house.

Still, assorted bad guys and homicidal types could hide in cute houses as easily as they could hide in crumbling tenements.

I could call the police, I supposed.

But if they decided to respond to my report of a break-in and found no signs of forced entry and nothing stolen, I'd end up spinning colorful lies to an audience of unimpressed cops, and that never ended well in my experience.

No. Better hold off until I had some idea of what to expect.

A quick trip around the side of the house to the small potting shed saw me armed with a hammer and a pointy-edged spade, which I tucked into the waistband of my skirt. Not the Glock 43 I had unwisely turned down as a graduation gift, but better than nothing.

I kicked off my shoes and proceeded through the grass barefoot. Finding the back door locked, I walked around to the front and tiptoed up the steps and through the front door.

The little green light on the security system panel in the entryway had turned a dull, dead gray. It hadn't just been disarmed.

It had been disabled.

I stood and listened to the house's familiar hum. Fridge compressor buzzing in the kitchen. The air conditioner breathing cool air through the vents. Somewhere, a ceiling fan stirred an artificial breeze.

I stood rooted to the spot not by what I saw but by what I didn't.

Not a thing out of place, but everything was ever so slightly . . . off.

A shift so minuscule I couldn't be certain whether I saw it at all.

I slid into the gardening clogs my mother had left by the door and felt the ghost of her feet there. The familiar high arches and the shape of toes she always complained were too stubby. I'd followed those footprints across beaches and over patios, through rain puddles and over sun-warmed sidewalks.

Now I walked in them through the strange landscape of her home.

One by one, I wandered through every room in the house.

Whoever had come here hadn't been looking for goods to hock. They'd been looking for something far more valuable.

Something my mother had hidden.

Like the fact that she'd had an appointment to meet up with Valentine after the graduation.

In that moment, I felt the weight of a thousand extra beats of silence I hadn't caught. All the times I'd seen my mother's smile slip for a split second and hadn't pressed her when she had said she was okay. The times she'd looked like she'd been crying and claimed allergies.

Next to the office, my mother's bedroom had clearly received the most careful attention. Her bed had been made in a rough approximation of the arrangement she favored, with the comforter tucked in at the bottom corners of the bed and the small army of throw pillows congregating in the center of the mattress. Her nightgown hung from a hook on the bedpost like a silky ghost.

I collapsed onto the bed beneath the canopy of fairy lights, the surge of adrenaline that had fueled my search well gone.

Exhaustion found me in its wake, bringing every contusion and abrasion on my body to vivid life. Scratched eye. Broken fingernails. Scraped knees. Stomach in the first phases of self-digestion.

All of which were dwarfed by my aching heart.

I balled the nightgown in my fist and tucked it beneath my cheek. In the deathly silence, I could hear the plucking sound my tears made as they soaked into the slippery fabric.

Many times had my troubles found their end in this same spot, my cheek resting against the slick material of my mother's nightgown, warmed by her skin.

The many, many nights I'd shrieked myself awake, the terrible sound of my mother screaming haunting my dreams.

*It was just a dream, Janey. Think of something beautiful to send it away.*

And what should I think of now?

What memory or idea could I now turn over in my mind to make this nightmare end?

What would she tell me if she were here now?

My mother's advice worked its way through my head no less than twenty times a day. All the things she had drilled into me over the course of my life.

*Always start with what you know, Janey. Then, figure out what you can do about it.*

I knew she had been in the auditorium until about 2:30 p.m., when my name was read. I knew her car had been broken into by someone who wasn't looking for valuable things to steal. I knew someone had searched her house, but had taken the time to at least blur their tracks. I knew my mother had made an appointment to meet Archard Everett Valentine before my graduation.

What I *didn't* know was what my mother might be hiding and who was looking for it.

Maybe I could do something about that.

Right after I did something about the ravenous hole where my stomach used to be.

I padded downstairs and washed my hands at the sink, using a brush to scrub at the gravel imbedded in my palms. Turning the tap to cold, I soaked a dishtowel and pressed it to the throbbing spot over my eyebrow until it no longer came back flecked with rusty blood.

Next, I retrieved a handful of ibuprofen from the medicine cabinet and washed them down with a few swallows of the whiskey my mother squirreled away in the seldom-used cupboard above the fridge.

I nearly wept when I spotted the unmolested maple bacon rolls on the counter beneath a blanket of foil.

After finishing off the pan along with several more swigs of whiskey, I pulled Valentine's business card out of my bra and stared at it.

Once upon a time, I'd thought Mom and I could tell each other anything.

She'd never once mentioned Archard Everett Valentine.

Okay, not entirely true. She'd pointed him out a couple of weeks before graduation when we were getting pedicures at our regular nail salon, handing me our favorite local gossip rag—*Mile High Grapevine*—along with a Coke she'd filched from the employee fridge. Thus began our weekly ritual.

After we'd read the most cringe-worthy personal ads aloud, Mom handed the tabloid over—the rumpled cover facing up—and turned on her chair's back massager.

"Have you heard about this guy?" she'd asked.

I followed suit, my voice colored by vibrations from what I presumed to be the Nuclear Kidney Slap setting on my remote. "That *guy* is giving the commencement address at my graduation," I reported.

"I hope they plan on sanitizing the microphone after he uses it. Especially after what they caught him doing down on Colfax last night."

I looked at the magazine sitting in my lap. "Looks pretty grainy. You can't even see his face."

"They got a positive ID on the license plates."

"Plates can be swapped," I said.

"I've taught you well." She lifted the Coke from my cup holder and took a swig. "But this guy's guilty. Went home and dirty-dicked his soon-to-be ex-wife after spending his evening with several local working girls. She was *livid*."

The petite, dark-haired pedicurist glanced up from her pumice stone.

"And thus he winds up on the front page of the *Grapevine*," I said.

"Which is the least of his worries." Mom's head dropped back against the headrest, and her eyes fell closed.

"What do you mean?" I'd asked.

"I mean that the hookers always come first. Then the blow. Then the embezzlement."

"Well, hookers and blow don't come cheap."

"Neither do defense attorneys," she'd said.

I jerked back to the present when the fridge clicked on, grabbing for the hammer. It twitched in time with my pounding heart. When no boogeymen rose up to throttle me dead, I set it back down and let my head fall into my hands.

Sitting in the kitchen of my mother's home—a place where every gleaming surface once testified to her calm and orderly presence—turned my all-encompassing sorrow into a fine, piercing ache at the base of my throat.

All the more irritating, then, when the muscular arm wrapped around my neck.

# Chapter Four

As the hairy forearm turned my head into a purpling balloon, I remembered my first real lesson in hand-to-hand combat.

My eight-year-old self rose up on the backs of my eyelids, wreathed in the charming branching of veins one sees before passing out.

I was a cute little squirt. A small girl with dark hair sprouting weedy and wild out of the meticulous french braid my mother had spent a full episode of *Care Bears* arranging.

In my lunch box, an uneaten brie-and-kiwi sandwich languished, the result of an unhappy hour spent in the principal's office.

In my hand, a surly note from the teacher about how I'd bitten Brandon Fike when he said I was lying about my father being killed by charbroiled janitor Freddy Krueger.

That Brandon was right and I was lying through my tragically bucked teeth did nothing to lessen my righteous fury at the time.

"Janey, this is unacceptable," my mother had said, licking a gob of cookie dough from her brass knuckles. She was a multitasker, my mother. "I thought I taught you better than this. You bit this boy, and you didn't even draw blood?"

I had looked up from the yellow ducklings on my ruffled socks to find her grinning at me.

"It's all about applying the proper pressure in the correct place," she continued. "And never bite unless you're going to bite hard enough to keep them from coming back for seconds."

Then she had explained to me that a swift kick to the nuggets was much more effective, a revelation that forever changed the way I felt about barbecue dipping sauce.

Fast-forward twenty years.

The memories swam into my head as what remained of the blood pumped out of it. From my current vantage point, with an elbow flexed beneath my chin and a hand pushing my head forward into the choke, I had no hope of a clean nugget shot. And digging at the ropey forearm beneath my chin would only serve to waste precious oxygen and energy.

My best shot at surviving this was to stop my unseen assailant from doing what he was doing, and the fastest way to do that was to inflict the maximum amount of pain possible.

I'd unwisely abandoned my hammer when I dove headfirst into maple bacon roll nirvana.

But I still had the spade.

I pulled it from my waistband and swung it up behind me at the approximate level of my attacker's head as hard as I could. It made a satisfying thwack when it hit bone.

My hair muffled an incoming jet stream of curses and pained grunts.

I repeated the action three times in quick succession like I was knocking on a door instead of a cranium, feeling a surge of victory when my assailant released the hand behind my head to get hold of my wrist.

The pressure behind my eyelids eased incrementally, and the lights in the room brightened. Hot blood surged up through my neck and into my head, where my pulse thundered in my ears with renewed vigor.

He jammed my hand hard against the stainless-steel fridge door, knocking the spade from my grasp. It fell to the floor with a clang.

I blindly searched the counter for a new weapon, which was when my hands closed on a handle I would have recognized by feel even in the pitch dark.

My mother's favorite crepe pan.

I drew my knees to my chest, waiting until we got close enough to a wall to plant my feet on it and shove away as hard as I could.

The unexpected momentum sent him reeling backward, his hand letting go of my wrist to steady himself against a fall.

At that moment, I visited my Teflon-coated vengeance upon his person with all the strength I had left, fortified by the memory of the many excellent breakfasts the pan had provided me.

My attacker lost either the will or the ability to arrest his earthward trajectory. We fell backward together in a heap of limbs and curses among broken dishes and cooking utensils on the kitchen floor.

I rolled sideways off him, grabbing the first thing I could and pointing it at him as I scrambled to my feet.

By the time I looked down at my hand and discovered I'd only managed to snag a wooden spoon, he was already on his way to standing as well.

I quickly inverted the utensil so at least the stick end was pointed at him.

"Stop right there, or I swear on my mother's name, I will shank the shit out of you."

At the word *mother* he froze, turning to look at me.

And I looked at him.

Trouble was, he didn't look like a bad guy at all. He looked like a friendly lumberjack.

He wore a red flannel shirt over a chest only beginning to lose some of its breadth and depth. Good jeans. Timberland boots. An ensemble that complemented the long silver hair drawn back in a ponytail at the base of his neck. Heavy rectangular brows shadowed eyes the color of good French roast.

But what chased the fight right out of me were the laugh lines cutting deep grooves into the sun-weathered skin around his eyes and mouth.

The man I'd just beaten about the head with a frying pan was *grinning* at me.

"Goddamn," the man said. "You're the spitting image of Alex."

"That's because I'm her daughter. Who the hell are you, and what are you doing in my mother's house?"

"Daughter?" Frank surprise migrated across his Marlboro Man features. "Alex didn't tell me that she had a daughter."

"Then she probably didn't tell you she taught her daughter six different ways to castrate intruders with a wooden spoon." I jabbed the spoon shank toward his nether region but mostly just to make sure he understood I was perfectly willing and able to give him dick splinters.

Wisely he lifted his hands skyward. "You've got your mother's spirit, I see."

"But not her charming personality nor disappointing lack of homicidal tendencies. Answer my question."

"My name is Paul Gladstone. I'm a private investigator and a friend of your mother's. If you'll allow me to reach into my pocket, I'll show you my license."

"Just exactly how stupid do you think I am, Paul Gladstone?"

"With all due respect, you're threatening me with a wooden spoon."

"My apologies," I said. "I'm afraid I didn't have time to search out a proper weapon while I was being *strangled to death*."

"I wouldn't have killed you," he said. "Just choked you out and handcuffed you to a chair or something."

"And they say chivalry is dead."

"What would you have done if you got to your girlfriend's house to find the door wide open, the alarm disabled, and some strange woman with a bulgy eye wolfing down baked goods at her kitchen table?"

I felt my blood pressure rise to about 140 over garden hose. "Look, my eye is—wait. Did you say *girlfriend*?"

"I take it you didn't know about me either."

"No, Willie Nelson, I did *not* know about you. She never mentioned you. Never once. I mean, it's been at least a decade since she even *had* condoms in her nightstand."

"That's because they're in her sock drawer." Paul retrieved a plastic bag from the drawer next to the fridge and proceeded to fill it with ice from the freezer, moving with the ease of a man who had clearly been in my mother's kitchen many times before. He pressed the makeshift ice pack to the pale goose egg of flesh erupting from his forehead.

My wounded eye began to jerk like someone had decided to brush away a stray eyelash with a cattle prod.

"Wait." I held up a hand and walked over to the counter to retrieve the whiskey. "Wait." Paul watched as I downed a few swallows. I snorted fire and whiskey fumes from my nostrils in a sound that was vaguely horselike . . . if the horse had galloped face-first into a street sign.

"Better?" Paul asked.

"That remains to be seen. Let's start small." I paused to inhale through my nose and exhale through my mouth. "How long have you been nailing my mother?"

If I'd had to describe Paul Gladstone's expression at that moment, it would have been something like "what happens when all your features suddenly discover they're allergic to each other." Eyebrows shooting upward, jaw fleeing downward, mouth ricocheting between shock and dismay.

"What the hell is wrong with you, asking a question like that?"

"Don't tell me you call it *making love*. I could never see Mom going for that kind of sick-making sentimentality." But then, I could never have seen Mom going for a guy like Paul Gladstone. A man who almost certainly cultivated a graveyard of fast-food wrappers in the back of his car and probably had never made a list in his life.

"Two years," he said. "Your mother and I have been . . . *together* for two years."

"Two years?" I pressed a finger to the vein pulsing rhythmically in my forehead, lest I stroke out before I could get the information I needed. "Two years. How could she hide something like this from me for all that time?"

"Looks like your mom is pretty good at hiding things." His glance darted around the kitchen in a way that suggested he too might have noticed the gentle *wrongness* of this place. "Speaking of which, where is your mom, exactly?"

I sank back into a chair at the kitchen table and exhaled so violently I thought I might have collapsed a lung. "Damned if I know."

Paul eyed me from beneath the ice pack. "You don't know?"

"She disappeared from my graduation earlier today. One minute she was making rude faces from the audience during the valedictorian's address; the next minute she was gone. Her car was still in the parking lot, but the front window had been busted out. Cops wanted to wait twenty-four hours to look into it, so I came here."

"City-paid pricks." Paul ran a large rawboned hand through his silver hair, winced, then moved the baggie of ice to the injury. The murky blue-green ink of an old tattoo peeked from beneath the cuff of his flannel shirt. "Did they find anything?"

"Just this." I plucked the business card from the glass baking dish where it had landed during our struggle.

As Paul examined the card, I examined his face.

I had learned to read people on rainy Saturdays when my mother and I used to go to the local mall to people watch. From our station at the edge of the unimpressive fountain smelling of chlorine and old pennies, we would pick random passersby and ask each other *the question*.

*What about that one?*

"That one," my mother would say, "is meeting his mistress later this afternoon."

"How do you know?" I asked around nibbles of my face-size cookie and slurps of white cherry Icee.

"First of all, he's got a Zales bag already on his arm, but he's stopped to buy jewelry at the discount kiosk. The real stuff is for his wife. The cheap stuff is for his mistress. Second, see how he keeps looking over his shoulder? He's afraid someone will spot him. Third, he's paying in cash, and fourth, I can smell his cologne all the way over here."

Small signs, these, but taken together, they made for a pretty vivid picture.

Paul Gladstone was proving far more difficult to decipher.

A subtle twitch of the lips. A slight eyelid tic.

"What is it?" I asked.

"Shit." Paul seated himself in the chair next to mine, maybe because it was closest, maybe so we wouldn't have to look each other in the eye. "Have you heard of Front Range Contractors?"

"Construction company, right?"

"Yeah. Well, a guy named Dexter Fairburn working on behalf of Front Range's owner approached me wanting to dig up dirt on Valentine. They thought if they could muddy him enough in the papers, he'd lose the bid for the million-dollar University of Denver building project they were competing for. Offered me a fifty-thousand-dollar retainer to get started. I told them to take their money and shove it."

"Why?" I asked.

"Because I'm not in any hurry to end up as aggregate material in the concrete for Valentine's next building."

"Valentine would do that?" I tried to reconcile this information with what I knew of Valentine, which, after today's commencement ceremony, now included ocular confirmation of the aforementioned bazillionaire's legendary ass.

From the prime vantage of the salutatorian's seat, I'd spent the better part of his keynote address creating a topographical map of gluteal perfection concealed beneath a $43,000 Brioni suit.

It was an ass I could easily imagine cheating with a hooker, but not necessarily a *homicidal* ass.

"Not directly." Paul scrubbed a leathery palm over his chin. "Valentine's not the kind of guy to get his hands dirty. But he could certainly arrange to have it done."

"I'd bet he can buy henchmen by the gross."

"Which is exactly why I warned your mother off when Fairburn approached her. But this," he said, tapping the business card on the table, "this is a bad sign."

"But if my mother was trying to turn up dirt on Valentine, why would she make an appointment to meet with him? Isn't it sort of counterproductive for her to research him on the down-low if he knows who she is?"

"For most private detectives, yes." Paul's smile warmed the room by several degrees. "But your mother isn't most private detectives. The stuff she's pulled off over the years, even my best guys can't get away with."

The compliment brought me a dram of relief. I knew my mother to be as capable as he described, and more. She always had a plan. A backup plan. A backup plan to her backup plan.

If she met with Valentine, she had a reason. Likely a damn good one.

So what was her reason for never telling me about Paul? And for never telling Paul about me?

"How did you know to come here?" I asked.

Paul pulled at a thread dangling from the sleeve of his shirt. "I tried texting Alex earlier to see if we were still on for tonight and never heard back. I decided to stop by and make sure she was okay."

"*Still* on?"

"Your mother and I have a standing . . . appointment on Saturdays."

My eyelid resumed its grand mal seizure. "Nope. Still not okay with the fuckbuddy thing," I said.

"What? You don't think your mother has needs?"

My eyebrow attempted to leapfrog from my face. "Words are still coming out of your mouth. I need them not to be."

The same strange prickles that had broken over my neck when Officer Bixby handed me Valentine's business card returned, this time traveling down my arms to raise the fine blonde hairs like small antennae.

I thought my mother and I knew each other better than any two people in the world.

What if I didn't know her at all?

"Paul Gladstone," I said, wanting to try on a name my mother supposedly knew. "How do I know you're who you say you are?"

"You have a cell phone?" he asked. "Look up PI Denver dot com and go to the 'About Us' page."

I pulled my cell phone from my bra and did as instructed. Sure enough, Paul's face hovered above the name Paul Gladstone, call sign . . . "P-Ripple?"

"Yeah, I know. It was a navy thing."

I scanned the short, blocky paragraph detailing his experience: navy seal, twenty years an investigator for the DA's office of Arapahoe County, specialist in campaign finance irregularities and police misconduct. To my mother, the words I read would have been as good as a love letter.

I put my phone facedown on the table between us and met his eyes.

"How do we find my mother?"

His hand landed heavy on my shoulder, warm through the fabric of my shirt when he squeezed. "Kiddo, finding people is what I'm best at. I'll give it everything I've got."

"Where do we even start?"

"First, I'm going to pay a call to Dexter Fairburn. Seems like he and I might need to have a chat."

"Good. I'll come with you."

"I don't think that would be a good idea."

"Look, spare me the 'I work alone' bullshit, okay? This is my mother we're talking about, and I'm not going to be sidelined just because you have some outmoded macho idea of yourself as Sam Spade."

"Actually, it's your face."

"Bite me," I said, not entirely without malice.

"No, seriously. You look like a walking poster for domestic abuse. I take you anywhere, and no one in their right mind will talk to me."

"I could wait in the car," I suggested.

"So people could think I was kidnapping you? No. The best place for you is somewhere safe and out of the way where I can call you the minute I get any leads."

"What will you do after Fairburn?" I asked. It was as near to acquiescence as I was willing to stray.

"One of the guys down at Denver PD owes me a favor. I'll put in a call and see if we can find out which towers your mom's cell has been pinging. I'll also need to get over to the University of Denver to see if I can get a peek at those parking lot security tapes."

"I already asked Officer Bixby about that. He said that requires a metric ton of paperwork."

"Or a little creativity," Paul said.

I was familiar enough with the private eye lexicon to know *creativity* was generally code for "tricking someone into giving me information they're not supposed to."

I had been a *very* creative child.

"What about Valentine?" I asked.

"I think it would be good to keep eyes on him from a distance. I'll call my top surveillance guy. He goes by—"

"Let me guess. Slamfactor? Gunsablazin'?"

"Shepard."

"Ahh, I get it. Because he keeps an eye on the flock, right? The one man standing between the wolf and the sheep."

"Because that's his last name."

"Right." Not for the first time, I mourned the fact that there was no default self-destruct mechanism that could fry my ass into a pile of powder before I humiliated myself one more time in a twenty-four-hour period. "So what do I do?"

We had come to the part of the conversation where the dean or the principal or the police officer usually told me what I wasn't allowed to do and I quietly figured out a way to do it.

Out of habit, I had already begun nodding with the gravitas of the recently reproached.

"You wait to hear from me," Paul said. "I know it's not the answer you want, but it's the right one. Do you have somewhere safe to stay?"

"My apartment is only a couple of blocks from the college. It's safe enough."

"You have roommates?"

"No, thank God."

"I don't like the idea of you staying anywhere alone. Is there someone you can call to come over?"

"Of course," I said without thinking. "Melanie Beidermeyer. We're like sisters."

"Good."

We exchanged cell phone numbers on the front porch after Paul locked up with his very own key.

*Really*, Mom?

"Straight to your apartment, right? And you'll call me when you get there." Something in the stern but warm cast to Paul's expression made me wonder if he might not have a daughter of his own. Grown, probably. My age or older.

"That's the plan," I agreed.

"And you'll stay there?" he asked.

I held up two fingers at an angle that felt trustworthy and resourceful. "Scout's honor."

As I watched the gray Jeep Renegade—not too new, not too old—pull away from the curb, it occurred to me that I might actually have made a pretty decent Girl Scout.

If my mother hadn't shot my troop leader twice in the chest.

# Chapter Five

In the slim rectangle of the rearview mirror, I watched Valentine exit the side door of his modest skyscraper in downtown Denver and stride toward the custom Rolls Phantom limousine parked at the curb.

Valentine made it about halfway to the car before television news anchors and a few second-rate paparazzi caught up with him, only to be swatted away by the security guards flanking him on either side. This unexpected distraction was an added bonus really. His recent tabloid coverage had already been kind to me.

From the video clips on local gossip blogs, I had discovered that Valentine's regular driver—a small silver-haired man named Louis—had a penchant for smoking Turkish cigarettes and waiting outside the limo while Valentine climbed aboard. I had also learned there was a precious thirty-eight-second interval—yes, I counted—between the time Valentine's entourage got him settled and the moment Louis flicked his brown cigarette butt toward the curb and got in himself.

This pocket of time proved more than enough to cozy up to Louis and bum a light. While he held his flame to my Virginia Slims cigarette, I held a pocket Taser to his leg.

I'd come a long way, baby.

He was slight enough that bodychecking him into the limo's passenger's seat and peeling him out of his jaunty little hat, coat, and gloves took no more effort than wrestling myself into my Spanx for the graduation ceremony earlier that morning.

The fine sheen of sweat on my lip helpfully melded with the spirit gum on the back of the cheap silver mustache I quickly tacked down while the security dudes opened the door for Valentine.

No one ever looked at drivers. Particularly at this one who, at that moment, happened to be folded down neatly into the space in front of the passenger's seat.

Plenty of legroom, these custom Phantom limos.

Along with an extensive driver-engaged security system and a wood-lacquered chauffeur's panel featured in a variety of YouTube tutorials, it was one of the vehicle's most celebrated features.

Starting the timer on my phone, I levered the car into gear and carefully pulled away from the curb.

Math had never excited me much, but I'd done a lot of it while folded over the blue light of my laptop at my apartment.

In downtown Denver, I could probably get away with about two miles before Valentine figured out that I had no intention of driving him toward the dinner his assistant had informed me he had scheduled that evening. A total of four minutes, if evening traffic followed its regular patterns.

With the aid of Google Maps, I'd determined that four minutes would get me to three different places where I could comfortably park the limo without drawing immediate attention. I'd settled on the Colorado Convention Center, as its proximity bought me two minutes and the chance to admire the auspicious omen of a forty-foot blue grizzly bear forever peering into the east-facing bank of windows.

Once I had us parked, I figured I had about five minutes before Valentine tuned in to the fact that I wasn't carrying a real firearm and decided to go ahead and summon his minions. Motivated by the fear of lost jobs and the fact they were *not* driving a stolen limo, they'd make better time to the Colorado Convention Center than we had.

This gave me a total of seven minutes to question Valentine about my mother's whereabouts, and I had every intention of making them count.

What I hadn't counted on was the alarming sounds the *real* Louis had begun to make behind his panty hose gag. I thumbed on the satellite radio and quickly located the opera station, where the odd soaring vocalization of male discontent wouldn't be out of place.

When the intercom buzzed I jumped enough to catch Louis's hat on the Roll's roof.

Valentine's voice filled the cabin, bare of the melodious smoothness he'd employed for the delivery of his commencement speech earlier that day. He sounded tired, annoyed, and infinitely more human.

"Louis, turn that shit off. You know the soundproofing in this thing isn't worth half of the extra ten grand I paid for it."

Rather than attempting to force a male voice, I poked Louis in the butt and hoped the resulting grunt would resemble approval.

Close enough.

I enjoyed another thirty seconds of silence before the intercom's little red eye winked at me again.

"You missed the turn. The Palace Arms is on Seventeenth, not on Curtis."

This time, I didn't bother prompting a response from Louis, whose eyelids had begun to flutter. We were two blocks from the parking garage, and my hands were beginning to sweat within their leather gloves. I relinquished my grip on ten and two and fingered the business card in the pocket of my skirt.

*Valentine's* business card. Had I not been wearing the gloves, I could have traced my mother's blue-ink pen scrawl, proof that she had spoken to the man growing suspicious in the back seat. Motivation to continue with my plan.

*Courage, Janey.*

"Louis, did you hear me?"

Louis heard him all right. The wiry driver had wormed his way off of the floorboards and flopped his torso onto the passenger's seat.

"Easy, Louis," I said. "You'll want to keep your head above your heart so you don't pass out. The panty hose tied around your wrists restrict the blood flow more than you know."

How *I* knew, I chose not to think about at that particular second, focusing instead on angling the Rolls into the parking garage and retrieving the ticket spit out by the automatic gate.

"Louis, what the fuck do you think you're doing?" It wasn't the intercom this time. Valentine's voice bled directly through the window separating the driver's compartment from the leather-and-wood-bedecked limousine cabin.

I steered the long black car into the first available slot and checked the timer on my phone. Five minutes and thirty seconds. Given the physical impediments I'd acquired in the course of this day, I'd allowed myself an extra half minute to account for limping in the getaway.

"I'm going to ask you not to move, Valentine." My pellet gun was the first thing through the window, followed by my shoulders and my head, then the rest of my body in a rapid, graceless lurch.

I managed to keep the gun trained on him as I righted myself, stripping off the hat, wig, and mustache. I wiggled my nose and mouth against the sudden, burning pain, vowing never to wax this part of my body even if it meant cultivating a full goatee postmenopause.

Valentine took his time looking me over. I found enduring his thorough gaze far more unnerving than tasing his driver or stealing his car.

Comparatively speaking.

"What did you do with Louis?" he asked.

"He's having himself a little rest in the front seat. He wanted to give us time to talk."

*About what?* would have been the predictable response to this statement. Valentine was not a predictable man. Neither was he a kempt one, upon closer inspection. Without the benefit of artistic overhead lighting, shadows bred in the hollows below his cheekbones and under his eyes. His dark hair had appeared carelessly entrepreneurial during his address but now bordered on homeless chic. His eyes, a color that evoked romance-novel descriptions of stormy seas or polished jade, were red rimmed and bloodshot. He looked less like a wildly successful architect and more like a playboy coming off a three-day bender—just as the papers had reported.

"I've seen you," he said, settling back into the leather seat. Valentine was one of those men who sat with his knees open wide, the gesture a brazen declaration of his dire need to make room for ponderously large testicles.

A declaration he supported by reaching for the crystal decanter full of amber liquid on the lacquered tray at his side without so much as a glance at the weapon pointed at his forehead. He poured three fingers into a Baccarat tumbler and held it out to me in wordless invitation.

I shook my head no, though my mouth watered in traitorous longing. Dutch courage and all that.

He shrugged in a lazy "suit yourself" fashion and swallowed a healthy slug of the drink. "I never forget a face." Half smiling, he tapped the glass with the silver ring on his finger. His *wedding* finger. Odd for a man whose estranged wife was doing her level best to crucify him via every available media outlet. "You were at the graduation today. Was my address really that bad?"

"I'm not here to talk about the graduation. I'm here to talk about what you did *before* the graduation." This felt like the place where I ought to cock my weapon for emphasis, but lacking this capability, I cocked my head instead. *Shrewd,* I coached myself. *Be shrewd and edgy.*

"You mean have lunch with one of your classmates?" He paused as if searching the memory's details. "Come to think of it, you were sitting next to her on the stage. Perhaps you know her. Melanie Beidermeyer?"

Oh, now I *really* wanted to pull the trigger.

But pulling the trigger was a monumentally bad idea for a multitude of reasons. As satisfying as pinging Valentine between the eyes might be, he would realize I was holding him hostage with a pellet gun, and I'd be facedown on the concrete before I could say *common law felony*.

Also, my mother had trained me better.

She'd trained all of Brownie Troop 621 from Plattsburgh, New York, better, to tell the truth of it. At the annual Spring Sunshine Jamboree, she'd squired the entire pack of giggling, brown-beanie-clad eight-year-olds out behind the canoe shed and pressed paintball guns into our sweaty hands.

"Balls and eyes, ladies," my pretty mother had said, demonstrating a quick double tap on the menacing male silhouette pinned to a nearby tree. "Balls and eyes."

We'd each splatter-painted the shadowy nards of about a dozen paper perverts when Mrs. Hooper came barreling over the hill, troop-leader neckerchief flapping below her pink face, creased corduroy shorts whistling their disapproval.

"Mrs. Avery," she scolded from thin lips the color of boiled liver. "What in heaven's name do you think you're doing?"

"Alex," Mom corrected. "And I'm teaching these girls a valuable skill." Violet Dupree—the smallest and meekest of our number—squeezed off a tidy nut shot, pausing to blow on the barrel of her gun before beaming a grin of unmatched brightness up at my mother.

"This is *not* part of the approved curriculum. These girls will follow me to their leatherworking class this very minute."

"Oh, great," Mom said, folding tanned arms below her breasts. "And when some letch tries to drag them into a van, they'll have a nice leather coin purse to whap him with."

Mrs. Hooper's close-set eyes went sly with dislike. "Not *all* mothers choose careers that would expose their daughters to that element of society."

And that's when Mom snatched the gun from Violet and popped Mrs. Hooper twice in the sternum.

"Would you look at that?" Mom held the pistol up and fingered a little switch on the side. "I must have left the safety off. See why I said it's always important to check?"

"Yes, Miss Alex," a singsongy chorus of girls answered.

Mrs. Hooper only blinked, her eyes watering, mouth opening and closing like an apoplectic fish before skulking off to the nurse's cabin.

So maybe Mom would have understood my itchy trigger finger after all.

A quick glance at my phone informed me I had only three minutes and twenty-three seconds left. Swampy with rage, I shucked off Louis's coat and fanned my face with his hat. "After lunch, but before the graduation. Say, at about one thirty?"

Valentine's eyes flicked over the thin cotton blouse clinging to my damp skin before finding their way to my face. I, of course, was already watching his. Waiting for the spark of recognition.

Valentine smothered it with another sip of whiskey. "Are you here to blackmail me too, then?" he asked, voice smoky from the alcohol. "There are better ways to pay off your student loans, believe me."

"Blackmail?" I parroted the word without thinking. Of the hundreds of responses and dozens of scenarios I had prepared for, this one hadn't even entered the realm of possibility.

"That's not what your mother called it, of course."

*Your mother.* He knew.

Valentine leaned forward, his elbows coming to rest on his knees. "Don't look so surprised, Miss Avery. I'm an architect. Good buildings begin as beautiful bones. Your mother has them. So do you."

"My mother would never blackmail anyone," I insisted.

"I'm relieved to hear that." Valentine shot the remainder of his drink and reached for the decanter. "Maybe you can tell me what she meant when she said she had information about me that someone was willing to pay big money for. Unless I paid her bigger money, of course."

I fought back more denials, all too conscious of the precious seconds each one would cost me. I hadn't come to haggle over my mother's relative guilt or innocence. I'd come to find out where the hell she was, and so far, I'd allowed Valentine to all but hijack the conversation. Time to steal it back. "Is that why you kidnapped her?"

"Kidnapped?" All traces of levity abandoned Valentine's face. His eyes went as blank and empty as a shark's. "Your mother is missing?"

"She disappeared during the graduation. She isn't answering her phone." I swallowed against the ever-present panic threatening to crawl up my throat.

Valentine set his drink aside and ducked across the limo's cab, sliding into the seat beside me. Awareness of his thigh alongside mine registered as prickling heat. I could smell him on the air between us. An intoxicating cocktail of whiskey and warm skin.

"Miss Avery, if I expended the effort to kidnap every person who claimed to have damaging information about me, I'd have to double my staff." The green eyes staring frankly into mine were fringed with those sable paintbrush lashes the average female would gut a supermodel for. "You, on the other hand, have kidnapped me and assaulted my driver. Fresh-faced law school grad that you are, I don't have to explain this to you. I could eat you for breakfast."

"But you won't." I resisted the urge to scoot away, knowing on some elemental level that yielding ground to a man like Valentine was tantamount to defeat. All future interactions would be governed by what I said in the next few seconds. No pressure. "If what you say is true, it sounds like we both need my mother found as soon as possible. And I'm your best chance at making that happen."

"Are you? I get the feeling you don't know your mother half as well as you think you do."

"That's still twice as much as you know."

Valentine was a man of many smiles. If I'd had to name the one he leveled at me just then, it would have been something like "cat contemplates sparing three-legged mouse for future fun and games."

"Perhaps," he said.

Someone tapped on the window nearest Valentine. Maybe a security guard. Maybe a police officer.

My time was up.

"I trust you'll keep in touch," he said. "It's better if I don't have to come looking for you."

Better for whom, he didn't say. He didn't need to.

"If you'll pardon me for a moment." I leaned back through the window to the front seat, trying not to think about which smile Valentine might be wearing as I reclaimed the panty hose that had served as both gag and handcuffs. Along with Louis's coat, hat, and gloves, I deposited two packs of Turkish cigarettes and a fifty in the driver's seat. "I'm really sorry about the tasing," I said, offering him my hand. "I just needed to borrow your boss. No hard feelings?"

Louis eyed the cash and smokes. "Keep your money," he said, voice raspy from lack of saliva and L'eggs control top in Misty Taupe. "I'm getting too old for this shit."

"I'll see that you're compensated for this evening's adventures, Louis." Valentine's voice was even and unperturbed.

Back in the rear of the car, I hiked up my skirt, slid my pellet gun into the holster strapped to my thigh, popped open the top three buttons on my blouse, and ran a hand through my hair to leave it appropriately tousled.

"Clever girl." Valentine gestured toward the door but made no attempt to move. I had half crawled over him on my way out when he caught me by the hem of my skirt and pulled me back. "Wait," he said, examining my face as he might a building schematic, eyes taking in several details at once.

Valentine dragged his thumb across my lower lip. That strange, sensitive flesh packed with blood and nerves, more than capable of feeling each and every ridge of his thumbprint sliding across what remained of my lipstick. Smearing it as if I'd been thoroughly, fiercely kissed.

And in a way, I had. The gesture had been just as deliberate. As possessive. Curiously intimate.

He sat back, admiring his handiwork. "Better," he said. "We'll talk soon."

I nodded, wondering why I hadn't made at least a passing attempt to bite the shit out of his thumb.

The door opened onto a fleet of black-suited men, all of whom cast each other knowing looks once they got an eyeful of my dishabille.

"He's all yours, boys," I said, adjusting my skirt. "I've had my way with him."

———

By the time I returned to my apartment overlooking the outskirts of campus, the sun had slipped behind the sawtooth ridge of the Rocky Mountains. My apartment looked its best in this light, with the last smudges of sunset gilding the walls and stretching interesting shadows across the floor.

Tonight I didn't wait for the light to fail before switching on my small army of lamps, which tended to soften the minimalist sensibility where exposed HVAC ductwork masqueraded as "industrial aesthetic" as opposed to "no room for drywall."

But it was cheap enough that I could afford to live there alone even though there were two bedrooms and two baths crammed into the seven hundred square feet I paid just under a grand a month for.

Priorities. I have them.

Unfortunately learning how to cook had never been one of them, so I was standing in sock-clad feet before the stove, supervising while a grilled cheese sandwich tried to brown itself, when my landline rang.

I stood there staring at it like I'd seen a ghost.

In the three years since my mother had insisted I get a landline— *it's quicker if emergency services ever need to find your physical address, Janey*—it had never rung. I wasn't even sure what the phone sounded like until that very second.

As far as I knew, only one person had the number.

*Mom.*

I floated over to it on watery legs and picked up the receiver.

"Hello?"

"This is Shepard. I work with Paul Gladstone. Listen carefully and don't interrupt. You need to get out of your apartment. Take the south stairs down to the laundry room and exit the building through the basement. I'll be parked out in the alley in a gray Hyundai Genesis, license plate 621 LAO. Go *now*, Jane."

My face felt like it had been swarmed by ants, alternately plagued by surging numbness and stinging needles. Why would Shepard—not Paul—call me? And how the hell did Shepard know the schematics of my apartment building?

Speaking of my building, why would I leave the safety of an apartment with a state-of-the-art security system—birthday present from Mom—to run out and hop in a car with a man I had never met? And all on the assumption that Paul, a man I hadn't even known existed until four hours ago, could be trusted implicitly, and by extension, Shepard too.

No matter what angle I examined the prospect from, it looked like a monumentally bad idea.

"Sorry, wrong number," I said, and hung up.

The phone shrilled again within seconds. When I didn't answer, my cell phone began playing the graduation processional—my mother's idea when I'd joked about forgetting to silence it for the graduation ceremony earlier that morning. A third and far less melodious sound joined the fray—the smoke detector howling its protest to the smoke billowing up from the grilled cheese pan.

Two things happened in quick succession then.

I swung around to douse the pan in the sink.

And saw two men standing in my living room.

Both wore black suits and blank expressions. One was completely bald, the other well on his way.

The banal and useless questions forming in my mind—*Who are you? How did you get in here?*—didn't have time to breach my lips.

It wouldn't have mattered anyway.

The men worked in complete silence. One launching himself over the counter as if it were the hood of a car. The other darting around the side. I backed myself against the fridge, reaching behind me for the butcher's block, trying and failing to lay hold of a weapon, not wanting to give them my back.

The one who had gone *Dukes of Hazzard* over my meager kitchen island grabbed me by the shoulders despite my ineffectual protests and spun me, driving me face-first into the fridge's black enamel surface. A cold blade bit into the flesh beneath my chin.

*One of mine,* I thought idly.

If it had been concealed on his body, it would have been warm.

He didn't bother threatening me. Didn't instruct me not to move. The knife said all that needed to be said. If I moved, he'd cut me. It was all very simple, really.

His partner pulled something long and white from a pocket. Shapes I could see only from the corner of my eye. In the next moment I felt serrated pressure around my wrists.

Zip ties. Far more effective than the panty hose I'd used on Valentine's driver.

Was this retribution then? Had Valentine set me free only so he could pay me back tenfold in his own time? Had my mother paid for her meeting with him in this same currency?

I'd find out soon enough.

The smoke alarm emitted a dying wail as one of the men pushed the override button.

I saw the bag coming. Velvet. I knew by the way it refused to reflect the light.

In those last few seconds before the fabric came down over my head, my attention shrank to a blurred edge beneath my cheek. A picture. Stuck to the fridge with some pizza place's magnet.

Mom smiling, sitting on the side of the tub, a cup of water poised to rinse the shampoo from my hair. Me squatting like a little frog amid clouds of bubbles.

I'd looked at it at least twice a day for the last three years but never actually *saw* it. Not until I had a knife to my throat had it occurred to me to ask myself one simple question.

*Who took the picture?*

# Chapter Six

Time.

There's never quite enough of it, is there?

One minute you can be contemplating the golden-brown perfection of a toasty grilled cheese sandwich, and the next, you've got a bondage hood over your head and a knife at your neck that you were going to use to cut the aforementioned sandwich into triangles, not rectangles, because you are a right-thinking human being and shit.

If I lived through this, I fully intended to take more time to stop and smell the browned butter.

Because roses were for basic bitches.

As were groveling and begging, candy-assed behavior my mother had long ago trained me against. Just as she had trained me on the finer points of breathing through cloth.

It was a little game my mother and I used to play called "what to do in a hostage situation." Okay, so it wasn't exactly "the floor is lava," but it had kept me entertained on long Sunday afternoons. I could hear her voice as clearly now as I had then, muffled through the cloth.

*Panic is what gets most people killed, Janey.*

*When someone attacks you, they've probably had adrenaline in their system longer than you have. They'll be twitchy. Edgy. Twitchy, edgy fingers on triggers can be a very bad thing. Breathe slowly. Think calmly. Then decide.*

Breathe slowly.

Think calmly.

I kept these two mantras in my head as I warred against the vertigo swarming through me.

The counter bit into my hip as I was marched past it into the living room, where I was guided down onto my knees on the carpet, knife still at my throat. The breath trapped beneath the velvet made my small dark world humid.

*Breathe.*

*Think.*

Shepard.

The name rang through my head like the tolling of a brass bell.

If he had really been in the alley at the bottom of the back stairwell, he could be at my front door within three minutes.

Not to say *I* could have been up four flights of stairs that quickly, but I thought it was only polite to give him credit for a better cardio routine than mine.

Three minutes.

If I could just stay alive that long . . .

"How are we going to do it?" a nasally male voice asked from behind me.

"We'll shoot her." His partner was a lifelong smoker judging by the tar-phlegmy wheeze. I heard a snapping sound like a briefcase opening.

"Wait," I mumbled through the cloth. "Why are we shooting me?"

They paid no more attention to my question than they would to a child squawking at a nearby restaurant table.

"But *before* we shoot her," said Wheezy, "I thought maybe we could have a little fun first."

Somehow I doubted that what qualified as fun for him would be fun for me, but close enough to fuck is close enough to fight. If I could manage to get my legs around his neck, I had a solid chance of sending him to Satan's waiting room pretty damn quick.

"Fun sounds good. I'm lots of fun," I said. "You guys don't even know how much fun I can be."

"But our instructions were to do her right away." The guy behind me had begun to loosen his grip on the knife at my neck, distracted by this unforeseen divergence in whatever plan they'd cobbled together.

"Instructions from whom?" I asked.

"From Val—" grunted the man behind me. Air whooshed out of his mouth like he'd been punched in the gut.

*Val,* he'd said. As in . . . Valentine?

"You want to watch your idiot mouth?" Wheezy asked.

"What? If we're going to splatter her brain across the wall anyway, what does it matter if she knows who ordered the hit?"

There were literally so many disturbing parts to that sentence, I didn't even know where to begin.

"It's exactly that kind of attitude that's kept you from promotions." Wheezy's voice was closer now. He might have been kneeling, sifting through the contents of his suitcase. "You have no appreciation for the details of the craft."

*Breathe slowly.*

*Think calmly.*

*Decide.*

"I really can't endorse any part of this plan," I said. "Particularly the brain splattering. But if I'm going to die anyway, I'd just as soon not die a virgin."

Now, I hadn't been a virgin since the tenth grade, but the word was enough to drag a spell of silence in its wake. I could practically *hear* the saliva flooding their mouths.

"I don't know," the knife wielder said, his thinning resolve pitching his voice higher. "They'll be expecting us back before too long."

"Come on," Wheezy cajoled. "We can both take a turn and still be done in less than ten minutes."

"I wouldn't brag about that." A gloved hand wandered up the naked curve of my calf, and I regretted my choice of plaid lady boxers and a tank top for dinner wear. If only they'd broken in in winter, they would have found me in baggy sweats I'd have defied any man to try and get a stiffy over.

"Oh, all right." The knife slackened at my throat. "But you can't look when it's my turn. I have a shy prostate."

When I heard a grunt and felt something warm spurt across the back of my thigh, I thought for one horrifying moment that someone's prostate wasn't shy at all.

This was followed by the unmistakable sound of a body crumpling to the floor. A gasp. Another thud.

My wrists were suddenly free, my hands stinging from the rush of blood into numb fingers. The darkness around my head evaporated, leaving me squinting, scrambling backward like a spastic crab until I backed into the coffee table. I blinked against the blinding influx of light, making out the shape of one large dark figure and two dark blobs on the floor.

"Miss Avery?"

Shepard.

Though I'd only heard a handful of words spoken by this voice, I recognized it immediately from the imagery of army fatigues and dog tags it conjured. A voice for which "drop and give me twenty" wasn't an altogether unpleasant prospect.

"That would be me." I pushed damp tendrils off my cheeks, my eyes finally beginning to focus.

"I'm Shepard."

*Yeah* he was.

I may have thought I was being facetious earlier when I'd conjectured about the man's call sign being derived from some self-styled hero complex, but this was precisely the image that Shepard's face evoked. He had a jaw made for offsetting the bold slopes of a fireman's helmet.

Hazel eyes made to search smoky rooms for stranded puppies or hanky-waving women. Biceps that could have easily carried a score of orphans. That these biceps were also branded by all manner of military tattoo did nothing to lessen the effect.

"Are you hurt?" he asked.

*Good question.*

I glanced down at my body, newly liberated from its bonds, and that's when I saw it.

Blood.

All over my legs. Soaking my socks.

"Oh my God." I instinctively searched myself for the wound, my fingers quickly slick and red as they slid up and down my legs. "I'm bleeding. I'm—"

"No, you're not," Shepard said. "*He* is."

I followed his casual glance to the pair of legs sticking out from behind the coffee table. Peering over the top, I found one of the assassins staring glassily at the ceiling, tongue protruding from the side of his mouth in a comically stereotypical rendering of death. His chrome-domed partner lay at a perpendicular angle, blood gushing through the fingers clutching his throat.

"What the fuuuuuu . . ." My vision shrank to a pinprick as the sound of my own voice went muffled. My heartbeat was a distant drum.

Darkness erased all.

———

I must have been ovulating.

This was the only explanation I could come up with for how it came to be that, upon waking to Shepard's mouth upon mine, my legs scissored themselves around his waist while my hand anchored itself in the short silky hair at the nape of his neck.

In my defense, grunts of surprise and alarm did sound almost exactly like groans of unrestrained passion and fathomless desire to my ears, which were muffled by carpenter-rough palms fastened to either side of my head.

Also, seeing as the only action in my bed for the last two years had been of the battery-operated variety, it was possible I may have been the *tiniest* bit out of practice in identifying signs of male arousal.

Shepard managed to peel my grabby paws away from the soft, well-worn T-shirt fabric covering his Captain America pectoral muscles and pin them to the floor above my head. A move that did nothing to quell the vivid fantasies already unspooling in my sex-deprived brain.

He too was gasping. Not because of a fainting spell like mine, but because I'd sort of sucked all the air from his lungs while I was going after his tongue like a baby bird.

"What was that about?" he panted.

"You tell me," I said. "Why did you kiss me?"

"I was giving you mouth-to-mouth," he stated matter-of-factly. "You stopped breathing."

"Oh," I said. Then, seeing my bloody socks locked together behind his narrow hips, "Ohhhhh."

Several facts crashed through my brain at once.

One quick glance toward the coffee table confirmed the hastily sketched memory. One bald fucker, very dead, marinating in a spreading halo of blood on my area rug. Additional fucker lying at his feet like a dog.

I disengaged myself from Shepard and shot to my feet, unsure of what to do, but sure I ought to be doing something. "What the fuck is wrong with you? You can't just storm into someone's apartment and start killing people on their antique Persian rugs!"

Shepard executed a perfect kip-up, transitioning from the flat of his back to his boots without the aid of hands. "That rug is from Ikea."

"But it *could* have been antique," I insisted. "Did you even think about that before getting all stab-happy?"

"Mostly I was thinking about keeping them from killing you. Which they were definitely going to do, by the way." Shepard slid a wicked-looking blade back into the leather holster strapped to his leg above his boot.

"You don't know that." Of course, *I* knew that, but then, I'd been there while they debated in what order to perform their heinous to-do list on my general person.

"Pretty sure I do. What do you think that stuff is for?"

We both looked down at the briefcase lying on the carpet, two halves opened like a book, the wicked instruments contained therein looking like a portable tool kit for recreational vivisection.

"Still," I said. "Next time, I'd prefer you do the killing somewhere I've had the chance to Scotchgard. Blood never comes out of berber."

"And you know this how?" he asked.

"None of your fucking business, Rambo." Disappointment deflated my chest as I lifted the frying pan from the sink and shook the blackened sandwich into the trash. "Oh, grilled cheese," I sighed. "You're the real casualty here."

Shepard wandered over from the living room to watch me through the cutout rectangle above the breakfast bar.

"Has it ever occurred to you that your priorities are seriously fucked up? Two guys busted in here ready to torture and kill you, and you're bitching about your rug and a burned-ass grilled cheese sandwich?"

"I'll have you know that until *you* called me, that sandwich was on its way to golden-brown perfection." I peeled the damp socks from my feet, padded over to the nonbloodied assassin, and grabbed him by the ankles.

It only seemed fair to let Shepard have the wet one.

"All right, Carl," I said, dragging him toward the bathroom. "Time to go."

"What are you doing?" Shepard asked. "And how do you know his name?"

"I don't. But he looks like a Carl, doesn't he?" I stopped to snatch a breath as I maneuvered Carl around a tight corner. "Also, these bodies aren't going to hide themselves. Are you going to help me or what?"

"Hold the fuck up." Shepard insinuated himself between me and the kitchen entryway. "I don't *hide* bodies."

"No? And how do you usually deal with dead guys in your apartment?"

"By calling the cops like any normal person. In fact, they're already on their way."

Something about this revelation set my still-stingy eye to twitching.

"One could take issue with the word *normal* being inserted into a conversation about proper protocol for dealing with the inconveniently deceased." The dead man's arm caught on a stool at the end of the kitchen island as I attempted to drag him around Shepard. I reached down to disengage the limp hand. "Goddamn it, work with me here, Carl."

"Are you saying you've done this before?" Shepard asked. I tried not to notice how the entryway volunteered itself for a comparison to his proportions. How the walls seemed just barely wide enough to accommodate his broad shoulders. How the ceiling's height would almost certainly be at the extreme reach of his long arm. How boyish his face looked among the modern angles. Nose and cheeks that would go pink with cold. Pillowy lips that would go red with kissing.

"No," I said. "But I might as well tell you that even if I were saying that, which I'm not, it wouldn't matter if you told a jury that I had, which I didn't, because your testimony would qualify as hearsay, and be therefore inadmissible in any court of law." Sweat had begun to bloom on my forehead and chin.

Turns out dragging dead weight is great cardio.

"P-Ripple said you were a law student." The acknowledgment felt, no doubt unintentionally, like a pat on the head. Magnanimous animal that I am, I opted to offer one in return.

"And he said you were his best surveillance guy. How come you're watching me and not Valentine?"

"I *was* watching Valentine," he said. "Until you kidnapped him."

The heels of Carl's shoes clunked on the kitchen floor as I dropped them.

*Shit.*

"*Kidnapping* is a rather strong word." But already my brain was churning out bad news. What had he seen? Me squeezing myself unceremoniously through the window separating the driver's compartment? Me threatening Valentine with a pellet gun. *Please*, I prayed to the gods of retail and all else that was holy, *please don't let him have seen the—*

"A pellet gun?" He chuckled. "You seriously took on Archard Everett Valentine with a motherfucking *pellet gun?*"

*Ye gods be damned.*

"Don't get me wrong." Shepard wrenched open the fridge door and stooped to help himself to a beer. "It was a gutsy move." He knocked the top off using the counter's edge, took a swallow, and thumbed foam from his lip. The carbonation lowered his already deep baritone. "Stupid. Sloppy. But gutsy."

"Stupid?" I demanded. "Sloppy? I got to Valentine even though he's surrounded by an entire team of security guys, and—"

"And now they all know exactly what you look like. Stupid," he repeated. "Sloppy." His Adam's apple bobbed as he took another pull on the bottle.

"And what would you have done?"

"Exactly what I *was* doing. Watching him. *Without* letting him know he was being watched."

"So how come you're not doing it now?" I folded my arms across my tank top, conscious of the cleavage Shepard seemed to be *watching* now.

"Because I'm also P-Ripple's best security guy, and you seemed to need that more than Valentine needed watching."

"Says who?"

"Says Carl." Shepard glanced down at the dead man on the floor between us. "And his buddy. They were following you even before the parking garage. And they weren't the only ones."

Needles prickled over my scalp and crawled their way from my hairline down my face, neck, and shoulders. "Who?" I asked. "Who else was following me?"

"Don't know yet." Shepard shrugged. "Looked like three different operatives from what I saw. I was in the process of running plates when these guys moved on you."

I thought of myself tottering down the street in my best heels in the wake of exiting Valentine's limo, feeling proud of what I'd just pulled off, already planning my dinner of grilled cheese, and all the time, I was being followed. Not just by Carl and company, but by Shepard and some unknown quantity of "others."

All those eyes on me, that whole time.

I gripped the counter with clammy palms. "Why didn't you call me sooner?"

"If I had, the people watching you would have known something was up."

"But if you had *told* me I was being watched—"

"Right. Because following instructions is such a strong point of yours?" His face almost managed amusement. "Just like you did when I told you to get out of the apartment?"

"Look, I'm not exactly used to someone wanting me dead."

*"Someone?"* For the first time since I'd clapped eyes on him, Shepard looked genuinely concerned. "You mean you don't know who hired them to kill you?"

"No, Mr. Stab First and Ask Questions Later, I don't. I mean, I may suspect that it's a certain kinky gajillionaire, but that would have been a great thing to find out *before you fucking killed them.*"

Shepard nudged the thug with the thick toe of his combat boot. "The words you're looking for here are *thank you.* As in, thank you, Shepard, for keeping these two grisly bastards from quartering me like a Christmas turkey and fucking the warm parts."

Was it wrong that the parts in question got a little warmer despite there being two dead bodies within stick-poking distance?

A sharp rap on the door followed by a shouted, "Police!" brought our conversation to an abrupt conclusion.

"Come in," Shepard shouted back. And then, quickly to me, "You let me do the talking. Understand? I know these guys."

I was on the point of arguing when my apartment door swung open, and I muttered a quiet oath when I saw who stood in the doorway.

Officer Bixby.

# Chapter Seven

"Oh, fuck. Not you again."

"Well, hello to you too, Miss Avery," Bixby said. Then, seeing the dead man on the floor, he nodded over his shoulder. The other officer jogged back down the hall, presumably to retrieve a roll of crime scene tape and/or to radio dispatch.

Shepard's sandy brows drew together. "You two know each other?"

"I wouldn't say *know*." I shifted on my feet and tugged the bottoms of my boxers farther down my thighs.

"Miss Avery fled a potential crime scene I was processing earlier this afternoon," Bixby explained.

"I wouldn't say *fled*."

"You took off so fast you ran face-first into a pedestrian crossing sign."

"So *that's* what happened to your eye." From the way Shepard said this, I inferred that the matter had been the subject of serious consideration, which, given the two dead guys on my floor, was not altogether complimentary.

"As eager as I am to have one more fucking person comment on the state of my face, could we just go ahead and process this crime scene so I can get back to my evening?"

Bixby looked at Shepard, fatigue plain on his face. "Just give me something believable for the report."

"Wait. You two know each other?" I asked, borrowing Shepard's line.

"I wouldn't say *know*," Bixby said, borrowing mine. "Frequently meeting over crime scenes involving assault and/or death that I'll inevitably spend hours writing reports for but that will never be investigated by the DA because a certain person has been granted some kind of unofficial immunity by God or one of his direct reports would be more accurate."

"No wonder you never learned how to get rid of a body," I said, perhaps a little too wonderingly.

"What?" Bixby blinked at me.

"Nothing." I quickly turned to Shepard. "What was that you were saying about the totally plausible and defensible reason these two not-so-fine, not-so-gentle men needed to be not alive anymore?"

"Right." Shepard took another swig of beer and set the sweating brown bottle down on the counter before looping an arm around my waist and sandwiching me to his side.

I tried—and failed—not to notice how his latissimus dorsi nudged my shoulder like a great wing.

"So, my girlfriend and me were just—"

"My girlfriend and *I*." I gave Shepard a playful tsk-tsk gesture. "Remember how cute you find it when I correct your grammar?" I squeezed the Japanese dragon undulating up his bicep, felt my eyes go wide, and squeezed it again. Dear Lord but there was a lot of bro-beef in this apartment all of the sudden.

Shepard's jaw ticked. "My girlfriend and *I* were settling in for a nice, pleasant evening of Netflix and chill—"

"I said *believable*," Bixby said with a snort.

"Why is that unbelievable?" I asked. "You don't think I'm good enough to be his girlfriend?"

"I meant the pleasant part."

In lieu of karate chopping Bixby in the carotid artery and thereby running the risk of proving his point, I simply smiled, making my voice sweet and syrupy as baklava, which I would have shanked the average Greek restaurateur for right about then. "What's the matter? Don't you have pleasant evenings at home with your mom?"

It was back. That charming white line around his lips. More pronounced now than it had been earlier in contrast to the five o'clock shadow dusting his jaw.

"As I was fucking saying before I was interrupted *twice*," Shepard said, raking a censorious look over Bixby and me, "my girlfriend and *I* were settling in for a *completely mediocre* evening of Netflix and chill when someone kicked the door in."

"Are you sure they *kicked* the door in, babe?" I asked, giving his glute a pat. Purely for the sake of verisimilitude, of course. "Because I don't remember there being any loud noises."

"Oh, my little wildebeest," he said, tweaking my nose. "That's probably because all the loud noises were coming from you."

Nose tweaking was a close second to pet names involving ruminants of the African Serengeti in my list of dick-punchable offenses. By pure, iron-spleened will, I managed keep my expression mostly unhomicidal. I needed to see where he was going with this. "Loud noises? Coming from me?"

"Yeah," Shepard said. "You were screaming, 'Oh my God, Shepard, you're the best fuck I ever had! I've never seen a cock so big in all my life'—or something like that—then boom. There they were."

"Boom," I echoed.

"That one right there"—Shepard pointed to the guy with the gaping neck hole—"lunged for Jane, and I grabbed my boot knife and stabbed him. I was aiming for his shoulder, but you know how it is when your head isn't getting enough blood." He winked at Bixby conspiratorially. "Then Jane screamed, 'Save me, Shepard—'"

"Funny." I thought I could hear my jaw creak as I forced the word out through gritted teeth. "I have no memory of that."

Shepard tugged a lock of my hair. Chiding. Playful. "You know how forgetful you get after six orgasms. Anyway, when I heard you scream and turned around, the other guy had you facedown on the floor. I was only trying to put him in a headlock to drag him off you, but he freaked the fuck out, and wouldn't you know it? He broke his own neck."

"Damn shame," I said.

"How did he get into the kitchen?" Bixby glanced at Carl, whose arms were flung over his head like a deceased roller coaster rider. "Seeing how his neck was broken and all."

All three of us looked at the bloody slug's trail starting at the dark, damp stain in the living room and finishing in the kitchen.

"Slithered?" I suggested.

Officer Bixby's resigned sigh carried the weight of a hundred such nights, all of which had apparently ended badly for him. "That it?"

"That's it." Shepard smiled like a shark.

"Huh," Bixby grunted.

"Huh," I agreed.

"All right, then. Homicide should be here any minute. They'll want to ask you two some questions."

And ask they did. We sat on my couch, repeating different pieces of the story Shepard had supplied to Bixby while the detectives rolled their eyes and scratched down notes.

"Are we about done here?" Shepard finally asked. "We really need to get going or we'll be late for, uh . . ."

"Choir practice," I finished for him.

Bixby had wandered in from the kitchen, where the crime scene techs were packing up their equipment. "I'm sure *the choir* could deal with the disappointment of not having you there for one night."

"But it isn't the choir we'd be disappointing," I chimed in. "It's Jesus. You wouldn't want us to disappoint Jesus, would you? I mean, without Shepard's wicked flute solo, 'Rock of Ages' is more like a pebble."

"For Christ's sake." Bixby scrubbed his face with a square hand.

"Exactly!" I said.

The detectives exchanged dubious glances. The foremost of them, a man with a softening middle and thinning hair, folded his notebook closed and slid it into a pocket. "We know how to get ahold of you."

"Should we hit the road?" Shepard asked, squeezing my knee.

"I'll just grab my purse," I said.

"I think it would be best if you stayed at my place tonight—don't you, babe?"

*Babe.*

Somehow this appellation bothered me more than anything else Shepard had said. It was just fake enough to mock and real enough to sting.

"Oh, I don't know," I said, hesitating. "I was thinking I might just zip up to my great-grandmother's ski chalet. The butler was expecting me later tonight, and he'll be so worried if I fail to show . . ."

"Did I forget to tell you?" Shepard slapped his forehead with the palm of his hand. "I already called and told him you'd be with me. I gave him the night off so he could spend it with little Ubuntu. You remember the Malawian orphan he adopted? His chemotherapy treatments haven't been going so well—"

"Just get your shit and get out of here, will you?"

At the twitching of Bixby's eye, I felt a small stab of victory.

"You heard the man." Shepard swatted my behind, the gesture as playful as his eyes were serious. "You might want to pack extra. Just in case you don't feel safe coming back here for a while."

I shuffled off to my bedroom, changing into jeans and a T-shirt before dragging a dusty duffel bag from my closet shelf. Stopping in the adjoining bathroom, I swept in all the necessary toiletries. After tossing in a couple of pairs of jeans and a few T-shirts, I contemplated the contents of my panty drawer.

Thongs seemed too provocative. Briefs, too casual.

How the hell did one pack for this kind of sleepover, anyway?

"The black ones. Definitely."

I spun around to find Shepard standing in my bedroom doorway. It was downright unnerving for a man that large to be so quiet.

I dropped the black lace thong I was holding and grabbed an assorted wad of underthings, jamming them into my bag. "Killing two assassins in my apartment doesn't give you the right to weigh in on my choice of underoos," I said.

"But I'm your boyfriend now, remember?" He walked over to the window, fiddled with the shade. Tested the lock.

"About that." I riffled through my drawer of sleepwear and grabbed several T-shirts and shorts, dropping them in as well. "I feel like I really need to work on myself right now. We're just on two different paths, you see. We've been growing apart for a while now. You deserve someone better. I think we should see other people."

"Our connection was mostly physical anyway." He closed the bedroom door. Locked it. Jiggled the handle. Unlocked it again.

"I knew you'd understand. Also," I said as I turned and raised an eyebrow at him, "*six* orgasms?"

"So I underestimated a little." He shrugged. "I would have gone with ten, but that just seemed like bragging."

"As opposed to the giant cock comment?" I asked around the golf ball lodged in my throat.

"Bixby said he wanted believable."

"You know what they say about guys with big egos." I made sure to amplify my snort so it could be heard from my bedroom's minuscule walk-in closet, a place whose clutter and disarray tended to reflect the general state of my life in ways I didn't like to consider overmuch.

"Where does this go?" Shepard glanced up at the small, square trapdoor in the closet ceiling I had always ignored.

"Could you not follow me everywhere?" I kicked a pair of panties behind the overflowing laundry basket as he brushed by, his front grazing my back. "Dude," I said. "Personal space."

"A luxury you no longer enjoy." He reached up and pushed the square, seeming concerned when it didn't budge.

"You're doing what, exactly?" I asked the broad muscles of his back.

"Discovering how ridiculously unsafe your apartment is."

"Unsafe?" I backed out of the closet and slung my bag down on the bed. "My mother checked this place out herself."

"That explains a lot."

"What is that supposed to mean?"

"It means your mother thinks like a good guy *trying* to think like a bad guy. Which isn't the same thing as knowing how someone who wants to hurt you would actually operate."

Now there was a disturbing thought. "And you're saying you do?"

"No," he said. "But even if I were, which I'm not . . ." He trailed off, leaving me to marinate in the memory of my own flippant words. Lord, how I hated any smart-ass who wasn't me.

"Shepard?" Bixby called from the other room. "Can you come in here a minute?"

"Go ahead," I said. "I'm almost done."

Truthfully I just wanted him gone so I could add one last item to my bag. I hurried over to my nightstand and pulled out the drawer.

Then stared at its contents for the longest minute of my life.

There, in place of the revolver I had been hoping to grab, was a note from my mother.

# Chapter Eight

With trembling hands I reached down and picked up the note, heart pounding as I traced a finger across my name. The same loops and curves that had graced a thousand brown-paper-bagged lunches. My mother's writing.

> *Janey,*
> *Needed to borrow Face-Gravy. I'll explain later.*
>     *XOXO*
> *—Mom*
>
>     *PS. Never keep your gun in your nightstand. It's the*
> *first place people look.*
>     *PPS. Lasagna in the freezer.*

The *how* didn't puzzle me as much as the *when* and *why*.

*When* had my mother come to my apartment? *Why* had she borrowed Face-Gravy—so named for the Magnum's ability to reduce the facial features of your average assailant to meat soup—when she had an arsenal most small countries would envy?

I closed my eyes and tried to feel her in the room. Tried to see her. To watch how she had come, how she had gone, and why.

*You're stopping by your apartment?*

Had it really been just that morning she had asked me that? It felt like another lifetime.

How content I had been sitting there at her breakfast table, not knowing she had an appointment with Valentine only a few hours later. Having no earthly idea she had a standing appointment with Paul Gladstone, longtime fuckbuddy. That she had a longtime fuckbuddy at all.

What had she been thinking when she'd asked me about my plans?

Had she been calculating when I'd be at my apartment so she could slip in when I wasn't around? Had she come by here before or after her meeting with Valentine?

Surely not *after* she disappeared from my graduation. Because if that were the case, she would have at least added some obscure line to inform me she was okay.

Wouldn't she?

Or was this just another thing I was incorrectly assuming about a woman I only thought I knew? And if I only thought I knew her, what else didn't I know?

Did I know *anything*?

I knew how she looked standing at the ironing board.

I anchored myself in the memory, letting the details superimpose themselves on the backs of my eyelids, that blood-colored screen.

The shape of her body. Her solid shoulders. Her small waist. Her round hips. The perfect union of utility and grace in that always-familiar form.

What alien mind lived beneath the bundle of that dark hair? What thoughts scuttled through its channels? It seemed impossible that she could hold me in it, and secrets too. That she could smile at me, look at me, touch me, and still feel like the woman I knew even with all those foreign thoughts in her head.

"Ready?"

I started and gave a little shriek. *Not* a good thing to do in an apartment full of cops, several of whom came rushing into my bedroom like something out of a bad police academy fantasy.

"Spider," Shepard said, waving them off.

"You do that again, and I'm putting a bell on you," I threatened, folding the note and tucking it into my bra.

"Who's Face-Gravy?" he asked.

He'd read the top of the note over my shoulder.

"My vibrator." The lie weighed less than a mustard seed.

"I'm just going to move right past that name and ask why your mom borrowed your vibrator."

"Hers must be on the blink," I said. "Desperate times, and all that."

"This is exactly why you shouldn't have broken up with me," he teased. "No such thing as desperate times in my bed."

"Pfft." I hoisted my duffel from the bed and looped it over my shoulder. "Face-Gravy sees your six and raises you seven."

Shepard transferred the bag from my shoulder to his. "I think he's bluffing."

"You gonna call?"

I had meant it as a joke, but neither of us laughed. It became something else in the silence that followed, crackling in the air between us.

Odd, I had never really counted on bonding over dead bodies as a potentially expediting factor for sexual tension.

———

If bonding over dead bodies is an inadvertent libido enhancer, evicting your stomach contents onto someone's crotch is about as close as you can get to an *an*aphrodisiac.

Honestly I never got clear on exactly how it happened. All I knew was I was trying to crawl out of the car, unsure of which way was up or down or out, and this mostly because I was in mortal fear for my life.

Not because a fresh crop of assassins had shown up with new and inventive ways to end my life, but because driving with Shepard was like being strapped into some kind of amusement park ride designed to relieve you of your corn dogs and cotton candy.

He darted in between vehicles, took unexpected turns and detours, punched it to eighty only to decelerate to a full stop just in time to narrowly miss creaming a pedestrian. He had insisted it was in order to disentangle us from anyone who might have been following, but I suspected it was a subconscious bid to underscore the size of his thunderstick.

A thunderstick right beneath the damp ground zero on his well-worn jeans.

"I'm really sorry," I said, trying to swallow my stomach back down my neck. "I have this inner-ear issue, and—"

"Let's just get inside so I can get cleaned up."

"Inside" was presumably contained in the nondescript apartment building on the outskirts of downtown Denver.

"I wouldn't have figured you for an apartment guy," I said, letting myself out of the car.

"I'm not."

"So this isn't your place?"

"Negative."

"But I thought I was staying with you."

"Women don't stay at my home," he said, retrieving both my duffel bag and his from the back seat. "I stay at theirs."

"How terribly original of you." I followed him up the sidewalk to the building's well-lit front door. "So what is this place?"

"This is a safe house." He punched a complicated code into the panel on the door.

"You're going to write that down for me, yes?"

"No." The panel beeped and the lock clicked open. We crossed the clean, empty lobby to the elevator, where Shepard plugged a black key card into the slot before pressing the key for the sixth floor.

"But what about a key card?" I protested. "I'm going to get one of those, aren't I?"

"Also no."

The elevator opened onto a long hallway, minimally decorated with sleek fake plants and boxy metal tables.

"But what if I need to get back in?" I asked.

"*Back* in implies you'd be leaving," he said. "You're not. Not the building. Not the floor. Not even the apartment."

Well, he was just determined not to make this easy on himself.

I had kind of been hoping for a dynamic duo situation. Where I was the mind to his muscle. I planned, he enforced. Hell, I would even have been willing to let him play the plucky sidekick.

But if he was going to be so wildly uncooperative, I was just going to have to plan *around* him. Which, I already suspected, would not end well for him.

I mentally retraced my steps, mapping the hallways, the fire exits, and the stairwells in my head. I saw again the unblinking eye of surveillance cameras. Certainly not an ideal situation for what I had in mind, but there was nothing for it.

Sacrifices would have to be made.

He paused in front of a door halfway down the hall and punched yet another code into yet another panel. As hard as I tried to memorize the trajectory of his fingers, he was fast and sly, and seeing past the wall of his back was nigh impossible anyway.

The place was pitch-black, and when Shepard flipped the light switch, I saw why.

Blackout curtains covered every window.

The furnishing sensibility was spare and distinctly masculine. A couch. A coffee table. I found the bedroom equally sparse. A bed with a simple blue comforter. A nightstand. A dresser. A lamp.

The relentless sterility of this place made me feel twitchy and tense.

I walked toward the window, determined to let some sort of outside light into the bleak space, even if it came only from streetlights.

"Don't," Shepard barked. "If you can see out, they can see in."

"You mean it isn't one-way glass? I'm a little disappointed." I withdrew my hand from the curtain like a scolded child, plopping down on the end of the bed, unsurprised to find the mattress about as yielding as a concrete slab. No doubt Shepard would cite something about it being best for lumbar alignment if given the opportunity. "So what happens now?"

"Now, I take a shower and change so I can head out and try to track down some of the people who were tracking you. *You* stay put."

"Stay here? How is that any better than being at my apartment?" A little jet of panic shot through me. I didn't like that I'd already begun to draw some measure of security from Shepard's presence.

"Because, unlike your apartment, this place is perfectly safe. There's no way to get up here without all the security information, and there's no way to get into the apartment from the outside."

"What about the windows?"

"Made from double-paned Lexan. It's nearly unbreakable."

"But what about my plans for the evening?"

"What plans?"

"I had a date."

It took me a minute to realize that the strange growly, gaspy sound Shepard was making was laughter.

I crossed my arms over my chest. "Why is that funny?"

"You haven't had a date in two years."

That this was exactly right did not a thing to quell the sudden onslaught of righteous indignation thundering through my veins. And yet, I couldn't ask him how he knew this without confirming its veracity.

"Your shoe size is seven, your bra size is thirty-four *b*, you have a gym membership you've signed up for but never used, you have four unpaid parking tickets and one warrant out for your arrest, and you tend to leave your bedroom blinds open even when you're changing."

I was doing my best impression of a gasping fish, mouth opening and closing to very little effect, when Shepard added, "Officer Bixby did you a solid, by the way. He could of arrested you."

"Could *have* arrested me."

"We broke up, remember? I no longer find it cute when you correct my grammar."

Shepard bustled efficiently from closet to dresser, retrieving a new pair of jeans, boxer briefs, and an identical black T-shirt. I suspected that if I allowed myself a peek in the closet, I'd find an entire row of them.

"I thought you didn't live here," I said.

"I don't."

"But you keep spare clothes here?"

"I keep spare clothes in a lot of places." He moved like a man with somewhere to be. Which, of course, he was.

With growing dread, I realized he'd be leaving soon and I'd be locked down in an apartment with more security than Fort Knox. Safe, but *alone.*

Alone.

Solo. Not a soul to lie to.

I knew this feeling. I hated this feeling. I had avoided all manner of therapist's couch just to make sure I never had to *talk* about this feeling.

And here it was, this lumpy, malformed bastard of a memory trying to crawl out of the tar of my subconscious. To tell me all about the childhood loneliness from whence it had sprung.

No way was I having that shit.

I kicked it down a mental staircase and tried to pick a fight with Shepard. Having him focused on what I was saying rather than what I was doing would be essential for what I had planned next.

"But I'm hungry," I protested. "Why can't I go out and get something to eat?"

"There's food in the fridge."

"I don't know how to work the remote."

"Google it."

"I forgot my nightgown."

Shepard stopped in the doorway to the bathroom and turned back to me, a small, strange smile tugging at the corners of his mouth. He stripped off his black T-shirt and tossed it at me. "Sleep in this."

It hit me square in the chest, sending up an intoxicating waft of *male*. Warm skin. Soap. Some kind of expensive aftershave.

Let those who have periodically accused me of an utter lack of self-control note that I didn't hold the shirt to my face and huff it like a tube of superglue until *after* the bathroom door was partially closed.

He showered. I paced.

Opening the fridge, I found *food* to be a loose approximation of its contents. For a guy who didn't live here, he sure seemed to have strong opinions about the comestibles on offer. Tupperware containers of poached chicken and greens. Brown rice. Fucking quinoa. Bottled water.

No dairy. No gluten. No dice.

I had to get *out*.

Returning to the bedroom, I sat down on the bed, watching as seductive tendrils of steam beckoned from a gap in the not-completely-closed door.

If you've ever seen cartoons where someone leaves a pie on a windowsill, you'll know what I'm talking about. There the hapless dog is, minding his own business, when those ghostly fingers of steam hook him by the nostrils and float him right over to the unattended pastry.

Sitting on the bed with Shepard on the other side of a not-closed door was a lot like that.

He'd left his duffel bag unattended at the foot of the bed, the silly boy.

It took me only three pockets before I found what I was looking for. "Bingo."

I toed off my shoes and crept toward the bathroom door, the shower scene from *Psycho* unspooling in my head along with its attendant nails-on-a-chalkboard screeching.

The door creaked, but it didn't matter. Shepard was a whistler.

It was when Shepard reached the chorus of "Rock of Ages" that I realized I had been standing there gawking while his face was tipped back into the shower's spray, eyes closed.

There would never be a more perfect time.

"Shepard!" I shrieked at a decibel that would have given Janet Leigh a run for her money. "Save me!"

As I expected, his reflexes were exceptional.

He was out of the shower, eyes wide, searching for the threat with single-minded focus that completely blinded him to the handcuffs closing over his wrist and the metal bar on the shower door simultaneously.

Snick-snick.

Done.

Shepard looked at the cuffs. He looked at me. Looked at the cuffs again. Looked at me.

I smiled in a manner both winsome and conciliatory. Just because I had triumphed was no reason for poor sportsmanship, after all.

"Jane, what *the fuck* do you think you're doing?"

"At the moment? Admiring the view. But in about three seconds, I'm going to leave your wet, naked ass and bounce."

"Very cute," he said. "Now go get the key."

"No can do." Okay, my smile might have been the *tiniest* bit smug when I said this, so his lunging for me was somewhat forgivable. I managed to leap back in time to avoid being grabbed, but only just.

Pretty impressive arm span, that Shepard.

He could reach the towel rack and did, swathing his hips in terry cloth while I feigned utter disinterest in his man meat.

Insouciance, thy name is Jane.

"Listen to me, Jane. The safest place for you is right here in this apartment—"

"My mother is *missing*. And so far you, P-Ripple, Bixby, and all the rest of the men concerning themselves with this case haven't turned up a goddamn thing. It's my turn."

"You can't just hit the streets unprotected."

"Who says I'm unprotected?" I pulled the Glock I'd found out of my bra. "Of course, it isn't as big as Face-Gravy, but I suppose it will do okay in the meantime."

"I thought you said Face-Gravy was your vibrator."

"And I thought you said you had the biggest cock I'd ever seen. Imagine my disappointment."

*Lie.*

Admittedly I wasn't a connoisseur of cocks (a cockoisseur?), but Shepard's had to be right up there. Well, right down there, at the moment. He wasn't finding this whole handcuffing business nearly as kinky as I was.

"You have a great evening, okay?" I tucked his gun back in my bra and turned to leave.

"Wait!" The clanking of metal on metal marked Shepard reaching the end of his tether. Literally *and* figuratively, I was guessing.

"At least leave me my phone so I can call someone to get me out when you're gone." He enunciated each word. Slowly. Clearly. The verbal equivalent of counting to ten. All things considered, he was doing a pretty bang-up job of schooling the rage from his voice despite the intriguing shade of purple it lent to his face.

I pretended to consider his request. "Also no."

His lunging for me a second time was my cue to book it.

Under a hail of not-so-subtle threats, I quickly changed into a black skirt, flat-soled sandals, and a tight knit top. Black skirt because that was about as fancy as I got and my best chance of blending into the place where Valentine would be supping. Flat-soled sandals, so I could hoof it if the need arose. And the tight top in hopes that a couple of inches of cleavage might distract at least a few people from a face that looked like it had been ridden hard and put away wet.

Thus prepared, I grabbed my bag, called out a friendly valediction over my shoulder, and slipped out the door.

# Chapter Nine

Archard Everett Valentine wasn't happy to see me.

True, I was technically trespassing as my name was not, in fact, on the guest list lorded over by the maître d' with a terrible attitude and equally problematic pedophile 'stache. Nor had there actually been a rat in the coat check as some anonymous party had shrieked mere seconds later. And it might not have been in the best interest for the patrons at the table adjacent to Valentine's to have their server's tray mysteriously upend its contents onto their laps.

And yet, it was precisely this confluence of events that allowed me to reach Valentine before any of the staff could stop me.

Now I couldn't be certain, but I suspected it was probably leftover resentment from the kidnapping thing that made him look at me like I had just shot a snot rocket into his glass of scotch.

Not his first, judging by the ruddy flush spreading over his high cheekbones.

"Anyone sitting here?" I asked, indicating the chair opposite his.

"Actually—"

"Good," I said, roosting down. I was comforted that the seat was not warm, which meant his date hadn't yet arrived as opposed to having stepped out to use the restroom. This might, conceivably, give me more time. I picked up the menu on my side of the table and perused it just for curiosity's sake. Call it culinary window-shopping. "So. What are we eating?"

"Liquid diet." Valentine raised his glass. "What I want isn't on the menu." His dark eyebrows lowered, eyes going both angular in shape and soft in affect all at the same time.

"Are you giving me the smolder right now? Is that what you're doing? Because you can save yourself the squinting. I'm impervious to sexual contrivances."

"Liar."

"Well, yeah," I admitted. "But not about that."

"What is it you want, Miss Avery?"

"We need to talk."

"Already?" He sipped his drink. "Usually women wait until after we've fucked to have this conversation."

"If you're trying to shock me, it won't work. I already know what you're into. I read the *Grapevine.*"

"The *Grapevine.*" Valentine snorted bitterly. "Believe me, Miss Avery. You haven't the first clue what I'm into."

"Well, that's why I'm here," I said. "To find out."

"And I was so hoping our delightful conversation this afternoon might have been sufficient to satisfy your apparently insatiable need for contact with me for at least a few days."

"It might have," I said. "Had you not sent a pair of goons to murder me."

Valentine's hooded eyelids raised a fraction. "Say again?"

"Archard—may I call you Archie?"

"Absolutely not."

"So, Archie, there I was, minding my own business, looking on with pride at perhaps the most expertly toasted grilled cheese sandwich in all creation, when a pair of guys broke into my apartment, dropped a bag over my head, and proceeded to argue about the order in which they'd like to fuck, torture, and kill me."

"And what did they decide?" he asked, stirring his drink with his finger, bringing it to his lips to suck the liquid from it. A man who appreciated how the salt of skin can improve the flavor of anything licked from it.

Interesting thought, that.

"Why do I get the feeling you're not taking this seriously?" I asked.

"You're here, aren't you? You lived to pester another day." When he reached for his drink again, I snatched it from him and shot the contents. In my mind, it had been a lethally cool gesture. In actual practice, however, it left me coughing and blinking away tears.

"Not a scotch person?" he guessed.

"I'm *totally* a scotch person." *Lie.* "I just . . . swallowed it wrong."

"Most people do their first time." Valentine signaled to the server, who darted over to the table as if yanked by an invisible leash. "I'll do this again," he said, pointing to his empty glass.

"And anything for you, miss?" the server asked.

"Nothing for her." Valentine preempted me. "She won't be staying."

When the server was gone, Valentine leaned in closer, the candle between us lighting twin flames in his eyes.

"Miss Avery, had *I* sent someone to remove you from my way, you wouldn't be sitting here right now. I have the means to pay for quality. Unlike whoever it is that obviously sent second-rate hired muscle to take care of a first-rate target."

"I'm a first-rate target?" In some more logical part of my brain, I knew this wasn't something to be proud of, but I couldn't help the little bubble of pride swelling in my chest.

"You'd have to be, as many people as you have following you."

The bubble quickly burst, leaking acid into my throat. "How do you know that?"

He only smiled.

My guess: his was one of the three groups Shepard had seen tailing me.

"Look, Archie. I'll be brief. I think the reason someone put a hit out on me has *something* to do with what you *allege* my mother was blackmailing you about. Whatever she knows, someone else must assume I know it too, and if I'm going to get killed for *something*, I'd really prefer it be for *something* I actually know. You dig?"

Valentine leaned back in his chair, his form graceful even in its laziness. His shoe slid between mine beneath the table. "I'm a businessman, Jane Avery. You want something from me? Make me an offer."

"An offer of what exactly? You don't need my money."

"You're right." His eyebrow arched as he glanced at my cleavage. "I don't."

"I'm not going to let you do lines from my ass, if that's what you're hinting at."

"Don't flatter yourself, Miss Avery. I wouldn't do lines from any part of your body. Not for payment. Not for pleasure."

"Why not?" The words were out before I could stop them. First Shepard not wanting me at my apartment. Now Valentine not wanting to inhale illegal drugs from my general person. This rejection was really starting to get me down.

"You're not my type."

"Paid by the hour, you mean?"

"Out of practice." Warm, smoky breath tickled my ear as he leaned in to whisper. "Two years in dry dock is a long time."

What. The. Shit?

How did everyone know this?

Just when I thought I'd reached my maximum density for humiliation in one day, I was proved wrong.

Again.

Valentine's hand had found my knee under the table. Carefully skirting around the abrasions, two fingers walked Yellow Pages–logo style up my thigh. "Shall we check if your cherry has grown back?"

This was the part where, in a movie, I would have stood up and thrown a drink in his face. But since I didn't have one, I did the next best thing. I picked up a piece of bread and chucked it at him.

So *this* was what it looked like to shock Archard Everett Valentine.

"Did you just . . . throw *bread* at me?"

"What's the matter? Is your vision as impaired as your morals?"

"In fact not." He gave me his shark grin. "In order for morals to be impaired, you must first have them."

"So what, if not sex, does a man without morals want in exchange for information?"

He ran a finger over the gleaming blade of his butter knife and adjusted it so it was perfectly parallel with its neighbor. "Your panties."

Shock leapfrogged from his face to mine. "Excuse me?"

"Give me your panties," he repeated. "Then I'll answer your question."

"You don't want to sleep with me, but you want my panties? What kind of perv are you, exactly?"

"If you really want the answer to that, we'll have to discuss additional *terms*."

"What? Like my socks?"

"You're not wearing any." He brought the cut-crystal glass to his lips and took a long swallow. I imagined I could see the smoky burn as it warmed its way down his neck and into his belly.

He set the glass down. "So what will it be?"

"I'd really rather not," I said. "Isn't there anything else I could do for you?"

"Like what?"

I thought about this for a moment.

A very long moment.

Turns out, aside from acing classes, pissing off faculty, and engaging in healthy bouts of misanthropy, I didn't really *do* much of anything.

"You win. Just let me go to the bathroom, and I'll—"

"No," he said. "Here."

"Here? But there are all these people. What if—"

"What if, what if, what if." Valentine's refrain was singsongy with booze. "What if everyone in this restaurant was only here to glut themselves on liquor and food and didn't give a shit what we were doing anyway? What if my date just texted me to tell me she was in the elevator on her way up?"

"Date?"

"She'll be here any minute. In or out, Miss Avery?"

Well, shit.

This was happening.

I took a deep breath, laid the edge of the white linen tablecloth over my lap, and scooted to the edge of my chair. Ever conscious of Valentine's eyes on mine, the subtle roughness of his pants leg brushing my calf. I slipped my hands under the tablecloth and up my skirt, hooked my thumbs through the band of my panties, and drew them down inch by inch.

Awareness I didn't know my body to be capable of sizzled in every cell. I could feel *everything*. The chair's velvety fabric beneath the edge of my buttocks. Cool air kissing damp skin between my legs. My own knuckles grazing my thighs.

Of course, our server chose that precise moment to bustle over to our table.

I sat there, thumbs in panties, staring at Valentine across the table and mentally calling him every creative swear word I knew and inventing a few new ones besides.

"Are you two ready to order, or do you need a little more time?"

"I think we're ready," Valentine announced. "The filet of beef for two. Medium rare. Sautéed greens with mine and truffled fries with the other."

"And how would you like your filet?" she asked, turning toward me.

89

"It's not for her," Valentine interrupted. "She'll be departing momentarily. Make them *both* medium rare."

"Very good. Can I take your menu?" And of course, she held out her goddamn hand.

"Yes, you *may*." I hoped she'd detect the serious note of censure in my grammatical correction.

Valentine finally came to my rescue, lifting both menus and handing them over.

"You exquisite bastard," I said when our server had departed.

"Yes," he agreed. "Continue."

Hearing a rise of laughter from the next table, I glanced over, only to be snapped back when Valentine slapped his palm on the table.

"No." His knuckles were pale on the hand gripping his drink. "Look at me while you're doing it."

And so I did.

I looked at him while the scrap of fabric cleared my knees, while it brushed past my calves. I looked at him when he pulled his foot from between mine so I could drag the panties over my sandals. I looked at him while his hand met mine under the table, warm and strong, prying my fingers apart to get at his prize.

I looked at him while all this happened to the knowledge of no one but us.

He sat up straight and glanced down. I knew he had my panties in his lap purely by the expression on his face. An amused, yet genuine, smile. "Wonder Woman?"

My ears burned like atomic torches.

"They're my lucky panties."

"Then let's hope they work for me better than they've worked for you." Valentine tucked them in his front suit pocket, adjusting them so a precise little triangle of red and blue poked out like a handkerchief.

"A deal's a deal, Archie."

"So it is. Your mother told me that someone had hired her to dig up incriminating evidence about a mistress of mine. She wouldn't tell me who, or when. Just that she had enough information now to put me in a very dark hole for a very long time. Savvy businesswoman that she is, your mother offered to suppress the information. *If* I paid her more than they were offering."

I tried to imagine my pretty mother sitting across the desk from Valentine in the cheery blue dress with tiny red polka dots she had purchased specifically for my graduation, saying these things. Doing these things.

I couldn't.

"What did you do?" I asked.

Denver was full of rumors about Valentine's ability to shrivel the gonads of any underling with one flash of his unnatural green eyes. I had personally overheard Dean Koontz's secretary kibitz with a colleague over the copier about how her husband's cousin—a contractor on one of Valentine's high-rise buildings—had once earned such a look and found out he had colon cancer the following day.

I had thought it the idle talk of simple minds.

Right up until he skewered me with the full force of that gaze and every muscle south of my belly button and north of my knees clenched. My body's natural reaction against Valentine's peculiar power, perhaps?

"I paid her," he said.

"How much?"

"Three hundred thousand dollars. Cash."

It was a good thing Valentine hadn't ordered a drink for me. I would have choked on it.

"Half the amount she was asking for. She'd get the other half when she handed over the information."

"And when was she supposed to do that?"

"An hour ago. That chair you're sitting in? She was supposed to be sitting there. She never showed." Valentine's mouth twisted in an ironic smile. "After you *dropped in* this afternoon and told me she was missing, I thought maybe she just needed to get free of you for a while so she could meet me here without your relentless *interference*. But no." A small, bitter laugh. "She did the same goddamn thing every woman in my life does once they get what they want. She disappeared." He raised his glass to me, half salute, half "up yours," before tipping the remaining contents down his throat.

He clunked the glass hard on the table, a sound that summoned our ever-eager server.

"Another?" she asked. I detected a note of worry creeping into her tone.

Valentine rotated a finger in the air.

My head was a hurricane of thoughts. My mother. Blackmailing Valentine. Disappearing with three hundred thousand dollars of his cash. She couldn't have left town. *Wouldn't* have left town. Not without giving me some kind of clue that she was okay.

This wasn't like her. Any of it. I didn't care what Valentine said. She couldn't have done this on purpose. She couldn't have been planning to skip town this whole time. Pretending to make plans with me for a sushi dinner and a weekend away, knowing she'd never be doing any of it.

She wasn't that good of a liar.

The thought that arrived next dragged with it a blanket of silence that killed every sound in the restaurant.

*Then who taught you?*

The memory was back. Oozing up the pipes, dragging words with it. Images. Sounds. Smells.

Red and blue flashing in the windows.

Banging at the front door.

My nimble mother sliding out the back window.

*Hide, Janey. They can't come in without a warrant. I'll be right back.*

But she hadn't been.

Not that night and not the next.

Two days.

Two days of keeping the blinds closed.

Two days of foraging for food in the fridge and cupboards.

Two nights of sleeping with my face pressed tight to my mother's pillow, holding her in my lungs the way I couldn't hold her in my arms.

She returned like spring. Pale and beautiful, full of apologies if not explanations. Staying away had been the best way to keep me safe.

My loneliness quickly forgotten. Quickly forgiven.

She was everything. She was the whole world.

Valentine cleared his throat, my twelve-year-old and twenty-eight-year-old selves colliding in the present.

I knew by the tectonic shift in his facial features that his date had arrived. Any semblance of sincerity the scotch had lent him was quickly chased away by the sly playboy grin he favored in public appearances.

I quickly stood, not wanting to have to be introduced to whatever small-brained, big-titted slut Valentine was entertaining himself with for the evening. But when I turned to leave the table, I ran straight into Melanie. Fucking. Beidermeyer.

Hadn't Valentine said they'd had lunch earlier? Now dinner too? What next, an engagement party?

I told myself it wasn't jealousy, this fiery poison burning through my veins. Dislike? Sure. Resentment? You bet. Loathing? Hell to the yes.

But jealousy?

Who the hell would've been jealous of Melanie Beidermeyer? Really, I felt sorry for her. With her glossy blonde hair piled into that idiotic doughnut atop her head. And that ridiculous black silk gown clinging to her bony mannequin body. And her glittery evening bag crammed with Daddy's credit cards. And her stupid face with its annoyingly delicate features. And that bizarrely long, smooth neck that had probably never, ever had a knife held to it.

I didn't even understand where she got the guts to come out into public, a mutant like her.

"Why, Jane!" She grabbed me by the elbows and made a smoochy noise toward both sides of my face. "Whatever are you doing here?"

"Just warming this up for you." I patted the seat of the chair where my bare ass had been moments earlier. "And giving my panties to your date," I said under my breath.

Melanie batted her dark eyelashes. "Pardon me?"

"She was just leaving," Valentine said, rising. "You look absolutely lovely, Melanie."

Her head dipped demurely, a gesture I would not have been able to master given a thousand years and an endless supply of Disney princesses for tutors. "Thank you, Rhett."

"Rhett?" I snorted. "Does that make you Scarlett?"

"Rhett is short for Everett," Melanie explained in tones usually reserved for idiot children and small animals.

"You go by your middle name?" I asked Valentine.

"For southern belles, I certainly do."

Melanie's cheeks stained a perfect pink. Which led me to wonder what color they'd turn if I slapped her good and hard.

"Well, I'll leave you lovebirds to your din-din."

"Lovebirds?" Melanie executed a perfectly self-effacing giggle. (Side note: Who the hell even knew giggles could do that shit?) "Goodness, no, sugar. Rhett is just giving me a few pointers. He was telling me over the valedictory lunch today how Gary Dawes is one of his oldest friends." Melanie winked. "How lucky is that?"

*Right,* I thought. *Just like it's lucky that Dean Koontz and your daddy are old golf chums.*

"Oh so lucky!" I said with the forced zeal of a cheerleader on meth. "You two have a good evening. And be sure to use protection," I stage-whispered to Melanie. "You don't know where he's been."

"Miss Avery," Valentine called after me. "I *wonder* when we'll see each other next." He patted his coat pocket for effect.

*Bastard.*

"Oh, you know me, Archie." I shot Valentine a smile as disingenuous and predatory as his own. "You never know where I'll pop up."

"That would be *wonderful*, Miss Avery. Enjoy your walk home. I don't know about you, but there's nothing I like better on a night like this than the feel of cool air against my *bare* skin."

"Thanks for the tip, Archie."

"And Miss Avery? Make sure you *follow* the sidewalks. Wouldn't want you to get *hit*, now, would we?"

This last sounded as much like a threat as I had heard in a long time.

Biologically incapable of allowing anyone else to have the last word, I felt compelled to lob a parting salvo over the fence.

"And just so you know, this ass"—here, I gave my own rear end a solid whack—"earned a four-point-oh despite Dean Koontz doing his best to bury me at every turn. This ass worked three jobs to put itself through law school. This is a tenacious ass. A victorious ass. You would be *lucky* to snort coke from this ass."

By the end of my impassioned speech, all diners within a three-table radius had frozen with forks halfway to their mouths, demi-glace and hollandaise slowly dripping like lazy tears.

Then Valentine said something more shocking than anything he'd come up with yet that evening.

"I know."

# Chapter Ten

If my life had had a theme, it would have been choosing the wrong shoes.

The flat-soled sandals I had thought would enable me to run should the need arise had already given me five separate blisters, and I could feel every one of them by the end of the second block.

I'd been known to say that the only time I ran was if I were being chased, and even then, only if I were being chased by a *Tyrannosaurus rex*. Or by zombies. Or by a zombie riding a *Tyrannosaurus rex*.

Recent events had warranted an amendment to that short list.

*Tyrannosaurus rex*, zombies, or Shepard.

When I exited the restaurant minus a helping of dignity and one pair of skivvies, I saw the man I'd left safely fastened to the shower door barreling down the sidewalk toward me like an enraged bull.

It helped not at all that I now knew Shepard was similarly endowed.

The small lead I had on him wasn't likely to last me long if I didn't get creative in a hurry.

I cut across an open courtyard and darted into the nearest building, one of those vague office/apartment jobs with a secure lobby and decent foot traffic. Putting the large indoor fountain between us, I watched Shepard through the scrim of artificial rain dripping from a bronzed umbrella held aloft by one of the figures at its center.

The proverbial mulberry bush between the monkey—me, definitely—and the weasel, Shepard. Totally Shepard.

He stalked me from side to side, watching my every twitch and hesitation. Employing counter measures seamlessly and without effort.

This was not at all going to plan.

The way I had imagined it, I was going to simply melt into the crowd. Maybe even swipe a hat or scarf to disguise myself and scuttle away with Shepard scratching his head in my nonexistent wake.

The problem with borrowing escape inspiration from *Scooby-Doo* was that the dull-witted monster was always some guy in a suit, and the guy in a suit was more often than not Old Mr. Smithers or something like that. *Not* six feet and then some of tattooed, pissed-off ex-army dude trained to change tank tires with nothing but a socket wrench and the spinal columns of his enemies.

*Think fast, Janey.*

Digging one hand into my bra, I took out Shepard's pistol and tossed it to him, taking off again as soon as his eyes were fastened on the weapon.

Clearly, along with a better cardio routine, Shepard also had far superior reflexes, because my stunt bought me approximately three seconds.

I had barely flung myself through the revolving door when Shepard caught up with me and stopped it cold, trapping me in the glass chamber between entry and exit.

Watching his face through the glass—all flared nostrils and downturned mouth—I felt a flash of sympathy for male silverback gorillas I'd once seen at the San Diego Zoo. All that raw power and masculinity forced to endure the sticky faces of school-age children smashed against the barrier.

No wonder they always looked so testy.

"Can't we just . . . talk about this?" My words were filtered out on puffs of air as I tried to regulate breathing made riotous by the unexpected aerobics.

Shepard was panting too, but something told me his had less to do with cardio exhaustion and more to do with black-brained rage. *"You,"* was all he said.

"Pronoun. A part of speech that takes the place of a noun. See how we're bonding over what brought us together in the first place?"

How often had the fifth-grade creative writing teacher I'd idolized admonished that dogs growl, men talk?

Next time I saw her, I was calling bullshit.

Growl was the only accurate word for the low, threatening rumble emitting from deep in Shepard's chest. "I'm going to strip you naked and cuff you to a fire escape. We'll see how the fuck you like it."

"How is that even fair?" I fought a wiggle of excitement at the prospect. "I cuffed you to a *private* shower."

From the way the fat vein rose in his temple, I surmised this was *not*, in fact, the commendation of my thoughtfulness I had hoped it would be.

"Aren't you supposed to be protecting me?"

"I told P-Ripple I wouldn't let Valentine hurt you." The hot breath from his nostrils fogged the glass between us. "I made no promises about myself."

"Sir. *Sir*, please exit the revolving door." One of the security guards tapped impatiently on the glass with his baton, but jumped back when Shepard turned and bared his teeth.

I used the distraction to throw all my weight against the opposite door, trying to budge it enough to sneak out of a crack onto the street.

And that's when I saw her.

*Her.*

A woman with dark hair peeking out from under a knit cap. Sunglasses shading her striking cheekbones. Solid shoulders inside a gray hoodie. Rounded hips in dark jeans.

I might not have looked twice were it not for the way she *moved*.

A figure out of place among the mindless, milling Saturday-evening bar traffic. Weaving among them like a wolf moves among sheep.

"That's my mother!"

"Nice try," Shepard said.

I slapped my palm hard against the glass. "Shepard, *look!*"

Reading the desperation written plain on my face, he scoped the street over my shoulder.

"Hey! That's your mother."

"I fucking told you!"

Then I was hurtling forward, barely getting my feet under me and tumbling out onto the sidewalk only to be hauled up by my shirt.

"Mom!" I shouted the word with every ounce of desperation I held, which, by this point, was a lot.

The figure only wove through the foot traffic faster, ducking into an alley.

"Come on." Shepard kept a hand at my back as I half jogged, half sprinted to keep from being dragged along at his pace.

We reached the alley's mouth just in time to see a set of sneakers disappear into the open side doors of a white van. The vehicle screeched away fast enough to leave the smell of burned rubber in its wake.

I tried to run after it, but Shepard still had me by the waistband of my skirt, steering me back the way we'd come despite my resistance.

"They took her!" I couldn't stop the words from bubbling out of my mouth. "They took my mother."

Shepard wasn't listening to me. He had his phone out and was barking into it. Street names. Terms I vaguely registered.

"I need a hot pickup on Seventeenth and Lincoln. Tango is a white van, tinted windows, no plates. Headed eastbound toward Coors Field."

"What are you doing?" I demanded, leaping at the end of my brachial tether like a spastic trout. "They're getting away."

Shepard pocketed his phone and spoke in clear, calm tones antithetical to panic. "Jane, listen to me. We'll never catch them on foot, and my car is two blocks in the opposite direction. My partner is around the corner. He's going to pick us up. I have another guy stationed two blocks north with visual confirmation of the van. A lot of shit is about to happen in very short order, and if you're going to be any use to me, I need you to. Calm. Down."

"Okay." A gusty exhale. "Okay. I'm calm. I'm calm."

*Lie.*

The inside of my head felt like an anthill at present. Thoughts swarming down various tunnels, stinging and biting as they vied for position.

What did this mean?

That my mother *hadn't* been kidnapped before, and now she had? That she had escaped her captors only to be captured again? And if she had been free, why hadn't she met with Valentine as scheduled?

Because of me? Because of something I'd done?

I wanted to scream. I wanted to cry. I wanted to fall down in the street and pound the pavement with my fists until the whole fucking world stopped and someone gave me some goddamn answers.

But it didn't seem like any of those courses of action would be available to me, because at that very second, a gray Honda squealed to a stop at the curb.

Shepard hustled me toward it with a grunted, "Get in."

I scrambled into the seat behind the driver and was surprised to see Shepard right on my heels. I had assumed he'd take shotgun, but running around to the front of the car apparently would have required more time than he was willing to spend.

"Go, go, *go!*" he instructed the driver before he even had the door closed after us.

I was still trying to negotiate the back seat, cluttered as it was by the same implements I was used to seeing in my mother's vehicle—duffel bag, camera case, bottled water, a tub of unsalted mixed nuts—when Shepard climbed over me and into the front seat.

Seeing how nimbly he performed this operation made me wonder what else he might be able to do in the limited environs of a car.

"Hey, watch the leather," the driver admonished.

But Shepard didn't seem to hear him as he was already on the phone again. "Professor, you still have visual? What do you mean *no*—fuck! There they are!"

I looked through the windshield just as the white van turned the corner onto Wynkoop three car lengths ahead of us.

"I see them," the driver said.

I wanted to ask his name but figured this might not be the most opportune time, so I contented myself with silently sizing him up.

He favored an aesthetic I'd call *Starsky & Hutch* Chic, which is to say, he looked like the rebellious Italian detective on any number of '70s cop shows. Wavy black hair shot through with silver and long enough to curl at the nape of his neck. Brown leather jacket. Dark jeans. Though I couldn't see his shoes, I'd have bet my best set of brass knuckles they would be cowboy boots.

And he knew how to apply them to the gas too.

"Watch it, D-Town," Shepard said, still keeping the phone to his ear. "This cat's going to screw you at the light."

The Civic cut a sharp diagonal to shoot past a Lincoln town car and straight through a blinding-yellow stoplight.

"D-Town?" I hadn't meant to ask this out loud, but a filter between brain and mouth has never been one of my strong points.

Shocking, I know.

"You can call me Danny B. Only this fool insists on using call signs." He jerked a cleft chin at Shepard, whose knuckles were white from the effort of not grabbing the steering wheel.

I may have been enjoying his distress just a *shade* too much.

"Stay in his blind spot!"

"You telling me my business, *Junior*? Do I need to remind you that if you hadn't fucked up and gotten out of your vehicle, you wouldn't have asked me to pick you up in the first place?"

"That was actually my fault." I raised my hand to indicate ownership of the suboptimal deed.

"How is that your fault?" Danny asked.

"That's not important—"

I ignored Shepard's attempt at interjection, feeling the need to unburden myself to Danny B., who had the kind, compassionate eyes of a priest.

"If I hadn't handcuffed Shepard to the shower door, he wouldn't have been so pissed off. If he weren't so pissed off, he wouldn't have felt the need to chase me down the street."

"Handcuffs?" Danny cut a disapproving look toward Shepard. "What the hell did I tell you about boning clients?"

"Oh, no," I clarified. "It wasn't a sex thing. I just didn't want him following me."

And that's when I discovered one of my new favorite sounds in all the world—Danny B.'s laugh. Loud. Raucous and contagious as all get-out. Back in the days of radio shows, he could have made a mint as "guy busting a gut."

"Let me get this straight," Danny said, wiping a tear from the crinkled corner of his eye with the back of his hand. "*You* managed to smuggle handcuffs into a safe house, cuff Shepard to the shower, and *get away?*"

"Not exactly," I said. "They were Shepard's handcuffs."

This produced a whole new gale of hysterics during which Danny actually slapped his knee.

Meanwhile, Shepard's jaw was demonstrating muscles I didn't even know the average human had. "Just keep your fucking eyes on the van."

Danny sighed as the last wave of mirth ebbed out to sea. "Shepard, my boy, I know what I'm doing. I was following targets while you were still praying for your balls to drop."

"Which is why you drive like my goddamn grandmother," Shepard muttered.

"How are you going to talk about your grandmother like that?" Danny B. looked at his cohort like he wished he had a wooden spoon to thwack him with. "That's so disgraceful."

More mandibular flexing from Shepard.

"Your face is disgraceful," I offered a few seconds too late. "No offense, Danny B. I like your face. I was just trying to help. Shepard doesn't seem to be all that good at this back-and-forth thing."

"None taken."

"What the—" Shepard lurched forward in his seat. "They're turning. Why the fuck are they turning?"

"I'm on it." Danny gunned the Civic's engine as soon as the van cleared the corner, then slammed on the brakes hard enough to clack my teeth together.

A city bus came roaring out from beneath the bridge, slowing only once it had us blocked. The bus driver looked at us a good long while as he passed.

Then he was gone and so was the van.

# Chapter Eleven

There are a few things I know I'm good at.

Lying.

Blow jobs.

Memorizing and regurgitating obscure legal terms.

Before today, I might have been tempted to add swearing to this list. Not anymore.

Shepard had me beat by an order of magnitude.

The man could string together profanities like Louis Comfort Tiffany could string together chandeliers. Lighting up the night with florid, complex configurations that left even the most unflappable of spectators in gap-mouthed awe.

In fact, I can't even repeat half of what he said, because I'm a motherfucking lady.

We'd spent the better part of the evening driving in ever-expanding squares all over downtown in search of the van.

Finally forced to admit defeat, Shepard had blown several gaskets, going as far as to kick a trash can hard enough to evict its guts onto the street.

"I don't even know what you're so upset about. It was *my* mother in that van."

My attempts to hail him from my own berg of frustration were unsurprisingly ignored. I resigned myself to taking a spot next to

D-Town on the stone steps of a nearby office building. It took a minute of doing to fold my legs just so, making sure I wasn't casually flashing passersby.

"He's never not completed a mission successfully." Danny B. clicked his lighter closed and exhaled a cloud of silvery Marlboro smoke into the spring night. In a world where it was damn near mandatory to be gluten free and vegan just to be considered a responsible human being, you had to sort of admire a guy who voluntarily took toxins into his body just for fun. "Of course, to my knowledge, he's never been handcuffed to a shower by someone he was supposed to protect either."

I winced.

"Okay. I probably shouldn't have done that. But he was being a total shitshark. Trapping me in that safe house. Telling me *no* not once, not twice, but *thrice*."

A smile creased one half of Danny's face. "You're Alex's daughter all right."

I felt my heart give an involuntary lurch.

"You know my mom?" Earlier today, this revelation might have banished me deeper into my pocket of dread. Now, recovering bits of information she'd squirreled away from me felt like progress, strange though it may have been.

"*Everyone* knows your mom." He must have heard my jaw unhinge, since he hastily added, "Not in the biblical sense, I mean. In the industry. Not that plenty of guys haven't tried. Not me, of course. I'm an old married guy. But if I wasn't . . . and I should probably just shut my face about now, because if P-Ripple heard me say that he'd be hanging my balls from his rearview mirror."

"He won't hear a peep from me."

We watched as a bicycle-drawn rickshaw whizzed by, bleeding bits of overloud conversation from its inebriated passengers. Giggling girlfriends staggered by arm in arm, supporting each other on towering boots as ill-suited for the evening's pursuits as my sandals had been.

They all looked so hopeful.

So young.

I bet not a single one of them knew how to drive someone's nose into their brain or wire a pipe bomb.

"It's funny," Danny said.

"What is?"

"See that rail over there?"

I glanced across the street to the concrete wheelchair ramp where a handful of skate punks were practicing their various grinds along the metal handrail. "Yeah."

"I once saw a guy tossing his mistress's salad over that rail."

"At least you got proof for the wife. It's better than wondering, I'd say."

"That's the sad part." Danny dragged on his cigarette and blew a perfect smoke ring. "It was an insurance case. He was claiming whiplash from a car accident. His wife wasn't the one who hired me. She didn't even know."

In days past, I might have pitied the woman. Even judged her an unobservant fool. Now I felt her pain acutely. The resonating ache of realizing the person you thought you knew best in the world was, in fact, a stranger.

"Someone should tell that kid to brush his teeth," I said, witnessing one saggy-jeaned unfortunate become physics' bitch. "Because he just ate that rail."

"Point to just about any spot in this city, and I can tell you about a case I've worked there. After a while, the whole city is a memory." Danny stubbed out his cigarette and flicked the butt into a nearby ashtray. "Taco?" He held out a brown paper bag spotted by grease and smelling of heaven.

So we sat on the marble steps, eating tacos beneath the buzzing streetlights. Every now and again, a staccato shrill of distant laughter punctured the night.

Shepard stalked over to us at last, looking no less bulky for the steam he'd jettisoned.

"What's the plan?" Danny crumpled the yellow paper he was holding and dropped it back into the taco bag. We'd slayed about three apiece.

"The plan is, I'm taking Jane back to the safe house, where she will *stay* this time." The look Shepard inflicted upon me could have cut glass. "Then I'm going to check in with P-Ripple and see if he's heard anything."

I'd have much rather stayed at my own place and pestered Paul Gladstone myself, but a warm belly full of tacos disinclined me to argue.

Tacos are good like that.

"What about you?" Shepard asked Danny. "You working tonight?"

"Not me." The illustrious D-Town stood and stretched. "I was on all last night, and there's a nap with my name on it. Call me if you need me."

"Will do, brother."

They did some sort of complicated handshake/back-pat ritual; then we parted ways, heading toward our separate vehicles.

It was slower going for me, blistered and exhausted as I was.

Though I didn't indulge in muttering florid curses with every step, I was certain Shepard heard each sharp intake of breath.

"You want a piggyback?" he offered.

"Pass." Though I knew it to be impossible, I was somehow certain Shepard would be able to feel my naked ladybits against the small of his back.

Now there was a thought powerful enough to distract me from the pain for a good five seconds.

"Do you always have to be so stubborn?"

"Yes," I admitted, heaving a huge sigh of relief when we reached the car.

All I wanted was a bed.

*Lie.*

All I wanted was a bed and my mom.

————

"*Jesus Christ.* Your feet."

Shepard stared at the angry-looking constellation of sores as I limped past him into the bathroom, shoeless and graceless and past caring about either.

"I've had worse," I said.

"I haven't. And I had to break in leather combat boots on a three-day hike in the Iraq desert."

"Army?" It wasn't so much a guess as an attempt at conversation. Though it hadn't been officially confirmed, I'd have wagered my newly acquired doctorate of jurisprudence on it.

He nodded.

"That explains a lot."

"Sit."

Too tired to argue, I plopped down on the closed toilet lid while he riffled through the medicine cabinet for bandages and ointment. Ever the magpie, my eye riveted on the glint of silver protruding from the towel at my feet. I leaned down and picked up what turned out to be the shower door handle.

I allowed myself to dip into a fantasy of Shepard naked and making a screwdriver out of soap or some other MacGyver shit before deciding the bathroom was entirely too small to be entertaining such lines of thought.

"I'm sorry about this," I said, placing the handle on the sink. "That was a dick move on my part."

"Was that an apology?" Shepard turned to me, hands full of boxes and tubes. "Somehow I didn't figure you for the apology type."

"Just because I'm a vexatious nuisance doesn't mean I can't also be self-aware. The two are not mutually exclusive, you know."

"You are a strange human being." He set his wound-dressing accoutrements down on the counter and, as he sank to one knee, I realized with dawning horror what he was planning.

"No!" I insisted, catching him by the obscenely rounded shoulders. "Don't help me. I can do this myself."

"Are you physically incapable of accepting assistance?"

"No. Well, yes. But it's not about that. I've been such a pain in the ass. I can't let you do this for me, or the guilt would crush me."

*Lie.*

"I'm willing to risk it."

He grabbed me behind the knees and scooted me to the edge of the toilet, at which point I both squawked and grabbed a towel from the nearby rack to cover my lap.

"Relax, would you? It's not like I'm gonna look—"

"I'm not wearing any panties!"

The changes in Shepard's face were so subtle, anyone not trained from toddlerhood to read faces might have missed them.

Dilation of pupils. Incremental lowering of brows. Subtle expansion of nostrils. Predatory instincts all and relics of a time when an animal nature was not only useful, but also necessary. The hunt.

I felt each of his eight fingers on the backs of my calves, his thumbs on the outside of my knees. One swift movement, and he could have my legs apart. Knowing this, knowing I couldn't stop him, sent a skittering pleasure from my neck to the base of my spine.

"You went commando to go see Valentine?"

"Of course not."

A measure of tension seemed to ease from Shepard's hulking shoulders.

"I traded him my panties for information."

I'd have given my best pair of stretchy pants to know precisely which emotion caused Shepard's eyes to darken. Anger at my recklessness? Jealousy? Irritation? Some potent mix of all three?

"You *what*?" His fingers dug into my calves in a manner not altogether unpleasant, stiff and sore as they were from the day's misadventures.

"In the limo this afternoon, Valentine claimed my mother was blackmailing him. I wanted to know why. He wouldn't part with the information unless I parted with my panties, so . . . I parted."

Shepard's eyes narrowed at this revelation. "And what did he say?"

I briefly debated whether I should keep what I'd learned to myself, but the earnest concern radiating from the man kneeling before me unraveled what little resistance remained.

The whole transaction summarized surprisingly easily. "Trouble is," I finished, "none of this really helps me, because I still don't know which mistress she was investigating or what client paid her to do it."

"Fuck." Shepard relinquished his grip on my legs and sat back on his heels. My skin felt colder without the borrowed warmth of his fingers.

"My sentiments exactly."

"No." He drove a hand through his sandy hair, causing it to stick up in endearingly disheveled spikes and whorls. "I know who it is. The mistress."

"You do? How?"

"I was helping your mother with daytime surveillance. She needed a point person who could stake out the someone-in-question's place of employment."

I sat there, face tingling like I'd been slapped.

"You've been working with my mother? Why didn't you tell me?" It made no sense, but somehow this felt like even more of a betrayal than finding out my mother had a longtime fuckbuddy. Paul Gladstone, I could almost understand. Everyone had needs. That biological itch that needed scratching.

But how often had she preached the virtues of working alone? How loneliness was a virtue because it meant you were a sovereign creature, self-sufficient and self-governed. How *friend* was just a word for someone who hadn't fucked you over yet.

"It was six months ago," he said. "I didn't think it was related."

"Tell me."

Shepard grabbed the box of bandages and antibiotic ointment and seated himself on the tile floor, his long legs folded one over the other in a pose decidedly yogic. His body loosened when he set to his task, relieved at having something to do with his hands while he talked.

I filed this information away for future use.

"She told me it was for a simple cheating case. The wife had been working late nights, going on extended business trips. We just needed proof that she wasn't where she said she would be. Well, I get set up to watch her and, on the first fucking day, guess whose limo comes to pick my target up for a *long* lunch?"

"Valentine?" I asked, before hissing as a cotton ball soaked with hydrogen peroxide fizzed when it came into contact with the first blister, then the next, and the next. Comfort came in the heat that followed that sting. A sensation my body associated with care.

"Bingo," he said.

With greater tenderness than I would have thought him capable, Shepard peeled open a bandage and smudged the center square with a daub of ointment before applying it to my heel.

He was a man who had dressed many wounds.

"Who was it?" I asked. "The woman my mother asked you to follow?"

"Kristin Flickner."

I blinked at him, stunned. "Not Kristin Flickner of Dawes, Shook, and Flickner?"

"Affirmative."

"But that's the law firm where I interned. I'll be a part-time associate there while I study for the bar. I start back the day after tomorrow."

Shepard, already several steps ahead of me, only nodded. "I imagine that's why your mother took the case. If something was going down in the firm where her daughter was working, she'd want to know about it."

My mind sorted through its limited memories about Kristin Flickner. I had never worked with her directly because, as part of her bid to make partner, she'd been away taking depositions for a major pharmaceutical case the firm had been gearing up for at the time. Flying somewhere different every week, it seemed.

On the few occasions I *had* seen her, I'd not been able to keep myself from staring with a dopey, puppy-eyed wonder. Equally as striking in a pantsuit as she was in jeans and cardigan, Kristin was lovely in the kind of effortless, understated way that made everyone around her seem vulgar by comparison. Hair of burnished copper and eyes a startling green-gold, every pale freckle in the galaxy pinwheeling across her high cheekbones and nose looked like it had been painted by an artist's hand.

It wasn't difficult to see why a husband could become jealous enough to have her followed. Or even a man like Valentine smitten enough to take foolish risks.

"So you think the cheating case was bogus?" I asked. "Did my mother find Kristin because someone had hired her to dig up dirt on Valentine?"

"It's the old chicken-or-the-egg question." Shepard continued to hold my foot in his hand like a little bird. "Whether your mother discovered the whole Valentine angle while following Kristin Flickner or vice versa, it amounts to the same. At some point, she decided to do something about it."

"And you think that *something* is blackmailing Valentine?"

"That I can't say. Alex Avery is a hard woman to read."

"No fucking joke," I said.

"Anyway, after the first day, your mom paid me off and told me she was going a different direction with the investigation. Whatever happened with the Flickner case after that, I don't know."

"Wait a minute!" I sat up straight as the idea hatched in my brain. "I could request Kristin as a mentor!"

"Absolutely not. It's out of the question." Shepard released my foot and looked me directly in the eye. "Whatever else your mother might have been trying to do, it's clear that she didn't want you getting involved."

"And I'll bet P-Ripple didn't want you getting involved with my mother's cases on the sly. Does he know you've been moonlighting?"

Shepard's cheeks colored in a manner both boyish and charming. "No. And he's not *going* to know."

"Provided you tell me anything you find out about Valentine when you talk to P-Ripple."

"Are *you* blackmailing *me* now?"

"Don't think of it as blackmail," I said. "Think of it as incentive to participate in a mutually beneficial exchange of information."

"If we're talking mutually beneficial, I think you owe me something in exchange for handcuffing me to the shower." Shepard's fingers tightened around my ankle. "I showed you mine."

I swallowed around what felt like a gumball of broken glass. "Technically, you didn't *show* me anything. Incidental nudity revealed in the course of an otherwise unrelated operation doesn't guarantee *animus contrahendi*, i.e., an intent to enter into a contract that might obligate me to reciprocate."

"I myself have always liked the sound of *quid pro quo*, i.e., tit for tat. And you've seen my tat."

About this, he was correct. His tat *and* his tats.

"What we have here is an unintentional exchange inter vivos. I *happened* to be looking into the bathroom, and you *happened* to be naked where I was looking." I was picking up steam now and adrenaline too. This had always been my favorite part. The bit when someone is rolling without brakes right into the trap they didn't even know I had prepared for them.

"But I *happened* to be naked because you threw up on me."

"And I *happened* to throw up because you drove like a maniac, thereby resulting in your need to take a shower and your subsequent nudity."

Shepard exhaled a disgusted sigh and dragged himself to standing with the aid of the sink. "Jane Avery, you *happen* to be fucking exhausting."

"It's better that you're learning this now. It'll save us trouble in the future." I helped myself up with the towel rack, testing my bandaged feet. They felt significantly better already. "Thanks for the first aid."

"An apology and a thank-you in a fifteen-minute period. Slow down, Avery, I might just swoon."

I found I liked him calling me Avery. It made me feel like part of some team I hadn't known I wanted to belong to. "Yeah, well don't get used to it. I'm still on a taco high."

"And here I thought that thing about the quickest way to someone's heart being through their stomach was just an expression."

"Actually, the quickest way to anyone's heart is between the ribs. Unless you have a seriously sharp blade, in which case—" Seeing the piqued look on Shepard's face, I thought better of finishing my sentence. "Never mind."

"I'm going to pretend I didn't hear that."

"Good call."

I followed him to the living room, where he armed the security system with his back turned to me.

"I don't suppose I have to tell you that I have guys stationed at every exit, so you might want to consider not taking off again."

"I figured as much." And I had. I also figured I'd spend what remained of the evening on my laptop, mining the interwebs for dirt on Kristin Flickner and Archard Everett Valentine.

He paused, turning around to face me. "That's what you did wrong, you know."

"Excuse me?" I could already feel my eyes begin to narrow at the unwelcome proximity of the words *you* and *wrong* in the same sentence.

"When you ran from me. You were doing okay until you ducked into that building. Never enter a building without knowing all the exits first."

I forced a, "Good to know," through gritted teeth.

"I'll be back tomorrow morning. If you need anything before then, you have my cell."

"Do I? I don't remember you giving it to me."

"Check your duffel bag." He grinned as he shut the door behind him.

Oh, I did *not* like the sound of this.

On feet tentative from emotional and physical discomfort, I padded into the bedroom and knelt down next to my duffel bag.

Only it wasn't my duffel bag.

Or it was, but the contents I'd hastily packed had been swapped for a pile of plain black T-shirts and boxer briefs. Shepard's spare clothes.

I pawed to the bottom, already having a decent idea what I would find.

Handcuffs.

Handcuffs and a note.

On one side, Shepard's number. On the other, two words.

*Your turn.*

# Chapter Twelve

I wondered how far I could get the pen up Melanie Beidermeyer's nose before anyone could stop me.

This wasn't a new thing for me, fantasizing about injuring Melanie in some fantastic way. What *was* new was the setting—the cavernous executive boardroom at Dawes, Shook, and Flickner.

In the past, it had been in the lecture hall (decapitation by encyclopedia), or at study group (suffocation via cheese pizza slice), or at the holiday get-together at my favorite professor's home (a mistletoe shank to the jugular). All richly provoked, I would have assured you.

As was my current homicidal daydream.

Over the course of the breakfast meet and greet with all the associates and partners both junior and senior, Melanie had managed to mention (*a*) my taking a leather folder to the eye during graduation, (*b*) her date with Valentine, (*c*) my missing mother—a fact I was pretty sure had come to her from item Valentine—(*d*) her new Hermes bag, and (*e*) my taking a folder to the eye during graduation. Apparently the story got enough laughs the first time to bear repeating.

Not only this, but Melanie had somehow welded herself to Kristin Flickner's elbow. Asking her thoughtfully sycophantic questions about her recent promotion to partner. "Discovering" that they shared a hairstylist, a masseuse, and a penchant for Bentleys. Complimenting her on her Antonio Melani suit and heels even though the skirt/blouse combo

Melanie wore probably cost twice as much and had most likely been hand-tailored by an army of child laborers housed in the capacious Beidermeyer basement.

Fueled by terrible coffee and stale bagels, I'd shuffled around the room, offering myself up like an hors d'oeuvre to any and every potential conversational partner but especially those whose proximity made it possible to eavesdrop on what Melanie and Kristin were saying.

Which is how I ended up in front of the bulging belly of Gary Dawes, who had never, not in the entire three months I had worked as a summer associate at the law firm *he* founded, managed to get my name right. And maybe I was off base here, but I felt I had extra cause to be insulted because my name was so damn common, it was literally the default moniker given to unidentified corpses.

Side note: thanks, Mom.

"Jennifer!" He pumped my hand up and down in his moist, fat palm. "Are you settling in okay?"

"Fine, sir," I said. "And thank you for asking."

"I sure am glad to have you aboard, Jennifer. Valedictorian of your class. I know you'll be a real credit to our firm."

"I was the salutatorian," I said, noticing just how much Dawes's nose, with its long, downturned tip and high-set round nostrils, resembled a penis.

"That's right, that's right. It's Melanie I'm thinking of." He glanced across the room, and he and the blonde show pony in question exchanged a nauseatingly fond little wave. "Still, if you have to come in second place to someone, you could do worse than Melanie Beidermeyer. Am I right?"

"Right you are, sir!" I gave him my biggest, toothiest smile. "In fact, it was such a pleasure losing to her that I wish she'd beaten me by three points instead of three-tenths of a point!"

Dawes waggled a Polish-sausage finger at me. "Valentine warned me about that rapier wit of yours."

"He did?" I felt my face go all hot and flushed despite my best efforts to affect a tone of abject disinterest. "What did he say?"

"Just that you were the sharpest woman he'd met in some time. A real 'wonder,' if I remember correctly. That we ought to make sure someone else didn't 'lasso you up' before you passed the bar exam."

*That son of a bitch.*

"Well, I'm mighty flattered that he saw fit to call you up just to chat about me," I said, sipping the last dregs of my terrible coffee.

"I'm afraid he didn't." Dawes gave me a pitying smile. "We were actually talking about Melanie, and Valentine mentioned he'd run into you at the same restaurant where they met for dinner."

"Oh." There was really no polite way to say, *Level with me, Cocknose: Did Valentine tell you about the panties or what?* So I went with the more mild but less specific, "Is that . . . *all* he mentioned about me?"

"Actually, no."

In the time it took him to take a bite of bagel—heaped with a small avalanche of cream cheese—chew it, and swallow, I'd managed to have a panic attack and a minor cardiac incident.

"He also recommended that you not be paired with Kristin Flickner as a mentor."

"What? Why?"

"Something to do with a clash of personalities. He has remarkable instincts."

"But he's not even a lawyer," I protested.

"Precisely." Dawes poked a finger in the air triumphantly. "That's why I asked his opinion. I often find it helpful to get an outside party's perspective when assigning mentorships."

"Listen, before you arrive at a final decision, can I at least make my case for whom I'd prefer to be assigned to?" Of course, "my case" was mostly a giant pack of lies that conveniently made Kristin Flickner the only logical choice, but Dawes didn't necessarily need to know this.

Dawes's eyebrows shaded his watery-blue eyes. "I'm sorry, Jennifer. But if you had a specific preference, you should have made it known via the mentorship paperwork. We certainly would have taken that into consideration."

"Mentorship paperwork? What mentorship paperwork?"

A fleshy crease appeared between Dawes's thick brows. "You should have received it several weeks ago. Judy sent it to the address on file."

And then I understood exactly what happened.

*Judy.*

The firm's legal assistant/receptionist/desk troll. Somewhere between a hard-worn forty or a very young sixty-five, Judy's hobbies included scowling, knitting, and misplacing documents I'd left with her to copy. She also had this cute habit of double-booking me for appointments and writing down the wrong numbers on my phone messages.

"I never received any mentorship paperwork," I said.

"I apologize for the oversight, Jennifer, but mentorship assignments have already been proposed and accepted for the remainder of the quarter. Of course, if you're dissatisfied with your assignment for any reason, we can always consider a change for the next quarter."

"When do I find out who I've been assigned to?"

"You mean you didn't receive a call from Judy about that either?"

"No. I didn't."

"Very odd," Dawes said. "She must have misplaced your number. Anyway, you've been assigned to Sam Shook. Valentine seemed to think you'd have a lot to learn from him. Just as he thought Melanie could learn a lot from Kristin Flickner."

"Wait. *Melanie Beidermeyer* is shadowing Kristin Flickner?"

"And a good decision it was too. They seem to be getting along famously."

We both glanced across the room, where Melanie was treating Kristin to a girly giggle while clutching her forearm like an old friend.

"Yeah," I said. "Famously."

"Well, I'd better be getting back to my office. You be sure and let me know if there's anything at all I can do for you, Jennifer."

I snagged him by the Armani suit sleeve before he could slide away. "Would you mind if I asked you what in particular made Valentine think I'd be a good match for Sam Shook? I mean, it's nothing personal, but I guess I was hoping for someone a little more . . . dynamic."

"Dynamic *how*?" Dawes asked.

"You know. Someone ambitious. Someone charismatic. Someone—" It was Dawes's smile that tipped me off. That, and the sound of someone clearing his throat right above my shoulder. "Who's not standing right behind me."

Fuckola.

"If you'll excuse me, I think I'll just leave you two to get better acquainted." Dawes grinned, revealing enough poppy seeds in his teeth to plant an entire field. A fact I chose not to mention just like he'd chosen not mention that Sam Shook had been hovering over my shoulder. Dawes turned to leave. "Good to see you, Sam."

"Good to see you too, Gary." His voice was melodic. Lilting. Ever so slightly accented. The *r* becoming a soft, silky *d* the way Shook pronounced it. English may not have been his first language, but I had a feeling he'd speak it far better than I did.

"Miss Avery, would you care to accompany me to my office?"

I took my time setting down my bagel plate, delaying the moment when I had to face Shook as long as humanly possible. Not that an extra ten seconds was likely to arm me with the right crowbar of words to extract my own foot from my esophagus, but hey. Every little bit would help.

I turned.

I smiled.

I died a little.

Shook was sort of beautiful.

And by "sort of" I meant ridiculously, devastatingly, insanely, and pretty much any other adverb which at any point had been used to describe the degree of a romance-novel hero's retina-scorching comeliness.

What he lacked in Shepard's rugged masculinity and Valentine's gritty danger, he made up for in finely calibrated allure. Dark, intelligent eyes. The skin below them ever so slightly darker than the rest of his face, which borrowed the color of milky tea with honey. His fine, straight nose brought to mind words like *aquiline* and *patrician*. Worst of all, a sweet, sensitive smile. Rightly, he should be giving me a thorough stink eye for what I'd just said.

"Of course." I nodded with the enthusiasm of a bobblehead doll.

I followed him out of the conference room and down the richly wood-paneled hall, fascinated by the way he walked. Silently, and with infinite grace. More like a ninja than a lawyer.

In the small corner office, he closed the door behind us and gestured to one of the armchairs across from his desk.

"Please. Make yourself comfortable." He shrugged out of his blazer and hung it on a hook on the back of his door. "Would you care for some coffee?" The long, slender vessel in his hand gleamed like an outsize bullet.

"No, thank you. I'm good," I said, the taste and texture of bitter coffee grounds still fresh in my memory.

"Are you certain?" Steam curled from the thermos's mouth as he decanted the contents into a coffee mug. A mug I couldn't help but notice had a handle like the butt of an AK-47 and the *Walking Dead* logo emblazoned on one side.

"I bring this from home. I find myself unable to drink what is provided at the community urn."

"In that case, I'd love some."

"Splendid." Shook retrieved a Styrofoam cup from the water cooler next to the file cabinet and shared it out.

"Thank you." I blew on the steaming liquid while examining the many, many framed diplomas wallpapering Sam Shook's office.

His name, as it turned out, wasn't Sam Shook at all, but Sahem Ashook, and he had not only a JD, but a PhD in psychology, a master's in applied physics, and a couple of bachelor's degrees in art history and the humanities. Just for fun, I guessed.

"You don't have to lie, you know," Shook said.

As openers go, this one was enough to drain the blood from my face like water flushed from a toilet.

Clearly we had a lot to learn about each other.

"What I mean is," he continued, "it's all right that you would have preferred Kristin to mentor you. She's an excellent lawyer with experience in areas that might be of greater interest to you than mine."

Shook had clearly spent time coaching all traces of an accent from his voice, and had succeeded, but for the subtle caress of tongue against palate when it came to his *r*'s.

"No, it's not that—"

He raised one dark eyebrow, and suddenly I found myself saying, "Okay, it is that. But it's nothing personal. At least, nothing personal to do with you."

Why the shit was I telling him this?

I began to wonder if this eyebrow thing was some kind of East Indian Jedi mind trick that rendered me incapable of lying.

Me, incapable of lying. Now there was a horrifying thought.

"You don't owe me any explanations, Miss Avery."

"Please, call me Jane." Because Miss Avery usually meant I was about to be on the receiving end of a lecture.

"You don't owe me any explanations, *Jane*. Nevertheless, I did agree to be your mentor, and I do think our partnership could be beneficial to you."

"So does Archard Everett Valentine, apparently. Don't tell me you're his best buddy as well."

"On the contrary." Sam matched the tips of his long, elegant fingers below his chin. "I'm his divorce lawyer."

# Chapter Thirteen

The sound of a needle scratching violently off a record echoed in my mind. "Mr. Shook—"

"If I am to call you Jane, you must call me Sam."

"Sam, when I was looking at potential law firms to apply to for internships last year, I specifically chose Dawes, Shook, and Flickner because it *didn't* handle divorces."

"Normally this is true. But as a relatively new partner, it is in my best interest to do whatever Gary Dawes would like me to do, and as you mentioned, Gary is close friends with Valentine."

"But Kristin Flickner is an even newer partner than you are. Do you mind if I ask why it is *you* ended up with this particular honor?"

"I practiced divorce law for a time before I left Chennai." He took a long sip from the zombie mug, consulting the bottom like he might be reading coffee grounds instead of tea leaves. "Also Kristin declined to represent him based on a conflict of interest." Despite the pause, Shook's face gave no indication he knew that the "interest" in question was Valentine pouring Kristin the pork.

Within the pocket of my *not* Antonio Melani blazer, my cell phone announced I had a text message. I quickly pulled it out and glanced at it, a little pop of adrenaline sizzling through my nerves when I saw Shepard's name on the screen.

**What the fuck are u doing in Shook's office? U were supposed to text me before u left the conference room.**

Shit.

Yesterday—a long, newsless Sunday I'd spent utterly alone in Shepard's safe house apartment—he'd called me to work out an elaborate code that would allow him to track my every move while I was inside the building. I was supposed to text him any time I changed location in the office. Naturally I'd managed to cock it up already. My question—how the hell did he know I wasn't still in the conference room?

**How the hell did you know I wasn't still in the conference room?**

"We can always talk later if you are otherwise engaged."

"What?" I glanced up to see Sam looking at my phone, his head inclined at a patient angle that filled me with instant guilt. "No. I just got a message from my building super about a potential invasion of naked mole rats in the basement." *Lie.* "I hear it's been an ugly one so far. Valentine's divorce." Not that I expected Sam to part with much information, but I figured a little nudge couldn't hurt.

"In that, you are correct." Sam smiled solicitously as my phone buzzed again in my lap.

I glanced down.

**I can see u.**

Now, there were several problems with this revelation, not even counting his insistence on abbreviating the word *you*.

The first: Sam Shook's office was on the fifth floor of the building, meaning there was no way Shepard could be watching us from the street. The second: the office's only window faced the building opposite across a two-way, six-lane main drag—too far away for me to make anyone or anything out with the naked eye. Which led me to problem number three: Shepard had to be watching me through some sort of high-powered scope. This thought should have been more alarming than it was erotic.

*Should have.*

A third text message arrived as I was composing a hurried reply.

Nice blouse. New?

I leaned an elbow on Sam's desk and conspicuously scratched my hair with my middle finger.

Fucker.

He knew damn well I'd had to rely on the new set of clothes dropped off by one of his random, black-clothed minions to replace the stuff he'd swiped from my duffel bag.

What had he given me?

A tight black pencil skirt and a blouse on which I had to leave the top two buttons undone lest my boobs bust them open Hulk Hogan–style. Also—and this was the thing that really chafed my cheeks—orthopedic flats. The kind worn exclusively by schoolteachers and church ladies with wicked corns.

"Are you certain you wouldn't like to talk another time? You seem most preoccupied."

"I apologize. It's been a stressful weekend." I took another swig of coffee and set my phone facedown on the desk. "About Valentine, though. I've only met the guy twice, but he seems like a piece of work."

Somewhere deep inside my brain, a little voice pointed out that on both occasions, my own behavior hadn't exactly been nonprovoking. What with the kidnapping and the cocktail crashing. So like any reasonable adult, I mentally duct-taped the little voice's mouth shut.

"And what makes you say this?" Sam asked.

"He hates orphans. He said so himself."

*Big, fat lie.*

And not even a good one. But better than admitting Valentine had asked for my panties, or worse, that I had ponied them up.

"Luckily, his feelings with regard to parentless children are not a prominent factor in these divorce proceedings."

*Bzzz.*

"I'm so sorry," I said. "Let me just turn this off." I picked up the phone and peeked at the text message.

Calling it now. Five years and homeboy's going to be bald on top.

How can you even know that? I hastily typed back.

Shepard's response pinged back instantly.

No way could I get a headshot in with that glare.

Headshot.

I hadn't asked specifically what Shepard had done in the army, and now I felt quite certain I didn't want to know.

Sniper. Try as I might, I couldn't put the word back on the shelf now that it had tumbled into my brain. I made a show of turning the phone off and putting it back in my pocket. "I imagine the whole nose candy and whore thing is a factor."

"You mustn't believe everything you read in the tabloids, Jane." Sam gave me a gently censorious look.

And as he said this, I knew why I had brought the extracurricular activities up.

Because I didn't believe them.

Despite Valentine's hammered-shit appearance and postured bad-boy aura, there was something about him that didn't gel with the whole paid-sex-and-stimulants vibe. Not class, exactly, but something deeper. Something darker and profoundly mysterious.

"Whatever else may be said about Valentine, he is startlingly generous." Sam toyed with a sleek black pen that probably cost more than my entire outfit, dexterously twirling it down his fingers like a baton.

"Oh?" I lobbed the single syllable over the desk like a shuttlecock, waiting to see if he'd swing.

Whether Sam knew it or not, this was a formative moment in our relationship. One where I got to determine how much information he was willing to part with, and how hard I'd have to work for it. When he leaned in with a sly, conspiratorial little smile, I nearly crushed my Styrofoam cup in the effort of not doing a spontaneous tap dance complete with jazz hands.

Sahem Ashook liked to gossip.

"He offered a complete fifty-fifty split of the financial and physical assets in addition to alimony and ownership of their summer home in Seattle and the Denver penthouse apartment. But his soon-to-be ex-wife believes she is entitled to roughly seventy-five percent of the monetary assets as well as sole ownership of the physical assets and all property accrued during the marriage as compensation for Valentine's alleged mental cruelty and verbal abuse."

Never was there a lawyer born who didn't pronounce the word *alleged* with special fondness.

"You sure as hell have your work cut out for you on this one."

"We have our work cut out for us. I thought you might assist me in deposing Mr. Valentine's character witnesses today."

I sat up in my chair like an Airedale catching the scent of fox musk. The day had become a hell of a lot more interesting all of the sudden.

"I'd be happy to assist," I said.

"Splendid. If you would be kind enough to meet me in the Woodshed at a quarter till ten, we'll go over who we're expecting and their relationship to Valentine before the first one arrives."

"The Woodshed?"

"This is the nickname I gave to the small conference room next to Dawes's office. He likes to avail himself of it for the many 'motivational one-on-ones' I seem to have a talent for earning."

"Sahem Ashook," I said, reaching across the desk to shake his hand, "I think we're going to get along just fine."

His grip was strong and warm from his coffee cup but not as smooth as I'd expected it to be. It left me wondering if he might also be a master carpenter in addition to all the various and sundry specialties declared by the paper on his walls.

"Jane Avery, I believe you are correct."

———

I had begun to think of them as the Not-So-Magnificent Six.

The Prostitute. The Burglar. The Gardener. The Cook. The Teacher. The Therapist.

Valentine's very own wildly dysfunctional Justice League of character witnesses, and each one of them more disastrous than the last.

By the fifth witness in, Sam looked like he wanted to throw himself out the window. Luckily for him and for me, there *were* no windows. That this setup drove Shepard certifiably batshit crazy was just an added bonus.

My self-declared bodyguard had insisted that I reschedule the meeting for somewhere he could keep an eye on me, but I politely declined. Politely meant suggesting several ways in which he could apply his donkey dick to his own person.

He'd responded by checking in with me approximately seventy-two times while I sat through interview after interview, frantically noting down things about Valentine that proved as interesting to me as they were useless to Sam.

For example:

From Rhonda Betts (bleached blonde, sooty eyed), lifelong working girl: "Abusive? Hell naw. I mean, he liked to do butt stuff sometimes, but he paid extra for that."

Here, Sam had shot his cuffs and rolled his sleeves to the elbow.

From Jeremy Blivens (balding, rat faced), childhood friend of Valentine and repeat guest of the state penitentiary: "When we was kids, Val was the most honest thief I ever met. Anytime we were gearing up for a job, he was always the guy that tried to get in without busting a window. Destroy as little property as possible. Thoughtful guy, right?"

Here, Sam had loosened the knot on his tie and unbuttoned his collar.

From Jarek Kozlowski (whiskey bloomed, sun leathered), Valentine's former topiary shaper and lawn mower: "Anytime he asks me to dig six-foot-deep hole on property, he gives me big tip."

Also from Rhonda, who came back for her purse: "Yeah, he always gave *me* his big tip too."

Here, Sam tore the top page off his legal pad and shot it into the trash. "Please strike that from the notes, Jane."

From me. "Sure thing."

From Phillip Billinghurst (apple cheeked, sweaty necked), Valentine's personal chef: "Well, of course he joked about poisoning his wife's soufflé, but who hasn't?"

Things started looking up around the time Mrs. Lickleider, Valentine's gray-haired, bespectacled eighth-grade teacher, primly perched in the hot seat.

"Little Archie was the best student I ever had. He'd stay after school every day to bang out the erasers." Here, Sam had sat forward in his seat, looking hopeful, only to have his face avalanche seconds later when she added, "And then he'd bang *me* in the coat closet."

As soon as the door was closed behind her, Sam dropped his pen on his yellow legal pad and commenced rhythmically thumping his forehead on the table.

Like, for real.

"Hey," I said, laying a hand on his shoulder. "Ease up there, fella. You're going to give yourself a concussion."

A round pink spot bloomed above his eyebrows when he turned his face to me. I did my best to squelch the errant smile threatening to hijack my face.

"We are screwed!" Sam's accent became thicker when he was angry, the diction of his country of origin more pronounced in the *w* turned *v* of *we*.

"Come on." I patted the flat of his back between his shoulder blades, trying not to notice the roller coaster of lean muscle my palm was currently riding. "It's not that bad. At least they all had something nice to say about him."

"Not that bad?" he repeated. "*Not that bad?* This is easily the least beneficial list of individuals that ever I have deposed. And these are the people who like him!"

"How about some tea?" I offered. "I think that's just the thing we need here." I had just begun to push my chair back from the desk when there was a knock on the conference room door.

"Come in," Sam said, the invitation mostly muffled by the table his face was pressed against.

The door opened to reveal a tall, slender woman in a sleek pin-striped skirt and blazer, her chestnut hair neatly tucked into a doughnut bun at the crown of her head.

"Sam Shook?" she asked through velvet-red lips. "The receptionist said I could find you back here."

Apparently I wasn't the only one for whom the infamous Judy harbored a grudge. Anyone else and she would have dialed into the intercom to *ask* if we were available for a visitor and perhaps even to give the visitor's name.

"Yes," Sam confirmed. His unfailingly polite, "How may I help you?" was a stark contrast to the *What do you want?* I would have given in his position. Noticing this contrast made me feel shabby somehow. Petty and ill-bred.

*Would it kill me to be more pleasant?* I asked myself.

*Probably,* I answered promptly.

"My name is Carla Malfi. I'm . . . well, I heard you might be in need of character witnesses for Archard Everett Valentine?"

Sam perked up, nimble fingers searching out his discarded pen. "Yes, in fact I am. Please have a seat, Miss Malfi."

"Call me Carla." She crossed the room with the grace of a panther, seating herself next to me and opposite Sam. When she crossed one shapely leg over the other and I felt a sudden surge of dislike, I knew.

Valentine had banged her too.

"I am Sam Shook, and this is my colleague, Jane Avery."

A shadow passed over Carla's face.

"You say Valentine sent you?" Sam asked, turning over a new page on his legal pad.

"No." She looked down at her hands. The cuticles had been bitten down to the quick. "Alex Avery did."

# Chapter Fourteen

"Jane? *Jane?*"

Sam's infinitely calm voice hailed me from some upper stratosphere.

I didn't know how long I had been fugued out or what I might have said or done aside from lasering a hole through the table with my unblinking gaze.

"Jane, are you all right?" He gave my shoulder a reassuring squeeze.

"Yes," I said. "I'm okay. I just got a little dizzy there for a moment." I turned my gaze to Carla Malfi, who was doing her best to gnaw her fingernails down to nubs. "Did you say that Alex Avery sent you?"

She nodded. "That's correct. Any relation?"

This question relieved me as much as it terrified me. Relief: Carla had obviously never met my mother face-to-face, because if she had, she would have *known* I was her daughter. Not just from the near-identical dark-haired, light-eyed coloring, but from the bones she had grown in my face. Terror: I'd have to perpetuate a major whopper to Sam Shook, who would promptly boot me from the interview, if not from the law office, if he knew.

"Nope. No relation." *Lie.*

Sam and I exchanged a glance, wherein permission for me to proceed was asked and granted. When he indicated my laptop in silent question, offering to take over the notes, I shook my head no. Not because I had some burning need to control what was written, but because in addition to getting down key facts about the witnesses, I had amused myself by trying to decide what I would name an eye shadow color based on Sam's entrancing eyes.

Lusty Mink was the top contender.

"Maybe you could begin by telling us exactly what your relationship is to Archard Everett Valentine," I suggested.

"I'm Valentine's therapist." The overhead lights rimmed her filling eyes with fluorescent crescents. "And his mistress."

Oh, snap.

Kristin Flickner, and now Carla Malfi. Valentine had something of a "professional women of Denver" collection going on.

"Okay. We'll come back to that," I said, employing my least judgmental tone of voice. "But first, I'd just like to clarify. When you say that Alex Avery sent you, you're referring to Alex Avery the private investigator, correct?"

Surprise lifted Carla's and Sam's eyebrows in concert, both sets of which, I had to note, were uncommonly well groomed above eyes both pretty and deeply tired.

"How did you know she's a private investigator?" Carla asked.

"Her name pops up whenever I google myself." *Not* a lie. My mom figured out the whole Google-ad words thing when the fusty, hard-boiled good ol' boys common to her profession were still paying for space in the Yellow Pages and engineering terrible cable TV commercials. "When did you speak to Alex Avery?"

"A couple of days ago."

Logically I had known she wasn't going to say something like, *Why only five minutes ago! In fact, she's just in the waiting room if you'd like to go say hello.* But still, my silly heart ached all the same.

"And how do you know her?"

"I don't. Not really."

"I'm afraid I don't understand," I said.

One tear escaped the well of her lower lid and slipped down her cheek. Sam nudged the box of tissues from the center of the conference table over to her.

Carla snagged one and dabbed her eyes.

"Would you care for anything?" Compassion softened Sam's gaze to melted chocolate. And we were talking the quality 86-percent-cacao shit. "Water? Tea?"

"Tea would be nice."

Sam pressed the button on the intercom. Judy's postmenopausal-excess-of-testosterone-deep voice came over the line.

"What is it?"

"Yes, good afternoon, Judy. Could you bring a cup of tea into conference room B, please?" Sam asked, polite as fuck.

"Can't," she snapped. "Too busy." The line went dead.

"It's okay, really," Carla said, embarrassment for us both plain on her face.

"I'll get it," I offered.

"Nonsense," Sam insisted. "You continue. I'll get the tea. Cream or sugar?" he asked Carla.

"No, thank you," she said.

"Okay." He beamed a reassuring smile at her. Lord, but that man was good with the smiles. "I'll be right back."

I watched in wonder as Sam slipped out of the room. A full-on partner getting someone tea so *I* could continue an interview?

"Right," I said, glancing at my notes. "You were telling me how you came into contact with Alex Avery."

Carla tucked the wadded tissue into the pocket of her blazer. "Two days ago, she called my office and introduced herself, then proceeded to make it clear that if I didn't come forward about my *relationship* with Valentine, she'd expose us both. I could lose my license."

"I see."

That Valentine had been plowing every available field didn't surprise me. But that my mother had felt it necessary to bully Carla Malfi into telling Valentine's divorce lawyer about it? There was no scenario in which this made sense to me. She'd always been a "bang and let bang" sort of woman, often insisting that what people wanted to do behind bedroom/closet/car doors was entirely their business.

"Tell me, Carla, when did you begin seeing Mr. Valentine?"

"Seeing?" she asked, pausing to daintily honk her nose into a new tissue. "Or *seeing*?"

"Either," I said. "Or both."

"He was assigned to me two years ago. He was my client for six months before . . . before the relationship turned intimate."

My brain fastened to one word in particular.

*Assigned.*

Assigned meant ordered by a judge. Ordered by a judge meant court records. Court records that I would have access to as an associate at good old Dawes, Shook, and Flickner, thankyouverymuch.

"And for what reason was he assigned to you?" I asked.

"Anger management."

*Yes,* I thought. That sounded about right. I'd seen flashes of it in the back of his limo. Across the table in the restaurant. That ever-present, hot-blue flame dancing just below the carefully contrived mask of control. Eyes behind which loose wires whipped and sparked like electric snakes.

"But it soon became my professional opinion that Valentine did not have an anger management problem."

"What brought you to this conclusion?"

"Shortly after Valentine began seeing me *professionally*, his wife, Miranda, insisted on coming to see me too. Of course, I had my reservations, but I thought perhaps if I worked with them separately, they might be able to transition to couples therapy at some point." She

135

sniffled and dabbed her nose. "But after several sessions with Miranda, I came to the conclusion that she was a serial manipulator the likes of which I'd never seen in my fifteen years as a therapist."

I glanced up from my keyboard to examine Carla's heart-shaped face more closely. Partially because I wanted to decide if she was lovelorn enough to be delusional regarding the quality of Valentine's character, and partially because she didn't seem old enough to have been practicing that long. In either case, I never would have credited Valentine of dallying with anyone remotely close to his own age, which I put somewhere between thirty-five and "will never not be hot."

I knew firsthand how charismatic Valentine could be. Women lied for men with far less to offer.

"So you think Miranda lied about the abuse?"

"I do," she said.

"What reason would she have to do that?"

"Money. Power. Attention. Take your pick. I'm sure you've seen how she's trying to smear him in the press."

"I have." I had just assumed the allegations were true.

The door squeaked open, and Sam deposited two steaming cups on the table. One before Carla, and one before me.

"I thought you might like some as well."

"That was very thoughtful of you." I picked up the cup and blew on the tendrils of swirling, bergamot-scented Earl Grey steam. "Thank you."

Polite as fuck *and* thoughtful. Damned if I didn't look like a goddamn slouch by comparison.

"So you came to believe that Miranda was lying about the allegations against her husband." The prompt was designed not only to get Carla talking but also to bring Sam up to speed.

"Yes," she said. "The more I learned about Valentine, the more I grew to admire him. Eventually, that admiration grew beyond the bounds of a simple therapist/client relationship and into something more."

*More* like banging on the leather couch in her office.

"Was it you or Valentine who initiated *contact?*"

"Me," she admitted. "He was never anything but respectful." Her eyes went all sly, her lashes lowering over her caramel irises. "Well, except for the time when he asked for my panties."

"You too?"

Carla and Sam both swiveled to look at me.

I took the longest sip of tea in the history of the universe while my brain scrambled for recovery.

"What I meant was, did *you two* begin your relationship on the occasion that he asked for your panties? Or was it a different time?"

"A different time. I did *try* to maintain some semblance of propriety in the beginning."

"Did you give them to him?"

Carla blinked, clearly piqued by my priorities. "Pardon me?"

"Your panties. Did you give them to Valentine?"

By this point, Sam was also looking at me like I was out of my mind. And maybe I was.

Otherwise, why the hell would it smart so much that this panty thing was a serial habit with Valentine? Had I honestly believed there was something special about me in particular that would make a man like Archard Everett Valentine covet my underthings?

"Not on that occasion, no."

"But on a different occasion?" I pressed.

"Yes," she admitted. "It was during a particularly difficult phase of his marriage, and I wanted to establish trust—"

"Did Valentine ever tell you why he'd asked for your panties—ouch!"

I leaned down to rub at the spot on my shin Sam had not-so-gently nudged with the hard square toe of his dress shoe. Apparently he didn't approve of this line of questioning.

"No, but I assumed—"

"Thank you for sharing with us so candidly, Carla," Sam interrupted. "I think that is all the information we need for now. May we reach out to you if we have any additional questions?"

"Of course." She rose and shook his hand, then mine. As soon as the conference room door closed, Sam turned to me.

"Would you like to tell me what that was about?"

Uh-oh. The *v-w* had returned.

"Not especially," I said.

"I don't mean to tell you what to do, but in my experience, you must be very careful when interviewing potential character witnesses, especially when you rival them in terms of position and power. If you want to get them to open up, you must prevent the conversation from becoming adversarial."

*Adversarial.*

The lightning bolt of an idea flashed through my head. "Sorry," I said, jumping up from my chair. "I'll be right back."

I caught up to Carla in the hallway just down from Judy's desk. It was risky, what I was about to do, but all I could think about was the answer on the other side.

"Hey, can I ask you something? Strictly off the record."

She shifted on her heels, folding her arms across her chest. "What is it?"

"Are you doing okay? I mean, it must have been difficult for you, when Valentine moved on to a new mistress."

A fine furrow appeared between Carla's brows. "A new mistress?"

"I'm so sorry." I let my face fall dramatically. "I assumed you knew."

"Knew what?"

"About Valentine and"—I dropped my voice to a whisper as I leaned in closer—"Kristin Flickner."

I had prepared for a look of heartbreak. Had shored myself up against the guilt I would feel at having willfully inflicted distress on another human being just to suit my own ends.

Hilarity, on the other hand, I was completely ill-equipped to handle.

To say that Carla Malfi laughed in my face would be no exaggeration at all. She busted up royal, going so far as to press a hand to her midsection as if glee was going to pop out of her stomach like an alien.

"Thank you," she said, wiping a tear of mirth from the corner of her eye. "I needed that."

Sadly I found myself unable to join in on the abundance of jollity in the wake of my plan's epic failure. "I'm afraid I don't understand what's so amusing."

The levity on Carla's face was replaced by something like pity as she realized I obviously had no idea what the hell I was talking about. "I know for a fact that there's no way Kristin Flickner and Valentine are having an affair."

"How?" Now it was my turn to cross my arms over my chest. A gesture of irritation I was unable to avoid.

"Because she's his half sister."

# Chapter Fifteen

A pain hammered behind my left eye socket as Sam's excellent coffee crawled up my throat, dragging a wash of stomach acid with it.

Kristin Flickner. Valentine's half sister.

What the fuckety fuck?

I was beginning to suspect that the whole goddamn crowd of Valentine's friends and relations was one big inbred family, and my mother had been doing some rogue genealogical mapping.

Why the hell had I just assumed that Shepard knew what he was talking about when he'd said they were boning?

I was making up my mind to give him the rough side of my tongue—and not in the good way—when the soldier in question came barreling through the same door Carla had just exited.

In his arms, a giant beribboned bouquet of Stargazer lilies—my least favorite flowers.

I stalked down the hall and straight up to Judy's desk, where Shepard was presumably inquiring as to my whereabouts.

"Shepard," I said tightly. "What are you doing here?"

"There's my girl now!" he said, pressing the malodorous blooms into my arms. "These are for you."

"Well, isn't that thoughtful." I stood on tiptoe to press a mock kiss to his cheek while hissing a hasty, "What the fuck are you doing here?" in his ear.

"I just wanted to congratulate my *smoochypoo* on her first day," he said, loud enough for Judy to hear.

Judy, biologically incapable of being charmed, merely harrumphed and turned back to her computer screen, muttering under her breath about unscheduled visitors.

"That's very kind of you, *pumpkin*, but my first day isn't over yet."

"Are you sure, *cuddlemuffin*? Because I'm pretty sure we agreed I'd pick you up at seventeen hundred hours."

"You've got it all wrong, *lovedumpling*. I told you to come by at six p.m. That would be eighteen hundred, right?"

I was on the point of arguing further when Melanie came swishing down the hall, stopping so hard at the end of it that Kristin ran right into her back. The stack of papers Melanie had been holding spilled from her hands like an avalanche and fluttered to the floor in a flurry of white.

Melanie dropped to her knees, blushing furiously as she hastily raked them into a pile. It was the first time I'd ever seen her flustered . . . and I liked it.

Kristin ducked around her and made a beeline for the door, tossing a hasty, "Good night!" to no one in particular.

*Shit.* I'd been hoping to catch her. At least long enough to get a closer look at her face and mentally measure the features against Valentine's.

"Let me help you with that." Shepard squatted down and gathered the pages that had floated like leaves to his well-worn combat boots.

"That's mighty kind of you, sir." Melanie layered on the Scarlett O'Hara drawl thicker than cream cheese icing on a red velvet cake, batting her dark lashes against her cheek.

I was pretty sure if I ever tried that, I'd probably look like I was having some kind of obscure ocular seizure.

Not liking the way Melanie accidentally on purpose brushed Shepard's hand, I nudged him with my knee and cleared my throat.

"Shouldn't we get going, *pookiepants*? We'll be late for your grandmother's birthday party."

I could have lived for decades on the heady cocktail of shock and dismay clouding Melanie's face.

Shepard rose to my side, but not without a dubious glare, which I ignored. If he was going to show up to my place of business pretending to be my boyfriend, then he could damn well carry out the charade.

"Oh, how rude of me. Shepard, this is Melanie Beidermeyer, one of the part-time associates here at the firm. Melanie, this is Shepard. My *boyfriend*." I somehow managed to turn it into a ten-syllable word.

"Does he have a last name?" Melanie asked *me* while not taking her eyes off *him*.

"Just Shepard," I said, looping my arm through his. "Like Prince or Adele. He's just that good."

Melanie tucked a lock of blonde hair behind her ear. I noted with dismay that it was still as perfectly curled as it had been this morning. "Well, in that case, *just* Shepard, I'm very pleased to meet you."

"Likewise," he said.

"Jane, shame on you for keeping such a *big* secret." Her gaze flicked to the level of his crotch with the authority of someone reared to evaluate the virility of thoroughbred stallions. Then, standing with her slightly scattered bunch of papers, she reached out and mock pinched my arm. "Where *have* you been keeping him?"

"In my bed, mostly." I gave Melanie a lascivious grin and let my free hand wander possessively across Shepard's pectoral. "He'll hardly let me leave the apartment. In fact, he just can't keep his hands off me." I knew this declaration was somewhat compromised by my reaching out to wrap Shepard's hand around my waist, but went for it anyway. "Isn't that right?"

"That's right, my little wildebeest." Shepard's fingers dug painfully into my hip. "In fact, that's why I came by early. I was hoping we could grab a quickie in the car before the party."

"Oh, you naughty boy." I playfully punched his arm, then imagined Shepard's face as a giant doughnut so I could summon the proper degree of rabid hunger. "Of course."

At which point I popped up to peck him on the lips.

That had been the plan, anyway.

Foiled chiefly by Shepard's frighteningly fast reflexes. His hand was on the back of my skull before I could so much as utter a gasp.

Not that gasping would have done me any good, because the only air currently available to me was in Shepard's lungs. And even then, I wasn't so much thinking about the man's lungs as I was his tongue. How hot, how wet it felt sliding across my lips.

It would have been just plain rude not to open my mouth for him, and hadn't I determined to do something about my lack of manners during my time with Sam today?

I gave him an inch.

He took a mile.

His hand on my jaw, fingers trailing down over my jugular, mouth creating a rhythm deeper parts of me yearned to mimic. After breathless seconds I recognized it.

Shepard was kissing me in time to the throbbing of my own heart.

I wasn't exactly sure how a wall had materialized at my back, but there it was.

There *I* was.

Across the room from where we'd started. Dizzy, dazed, jelly legged, and kissed so thoroughly that I knew Shepard had a bridge, two crowns, and a few assorted fillings.

Melanie stared at us gap mouthed.

Twin rectangles of blue light reflected from the computer screen outed Judy, who had risen from her chair enough to see over the reception desk.

And of course, standing at the end of the hallway, his cheeks flushed the color of a stoplight, was Sam Shook. He held my laptop in one hand and the messenger bag I'd left in his office in the other.

I felt like taking a page from his book and repeatedly thumping my head against something harder than my skull.

Like a diamond.

"I . . . I thought I heard you say something about leaving," Sam said. "I didn't want you to forget your things."

It was Shepard who stepped forward to retrieve them since I seemed to have grown roots into the floor. "Thanks, guy."

*Guy.*

I wondered if Sam had picked up on the slight pejorative.

"Well," I said, stooping to gather the bouquet of lilies we'd crushed between us. "I guess we better be going. See you tomorrow, Sam. Good night, Judy."

Judy made a noise that might have been an acknowledgment or dislodging of excess phlegm.

Shepard steered me out the door and to the elevator, which I was relieved to find occupied by at least a few other business types. The space seemed entirely too small and enclosed after our full-contact tongue wrestling.

We exited into the parking garage, cool beneath the earth.

"So Kristin Flickner is Valentine's half sister," I announced as soon as we were closed into his Civic.

"The hell you say?" Shepard depressed the engine button, turned on his police scanner, and pulled a reflective folding cover off the windshield that had nothing to do with keeping out the sun.

"Truth." *For once.*

"I thought I told you not to go digging into Kristin Flickner."

144

"Here's where you'll be proud of me. I didn't even have to ignore what you told me. I assisted Sam with character witnesses for Valentine's divorce proceedings today."

"*Sam* is it?" Shepard's brows flatlined as his lips tightened. "I thought the firm didn't do divorces."

"They do for Valentine."

"That fucker gets more personal exceptions than the pope gets in Rome."

"You mean exceptions like an understanding with the cops that renders him inculpable for manslaughter?"

"That's different." He put the car in gear and backed out without looking either in the rearview mirror or backup cam. His judgment of spatial relationships was truly eerie in its accuracy.

I yawned as we pulled out of the garage into the early evening, the skyscrapers around us gilded by the sun's westward descent. "What's on the agenda for tonight?"

"P-Ripple, D-Town, and I had an idea, but I don't know if you'd be willing to participate."

"I'm up for anything that isn't going to the safe house."

"*Anything?*" The playful suggestion in his voice hinted at possible wild gorilla sex.

"Well, not *anything* anything." The lack of playful suggestion in mine belied my desperate need for the same.

"There's three of us, and three different groups of people following you. The easiest way to flush them out is—"

"To put me out for bait," I finished for him, having already arrived at this conclusion during yesterday's endless solitary sequestration.

"I warned them you probably wouldn't be up for it."

"Are you trying reverse psychology on me, Shepard?"

"That depends," he said. "Is it working?"

"Not really. But it just so happens that my impulsive nature suits the purposes of this particular operation."

"Mission," he corrected. "Operations are for doctors."

"Would I get a gun?" Fantasies of being a black-clad badass with an impressive sidearm strapped to my leg might have already begun to gallop way ahead of me.

"No, but you'd get a *weapon*."

"I thought I was the one who did the linguistic correcting in this relationship."

He cleared his throat and swiftly crossed three lanes of traffic without signaling—classic Shepard, as I was learning. "Speaking of the relationship . . ."

My head lolled back onto the headrest. I'd become very, very tired all of a sudden. "Don't tell me you want to talk about our feelings and shit. It was just a kiss, okay?"

"*Alpha*, that was just a kiss like Hiroshima was just a bomb, and *Bravo*, I want to know about the blonde."

It was inevitable, really. Anything I had, Melanie would get, and apparently this held true even for things I only *pretended* to have. "We've only been a make-believe item for forty-eight hours, and already you're eye-humping blondes?"

"Negative. I want to know why you started acting like a jealous girlfriend only when she showed up."

"You were the one who showed up toting flowers. I was just playing along."

"Please," he scoffed. "Voluntary cooperation isn't part of your MO. Who is she to you?"

The one who beat me out of the valedictory chair I killed myself to earn. The one who mocked me for studying when everyone else was celebrating. The one who met with Valentine before *and* after my mother disappeared. The one who somehow managed to finagle a position shadowing someone my mother had been investigating. The one who delighted in pointing out my every misstep and mistake since I'd met her.

"Just someone I know from school."

"Do you look at all your schoolmates like you want to eat their spleen on toast?"

"Gluten-free crackers," I corrected him. "With a good beluga caviar and crème fraîche. It *is* Melanie Beidermeyer we're talking about here."

"Jealousy, huh? I read you. Want me to dial it up next time?"

"Dial it up *how*?" I raised a hand to my still kiss-swollen lips. "Dry hump me on Melanie's desk?"

He shrugged. "If it would help the cause."

"How very generous of you."

"I'm a very generous guy."

I indulged in an eye roll and dug around in my laptop bag for the fortifying candy bar I'd been saving. I had a feeling I was about to need it. "So, generous guy. Tell me about this mission."

———

My threefold instructions were pretty simple, really.

Stay in contact. Be conspicuous. Don't do anything stupid.

Directives given to me by Paul Gladstone, D-Town, and Shepard, respectively.

Simple, right?

Hi. I'm Jane.

Have we met?

"I'm cold, and this is stupid."

"What did I say about talking?" Shepard's voice buzzed in my ear as it had all evening, a mosquito that had taken up permanent residence snug against my eardrum via a covert Bluetooth earpiece.

"People see you muttering to yourself on street corners, and it's a hop, skip, and a divorce from a shopping cart full of cats and empty wine bottles. Is that what you want?"

I felt no compelling need to mention that I already had the empty-wine-bottles part covered.

"What I want is something warm to eat, a chair to sit in, and not to have your voice in my head for five goddamn minutes. I'm beginning to have a whole new sympathy for schizophrenics."

"Get your hand away from your ear."

Truly I hadn't even realized that I had started to massage it. Only that I wanted to allay the ache caused by the foreign object, small though it might be.

"How much longer do I have to stand out here?" I shivered against a bone-deep chill, the result of an unseasonably cold spring storm settling over the city. The nearby alleyway was a damp, piss-scented mouth breathing the weekend's revels onto my neck at odd intervals.

"Has anyone ever told you that you have a real lack of patience?"

"And has anyone ever told you that you have a real talent for stating the totally fucking obvious?"

Shepard was silent for a moment. A silence into which I imagined him dumping florid mental curses by the bucketful and slowly counting to ten.

"Listen to me—"

"No, *you* listen." I cast an irritated look out into the city at large, having no idea exactly where he might be. "I've been standing on this godforsaken downtown street corner for two hours now. I've been mistaken for a prostitute three times, and not a single person has made an attempt to kidnap, assault, or otherwise maim me. This is damned disappointing is what it is."

"Now is when the real work begins, Jane. Use this time—"

"If you start up with one of your lectures, you're not going to have to worry about someone trying to kidnap me, because I'll smack my own head against this building until I'm dead." I patted the corner of the rough brick edifice for emphasis.

"Jane, do *not*—"

"Okay, GI Joe. I'm going inside to warm up. We'll talk in a little bit."

"Negative. Stay in position—"

*"Goodbye."* I affected the particular tones of an automated operator right before she disconnects your call after a couple of wrong menu choices. As far as I was concerned, Shepard had done just that. The breeze was cool in my empty ear canal as I pulled the bud from my ear and stashed it in my bra. If nothing else, the beating of my heart could witness to Shepard that I hadn't snuffed it.

A whoosh of warmth blasted my face as I pushed into the Tilted Tiger, a gastropub specializing in overpriced microbrews and perfectly good food ruined by hipsters. A cheer rose from the bar area, crowded for a Monday night. Likely a result of the hockey game unfolding on one of the many TVs suspended overhead.

I bypassed a hostess wearing a miniskirt and knee socks and took a seat at the bar as far away from the other patrons as possible but still in full view of the big windows. An awfully thoughtful nod to my trio of would-be co-operatives, as they couldn't set foot in the place without getting burned.

The bartender—Debra, her minichalkboard nametag announced—swiped the area in front of me with a bar mop and set down a recycled cardboard coaster and a small white dish of dusty-looking nuts. "Complimentary spiced raw almonds," she said when I dubiously eyed the proffered snack. "Our specials tonight are cauliflower kale tacos and vegan kimchi nachos. Can I get you something to drink?"

I glanced at the small menu card of house-special drinks. My eyes glazed over when I got to the words *Lavender-Infused Fig Thyme Old-Fashioned.*

"You hiding any plain old vodka back there, Debs?" I nodded toward the bottles glowing behind her like a backlit choir. "Preferably something that *hasn't* been made from locally sourced potatoes and strained through a hippie's sock?"

Debra's mouth looked like a coin pouch someone had just pulled the strings on. "We have the *regular* brands."

"Lovely. Dump some regular shit in a shaker for me with ice and three olives, shake it like an ass in a Lil Wayne video, and bring it back here, if you could."

She took herself off to see to my drink, and I let myself sag on the barstool, elbowing the armpit-scented almonds out of the way.

"Can I buy that for you?"

The feelings arrived in this order: Delight. Recognition. Despair.

"Fuck. Not you again."

"Is this going to be our standard greeting?" Officer Bixby set his bottle of beer down on the bar and slid onto the stool next to mine. He'd traded his patrol uniform for a polo shirt that showed off his guns to devastating advantage and jeans well worn enough to hint at thighs roughly the size of tree trunks.

"I was sort of hoping we wouldn't be seeing enough of each other to require a standard greeting," I said.

He almost managed to look offended. I say *almost* because his face was beer-rosy and more relaxed than I'd thus far seen it.

"And here I offered to buy you a drink."

"Poor judgment on your part."

Debra returned with the shaker and reached for a mason jar on the shelf above the beer taps. I cleared my throat and shook my head no when she glanced back at me. With a disgusted sigh and no small amount of eye rolling, she bent down to the literal bottom shelf to retrieve a regular old lowbrow martini glass. She sloshed the shaker's contents into it, adding a garnish of three olives skewered on a rosemary sprig instead of the classic plastic cocktail sword. I decided to let this small act of rebellion slide.

I ate an olive from the stick and sipped my drink, grateful for the instant warmth it kindled in my empty belly.

"I've been meaning to call you," Bixby said.

"About?"

"Your mother."

These two words lodged an icy stone at the base of my throat, the vodka refusing to trickle past it. "And why haven't you? Called me, that is."

Bixby scooted his stool closer to mine. "I wasn't sure you'd be alone."

I pretended an ease I didn't feel, stirring my drink with the twig. "Why would I need to be alone for you to call me?"

He consulted his beer's peeling label like it was the Delphic oracle. "How much do you know about Shepard?"

I didn't like this question. Not one bit. And in no small part because I didn't like the answers already forming in my mind.

*I know he's frighteningly good with weapons. I know he can judge visual distances better than a hawk. I know he's hung like a draft horse.*

Well, that part of the answer I didn't mind so much.

"I know he's an army veteran. I know he's working for Paul Gladstone. I know he's been assigned to keep me safe from the people who are following me." I reached into my bra, pulled out the earpiece, and held it up for Bixby to see, then dropped it into the glass of room-temperature water Debra had deposited along with my martini, knowing this would make me very unpopular next time I met up with the man in question.

Bixby gave me a knowing smile. "How do you know you're being followed?"

*Because Shepard told me.*

"What's your point here, Bixby?"

"He's not a normal guy, Miss Avery."

"Anyone who's seen me in my bra might as well go ahead and call me Jane."

The beer-blush deepened in color. "He's not a normal guy, *Jane.*"

I snorted and took another sip of my martini. "I could have told you that."

"What I mean is, he has a record."

"A record of being a pompous, overbearing ass," I said with a grunt. "I mean a *record* record."

I knew what he'd meant, of course, but was delaying as long as possible the inevitable moment when he would tell me something I didn't want to know.

Bixby leaned in close, beer sweet on his breath. "You have access to court records. Maybe you want to look into the restraining orders filed against him?"

The truth was, I couldn't. I didn't even know Shepard's first name, a fact I didn't want to confess to Bixby.

My heart fluttered up into my throat, pumping hard enough in my ears to drown out the sudden swell of cheers from the other bar patrons.

I felt the urge to defend Shepard, but I didn't because I knew why I wanted to. Not owing to some misguided notion of his innocence. Not even because I'd been stupid enough to trust him.

I wanted to defend him because I'd been stupid enough to trust *her*. My mother. And I'd done it in direct contravention to her lifelong, repetitive admonitions.

You *are the only person you can trust, Janey. Not teachers. Not police. Not even me.*

Hadn't she warned me?

Hadn't I decided that she was just being overprotective?

Hadn't this misguided belief inclined me toward the assumption that anyone who urged me to be cautious likely had my best interests at heart?

"Is that all you wanted to tell me?"

"No," Bixby said. "I've been looking into your mother's disappearance."

I let my anger rise to the surface as sarcasm, an old but familiar friend. "What, are the forty-eight hours up already?" I slid another olive off with my teeth, the resinous scent of rosemary on my fingers.

"I started digging into a couple of things even before that. About the time Shepard offed two guys in your apartment. Which you haven't returned to since, I've noticed."

Now why did he have to go and bring that up? I'd been hoping I might just live the rest of my life in blissful denial that two random thugs had been sent to torture and/or kill me and had been slaughtered by Shepard instead. This memory was totally going to screw with my ability to Netflix and chill there for at least a fortnight.

"Would you be in some big hurry to return to your mother's house if someone had killed two people in the living room?" I'd taken to shredding a damp cocktail napkin, making a little nest of the scraps and populating it with almonds in place of eggs.

"For the last time, it's *my* house, and you know that's not what I was asking."

"I've been staying at a safe house. Well, a safe apartment, really."

"Are you on parole tonight or something?"

"Or something." I felt eyes on me. Shepard's. Bixby's. Men at the bar.

"I don't know how safe it is for you to be somewhere only Shepard knows."

"You were telling me about how you started looking into my mother's disappearance?"

"Nice subject change."

"I've been practicing." I lifted the martini glass to my lips and drained it, trying not to notice how the rosemary had begun to steep a refreshingly woodsy counter note to the briny olive juice.

Bixby scrubbed a hand over his goatee like it was a Magic 8 Ball and he was searching for guidance as to where to begin. "I'm assuming Paul Gladstone has also been looking into your mother's disappearance as well. What do you know so far?"

"Something between squat and diddly." This had been a point of contention, as Paul had seemed reluctant to divulge any specific details when I had pressed him over the phone. His refusal had stung, as had his failure to stop by the safe house. I hated to admit that I'd wanted to see him again. To bask in a vaguely fatherly presence.

"So, after you booked it from the parking lot, I ran your mother's plates. Turns out, that car isn't even registered to her. It's registered to an LLC."

My chest filled with cold air, my lungs shrinking to half their usual size. I'd grown used to this feeling over the last couple of days.

"That's not so unusual," I said. "People register their vehicles to LLCs as a way to reduce liability in personal bankruptcy proceedings."

"If they happen to be an authorized agent of the LLC, sure. The name First Security Enterprises mean anything to you?"

It didn't.

"I tracked down their address of record, and it's a virtual office out in the Denver Tech Center."

"How do I explain this?" I motioned to Debra for a refill and swiveled to face Bixby on the barstool, giving him my full attention. "My mother has what you might call an inherent mistrust of government-operated institutions. She probably just didn't want anyone knowing what kind of vehicle she owned or where she chose to base her business."

"That isn't all." Bixby drained the last of his beer and clunked it down on the bar as punctuation.

"Get you another?" Debra offered with considerably more sweetness than she'd directed at me.

"Sure," Bixby said.

"*What* isn't all?"

"I also ran a background check on your mother."

I could feel my face stretching longwise like dough hung on a hook. "Look, I already know about the arrests. And as to the criminal charges—"

"I didn't find any."

"Oh." A measure of relief soothed my jangled nerves mere nano-seconds before they began jangling anew. "You didn't find any *what* exactly?"

"Records."

Debra deposited my martini and Bixby's beer.

"Criminal records?" I asked.

"Records *period*."

I couldn't have been more breathless if someone had knocked the air out of me with a baseball bat. Panic heightened my awareness of odd details. The neon streaked through Bixby's dark hair from the glowing bar signs. The tangled threads of gunmetal gray in his irises. The tender crease of his hooded lids.

"What does that mean?" I hated the sound of my own voice. Wobbly. Naive. Scared and stupidly hopeful.

Officer Bixby's voice, on the other hand, was smooth and reassur-ing. Practiced in the art of delivering devastating news. "It means, that according to the public record, your mother doesn't exist."

# Chapter Sixteen

"How is that even possible?" I asked.

"Beats the hell out of me." Bixby shrugged. "I've never seen anything like it. No driver's license. No traffic record. No registration. Nothing."

"Are you sure you did it right?"

Bixby gave me a first-class crusty look. Eyes narrowed, mouth a tight, mirthless line within the carefully clipped parentheses of his goatee. "Despite what you may have assumed, my brain is, in fact, slightly larger than the average walnut."

"I didn't assume that at all."

I'd credited him with a plum-size brain at least.

"I searched every possible spelling, abbreviation, and variation of your mother's name that I could come up with. I got no hits."

"What about her address? Did you try searching by that?"

"Way ahead of you. Your mother's residence is owned by yet another LLC with yet another virtual office listed as the HQ."

"What? No." Denial shook my head side to side like an epileptic bobblehead doll, useless words boiling from my idiot mouth. "I remember the day she closed on it. We went and had sushi to celebrate after she picked up the keys. She'd been saving for years. We cut pictures out of magazines together. She told me, she told me—"

"She lied." Bixby's flat pronouncement landed with the weight of a sledgehammer.

*She. Lied.*

I wanted to hurl more words at him. To make him understand.

*I* was the one who lied. Not my mother. Not the woman around whose words I'd constructed my entire life.

"I understand that all of this is probably pretty shocking for you. But that's why I wanted to talk with you. I thought that maybe if you came down to the station and—"

"Yoo-hoo!" The unmistakable, eardrum-bloodying coo of the one and only Melanie Fucking Beidermeyer.

I mentally measured the length of the rosemary twig in my drink and found it too short to brain myself with, even should it be shoved through the corner of my eye like my mother had once demonstrated with a cantaloupe.

Resigned, I slowly turned on my stool and spotted Melanie crossing the bar with the same show-pony prance she'd used to traverse the graduation stage. A gait I was certain she'd perfected in the many beauty pageants of her youth. Men's heads followed her, jaws dropping like flies in her wake.

"Who is *that?*"

"Satan." I closed Bixby's mouth with a flick of my index finger. "Or one of his lesser demonic minions. The jury is still out." I took a fortifying swig of my drink and gave Melanie a floppy, half-hearted smile.

She floated up to us in a pale-pink cocktail dress as short as it was tight, noisily kissing the air by both my cheeks. "Jane! Imagine running into you *again*."

"Imagine." I rudely slurped my drink, Melanie's impeccable manners always bringing out something of the rebellious barnyard animal in me.

"Well, this seems like the place to be tonight."

"How so?"

"First I run into Dean Koontz, then you."

"The dean is here?" I glanced around and spotted Dean Koontz hunkered down in a booth across from a woman whose tits could've doubled as floatation devices. "Didn't he lose his wife just a couple of months ago?"

"He did," Melanie confirmed. "I'm glad to see he's dating again. He's been awful lonely."

*Yeah,* I wanted to say. *Dating.*

"And what brings you to the Tilted Tiger?" I couldn't care less what answer she offered up, but something told me Melanie wasn't going away until I at least pretended to have a conversation with her.

"We were just having us a girls' night out." She gave a little finger wave to a table presided over by Melanie's own mother and my buxom classmate, Lauren Hayes, whose repeated invitations I had continued to dodge. Apparently Melanie had lured her over to the dark side along with the entire constituency of my study group. *My* acquaintances, now *her* friends. As if on cue, they all lifted mason jars full of pink liquid in silent country-club salute.

"And what about you? I thought you had a birthday party to attend with your *boyfriend.*"

"I do." *Lie.* "I did." *Lie.* "Nana called it an early night. She is ninety-seven, after all."

Melanie raised a perfectly microbladed brow. "So you decided to come have a drink with, with . . . well, who *is* this delicious hunk of masculinity?" She treated Bixby to a round of lash batting.

"This is Bixby." I really needed to start asking people's first names as an order of business. "Steve Bixby." I decided not to count this as a lie. His first name *could* have been Steve.

"And how do you two know each other?" Melanie asked. "He can't be your boyfriend too."

"He isn't," I admitted. Then, seeing the Cheshire grin spread across Melanie's face . . . "He's my *ex*-boyfriend." Oops.

*Lie.*

Bixby aspirated beer and coughed up a mouthful of foam. I slapped him heartily on the back to encourage respiration. "There, there, Steve. Steve's been so upset about the breakup," I stage-whispered to Melanie. "He begged me to come out for a drink. Just to talk, you know?"

Bixby's wide-eyed, querulous expression failed to stop me. I was on a roll now. In my element. Working in sedition the way some artists work in oils or clay.

"I'm surprised that Shepard fella of yours didn't mind."

"Oh, he did mind. He's insanely jealous. But I managed to calm him down." I winked at her, a gesture redolent of conciliatory bones-jumping and libidinous bargaining. My cell phone chirped on the bar. "That's probably him now. I'd better let him know I'll be headed home soon."

I picked it up, suddenly remembering why I'd left it facedown next to the discarded nuts in the first place. I hadn't wanted to deal with the slew of angry messages from Shepard I knew I'd have.

Only, there weren't any.

No messages from Shepard.

One from a number I didn't recognize.

Valentine's building site. Ten minutes. Come alone. Your mother is waiting.

The whole damn message was one big flaming red flag. Remote location. Expedited time frame. Emotional extortion.

And then there was the whole *come alone* thing.

Come alone. Code for *bad idea.*

I knew it then.

Just like I knew that I wasn't expecting some tearful reunion wherein I managed to rescue my mother with naught but my wits and the side-arm strapped to my thigh beneath my "conspicuous target" skirt.

Nope.

I was about to run headlong into danger, eyes wide open and metaphorical ass cheeks exposed to the wind.

Why?

Same reason I had commandeered Valentine's limo and cuffed Shepard to a shower.

Because I could.

Because I knew how to get myself out of trouble just as well as I knew how to get myself into it.

Because I was Alex Avery's daughter, goddamn it, and I wasn't about to sit around on an organic pleather barstool with a thumb up my butt while some ass-raptor firebombed me with obscure and vaguely menacing texts.

"Trouble in paradise?" Melanie asked hopefully, nudging me with her bony wing.

"Not at all." My smile felt brittle and unconvincing. Someone had left a dumb slab of meat where my face had once been. I'd forgotten how to make it do things. "I just need to visit the ladies'. Would you two excuse me?"

I could feel Bixby's eyes on me, but I refused to meet his gaze. The last thing I needed was for him to decide to do something stupidly heroic.

That was *my* job.

When I was out of sight behind the cavernously large wine rack, I broke right toward the kitchen instead of left into the ladies' room.

Plan B—wherein Jane ditches the babysitters—had officially been engaged.

The thing about people who have a highly developed set of skills in one area is that there are often glaring gaps in education about things they don't consider important.

Take Shepard, for example.

Tactical badass, surveillance ninja, and weapons aficionado. Absentee clothes-shopping buddy.

He had been so busy silently devising plans to kill every single person in the mall should the need arise that he hadn't been paying attention to the additional items I'd slid in my shopping bag while we hit the racks in search of my *conspicuous* outfit.

Like a wig and glasses.

Lest you be tempted to get all judgy here, I'd like to point out that I kept a running tally of where the items had come from and how much they'd cost so I could mail in payment along with an anonymous yet polite as fuck sorry-I-stole-shit-from-your-store card.

I'm a pathological liar, not a kleptomaniac.

In the bustling Tilted Tiger kitchen, I ducked into the walk-in fridge and proceeded to transform myself behind a metal rack of organic local produce. I shimmied out of my skirt, revealing the shorter skirt I'd been wearing beneath. Off came the blouse, under which was a plain black fitted T-shirt. Next I retrieved the pair of knee-high socks I'd secreted in the cups of my bra and pulled them on, sliding back into my nondescript black flats. From a pouch strapped to my thigh next to the disappointingly small pistol Shepard had lent me, I withdrew a spiky blonde wig, black-rimmed hipster glasses, a fake nose piercing, and a tube of matte blue lipstick.

When I was finished, I looked exactly like any and every other server at the Tilted Tiger, the spot P-Ripple had chosen as ground zero when we'd gone over plans earlier that afternoon.

Catching a glance at myself in the mirror, I decided my mom would approve.

*A disguise is like a face-lift, Janey. The better it is, the less people notice it.*

From a board next to the time clock, I swiped a nametag to complete the look, along with someone else's army surplus jacket, which I fully planned on returning the following day.

I was no longer Jane, but Billie, and Billie knew about a fire escape on the second floor.

Billie agreed with Shepard on one score.

Never enter a building without knowing all the exits.

———

I had scarcely hoisted myself over the chain-link fence on the perimeter of the building site when the smell hit me.

Acrid, metallic, and sweet by turns. Acrid—the searing muscle tissue. Metallic—the sizzling of iron-rich blood. Sweet—the evaporating cerebrospinal fluid.

The odor of a burning body was unmistakable.

I knew because I had encountered one at close range when I was ten.

Okay, it was a white-tailed deer carcass that my mother had used to make a point, but close enough.

We were three days into a trip Mom had pitched as "camping" but that had turned out to be survival training when we saw the smoke and followed it to the balder face of the mountain.

She had looked like an Amazonian queen that day, clad in camouflage cutoffs and a cactus-green tank top. She wore the length of rope and boot knife more elegantly than most women wore jewels. The dying sun cast half of her face in copper as she scrambled upslope, nimble as a mountain goat. Dark hair whipped around her ice-chip eyes each time she paused to look back at me. I thought my heart might burst from love and pride as she waited for me by the burning carcass.

"Now do you see why burning is a terrible way to get rid of a body, Janey?" Her calf flexed as she nudged the unfortunate creature with the toe of her hiking boot, revealing the wet, red mess spilling from a tear in the singed fur. The muscle tissue around it was gray and had already begun to cook. "Internal organs are too wet to burn, even if you use a gallon of accelerant."

"Who did this?" I asked, nose buried in the crook of my arm against the bitter, lung-blackening smoke.

"Poachers, probably. Looks like they hacked off the best parts and decided to burn the rest." Gently and with infinite tenderness, she had peeled my arm away from my face. "Learn this smell, baby. This is the smell of a burning body, and there's nothing like it in the world."

There had been a lot of esoteric things my mother wanted me to know. Facts now leaping through my head like a herd of startled rabbits as I stared at the blackened human body at my feet.

The skull was often the most charred due to the scant amount of soft tissue over bone.

The body had burned hottest and longest where the clothing had acted as wick, the fabric soaked and fueled by the melted fat.

Muscles and tendons shrank as they cooked, curling arms and legs into a pugilistic stance common to boxers. Flexion of elbows, knees, hip, and neck. Hands clenching into gnarled claws.

She was a woman.

*Had been* a woman.

The fire had eaten her face. Burned her hair away. Left her mouth a fearful rictus. Death's ecstatic grin carved into fleshless cheeks, the tissue beneath it slick and red in the places where it had split open.

Beyond recognition.

These words had always seemed like an expression. An exaggeration. But they weren't. Not really. What I was looking at could scarcely be deemed human but for the bones. Their long, delicate lines beginning to show beneath flesh that fire had stripped away.

Beautiful bones.

Where had I heard this phrase?

Valentine.

*Good buildings begin as beautiful bones. Your mother has them. So do you.*

So it was at Valentine's building site with the metal skeletons of his design rising from the earth all around me that his words circled back again and landed with a synaptic snap.

I went to my knees. Searching for something, anything that would render the idea impossible.

She was the right size.

*This is not my mother.*

The right shape.

*This cannot be my mother.*

Those could be her teeth.

*Your mother is waiting.*

The first drops of rain sizzled as they hit the skull. Cold on her cheeks, cold on mine, both of them warmed by the same fire.

I shouldn't be able to look at her this way. I shouldn't be able to look at *anything* this way. Feeling no horror. No grief. Only the cool blue flame of recognition that my life had been one long climb to an inevitable disaster. The sum total and purpose of all my mother's preparations.

"Jane!"

Floodlights and slanting rain hung a shimmering curtain on the air. I squinted through it, my mind dully arriving at recognition just in time to see him get shot.

# Chapter Seventeen

I'd never ridden in an ambulance before.

If Bixby had had his way, I wouldn't have been riding in one now.

Luckily the man in question was buckled to a stretcher, and the paramedics didn't seem as concerned about his protestations as they did staunching the bleeding from his hand.

Or what was left of it.

"I don't want her in here." He gestured to me with his crimson-stained gauze mitt, wild eyed and pale faced, whether from anger or blood loss, it was difficult to say. "She needs to go back to the building site for questioning."

About this, he was not wrong.

In the confusion resulting from the simultaneous arrival of cops and paramedics, Bixby had identified himself as an off-duty officer, and I had identified myself—out of his earshot, of course—as his fiancée.

They'd taken one look at the blood squirting from his wounded hand and hustled both of us into the ambulance, ignoring his insistence that they leave him behind to help process the scene.

Allowing myself to be thus escorted was in large part due to the discovery I'd made *after* I had dialed 911 and tied a tourniquet around Bixby's wrist but *before* the ambulance had arrived.

Namely, the body was not my mother's.

At least, I was reasonably sure it wasn't my mother's after I helped myself to a sneak peek of a mostly unscorched cell-phone holder/billfold a couple of feet from the body. The full significance of whom the driver's license inside belonged to didn't quite register until I had stopped gagging from relief.

Carla Malfi, Valentine's mistress-shrink.

"He's in shock," I said above the ambulance's howl. "He doesn't know what he's saying."

"Oh, yes, I do. I want her out of here. *Now.*"

The female paramedic, brusque, middle-aged, and brimming with efficiency, palmed Bixby's bicep and retrieved a blood pressure cuff of a larger size. "You know we can't stop the vehicle, Officer Bixby."

"Who said anything about stopping?" Bixby glanced at the back doors, a small, feverish smile tweaking a dimple into his cheek as he presumably imagined my ejection at full speed.

I dragged a hand to my chest, feigning hurt. "Just because we don't agree on the wedding venue doesn't mean I don't still care about you, Steve." I tenderly pushed a dark lock of hair from his forehead, which was clammy with sweat.

"My name is not Steve, and we're not engaged, goddamn it."

"Could he have traumatic amnesia?" I asked, giving the male paramedic my best concerned-spouse expression. "I've heard that's a thing."

"Possible," he allowed, his eyes widening as he shucked an IV port from its sterile packaging and examined Bixby's good arm.

Lifting had given Bixby veins like a porn star had tits.

A damn shame that he probably wouldn't be lifting anything more than hospital Jell-O for quite a while.

"I do *not* have amnesia." Bixby's knuckles were as pale as milk on the stretcher's side rail. "You left the bar, I followed you, I got shot."

"But I found your fingers. Doesn't that count for something?" I lifted the cooler in which four-fifths of Bixby's left hand—his thumb was still attached—currently enjoyed a refreshing ice bath. I had my doubts about whether they'd be able to reattach it, as what I'd picked up from the construction rubble mostly resembled a rawhide chew that had been gangbanged by a pack of pit bulls.

"If it weren't for you, my fucking fingers would still be on my fucking hand!"

"Please, try to stay calm." The female paramedic glanced at me over her shoulder. "We just gave him something for the pain. Maybe it would be best to let him rest for a while?"

"Of course."

Something for the pain.

I watched Bixby's eyelids sag, feeling an irrational stab of jealousy. Would that they could do the same for me.

Cold, hard facts were arriving at a speed faster than the shrieking ambulance could escape.

Someone had wanted me to find Carla's body.

Someone had wanted me to find Carla's body *at* Valentine's building site.

Someone had wanted me to find Carla's body *at* Valentine's building site so they could fire a bullet in my general direction, but Bixby had reached out to get my attention at the last minute.

Shepard hadn't texted me since I'd abandoned my position on the corner of Wynkoop and Sixteenth Street. The radio silence wasn't like him.

*Someone* had some explaining to do.

———

"We have a tentative ID on the body." Paul Gladstone, a.k.a. P-Ripple, seated himself next to me in the emergency room waiting area, the scent of rain and smoke riding in on his coat. His voice carried an edge I didn't remember. A hardness underscoring his native warmth.

"Carla Malfi?" After an hour of going over and over everything I had seen with a homicide detective from Bixby's unit and omitting this one particular detail, I was too tired to pretend.

Surprise stripped a decade off Paul's face. It was an expression I could imagine my mother finding endearing. "You know her?" he asked.

Ice water replaced the blood in my veins, numbing me from head to toe. "I interviewed her earlier today as part of Valentine's divorce proceedings."

A coldness crept into Paul's weathered features at the mention of Valentine's name.

I found myself pausing, deciding how much information I wanted to part with, given how little Paul had been willing to offer to me so far. That Carla claimed my mother had threatened to expose her and Valentine's relationship, I didn't feel especially compelled to mention. "She was his therapist. And his mistress."

"What did she say about him?" Paul asked.

"Mostly that she didn't believe Valentine to be the violent psychopath his hideous dragon snatch of a wife claimed him to be."

"Maybe she was wrong. If being a private investigator has taught me anything, it's that people are willing to believe all kinds of things about someone they love."

"Don't I know it."

"You were afraid it was your mother?" It wasn't so much a question as a statement. "Is that why you copped a look at the ID before the police showed up?"

I didn't ask Paul how he knew. For the moment, I wasn't nearly as concerned about that as I was about *what* he knew. And why he hadn't bothered to tell me.

"You think I should have waited for a comparison to dental records we both know my mother doesn't have?" I had thought of a dozen more elegant and subtle ways to mine information, but all of them seemed to have evaporated in favor of a ham-handed segue. The sure thing. "Why didn't you tell me that there aren't any public records for my mother?"

The reflection of white linoleum cast an eerie glare over Paul's cold coffee eyes. "How did you find out?"

"Bixby told me before I left the bar. He also had some interesting things to say about Shepard."

Paul examined his battered knuckles as if the answer might be hidden among the scars.

"I knew about your mother's records, or lack thereof, before you and I even met."

"Did she know that you knew?"

He nodded. "I asked. She didn't elaborate. I didn't push it."

"What about Shepard's criminal record? Did you know about that when you made him my armed babysitter?"

"Combat twists you in a lot of ways. Shepard is twisted in ways I can accept."

I folded my arms and turned toward Paul to give him my full attention. "I'm listening."

"When you're downrange, you learn things. Things you can't forget just because you come back."

"Such as?"

"You have enemies. Shepard served in the sandbox, where those enemies looked just like everyone else. Mothers. Children. Anyone and everything with a heartbeat is a potential threat."

"He was a sniper?" I asked, finally giving voice to my suspicion.

"*Is* a sniper." Intensity sharpened the dark wells of Paul's eyes. "That training doesn't go away just because he's no longer wearing the uniform."

"I see."

"I'm not sure you do." Paul sat forward on the waiting room chair, his ponytail a wolfish silver beneath the fluorescents. "After Vietnam, the Department of Defense did some math and figured out that they were spending about nine thousand dollars in bullets for every kill. So, they started training soldiers who could actually eliminate a target with a single bullet. One." He paused, holding up a finger. "Sometimes a sniper has to go days before pulling the trigger. Watching. Waiting. Civilians who have never been in that situation can find that kind of focus a little overwhelming."

"I can see where he'd be well suited to surveillance."

"Exactly," Paul said. "In all his years working for me, he's never lost a target. Until you."

"Ahh." I cleared my throat, making room for the crow I'd inevitably be ingesting. "I'll acknowledge that my lack of cooperation may or may not have contributed to his particular difficulties."

"You left a man who won't even sit with his back to the door naked and handcuffed to a bathroom fixture."

I sank down an inch or two in my seat. "Perhaps not the most considerate thing I've ever done."

"And dropped his four-hundred-dollar earpiece into a water glass."

"An insensitive gesture on my part."

"And that's to say nothing of entering a restaurant so you could—"

"Yes. Okay. I get it. I'm a dick!"

"You're not a dick. But you are your mother's daughter."

I sighed, heavy of heart and spirit. "I don't even know what that means anymore."

"It means you're not so good at letting anyone help you." Paul dropped his big warm hand over mine, the palm leathery and comforting against my knuckles as he squeezed. "But it also means you're stronger, smarter, and braver than just about any other woman I know."

Treacherous tears welled in my eyes. Stupid fucking compliments and kindness. "Where is she, Paul?"

"I'm doing everything I can to find her. But if you're determined to help, we need to work together."

"Does that mean you'll tell me what you know from now on?"

"That depends." Paul searched my face, perhaps looking for similarities to the woman we both loved. "Can I trust you not to lie to me?"

"Me?" The hyena/buzz saw laugh and I had a spontaneous and unwelcome reunion. "What would I lie about?" And on this episode of *Stupidest Questions Ever Asked in the History of the Universe . . .*

"You lied about being friends with Melanie Beidermeyer."

"Says who?"

"Says you. I saw how you looked at her at the bar tonight."

This was an unwelcome revelation. Paul had seen me—and at fairly close range—but I hadn't seen him.

"How did I look at her, exactly?" I tried for wide-eyed innocence but felt my face tipping perilously toward manic surprise.

"Like you wanted to smash her face and make a meat collage from the pieces."

I silently added this to the list of creative ways I'd come up with to end Melanie's unholy dominion upon the earth. "Maybe a little bit," I admitted.

"I need to know that I can trust you with information. And that you trust *me* with information if and when you find it."

Oh, I was going to find it all right. Beginning with Carla Malfi, whose life I intended to turn inside out like a bag of doughnuts. I'd scrape the metaphorical frosting off with my teeth if I had to.

And not just because metaphorical frosting didn't make my ass wobble.

"Listen, P-Ripple— may I call you Paul?"

"Makes no difference."

"I can't always control the first thing that comes out of my mouth, Paul. But I promise you that the second thing will always be the truth."

"Deal." He offered his hand and we shook on it.

"Mrs. Bixby?" A nurse stood at the double doors leading back to the intensive care unit.

"Here," I said, shooting up from my chair.

Paul raised a dark rectangular brow at me.

"That one doesn't count," I insisted. "It happened before you got here."

"Fair enough." Paul pushed himself to his feet. "Do me a favor?"

"If I can."

"Call Shepard to pick you up when you're done."

I hesitated in the doorway, the nurse impatiently shifting her weight as the automatic security timer buzzed.

"Do I have to?"

"I'm sure he'll have mostly cooled off by then."

Shockingly this failed to reassure me.

Just as shockingly, Bixby didn't want to see me. Not even when I explained to his closed door how one of his detective friends had come to the emergency room and I had disgorged everything I knew about the crime scene, so really my having hitched a ride with the ambulance wasn't a bad thing at all in terms of the investigation.

It was about this time that something crashed against the other side of the door in the general vicinity of my head, so I elected not to belabor the point.

I did, however, offer to bring back to Bixby whatever it was he'd thrown at me.

My offer was roughly rebuffed with an abrupt verb and an even shorter personal pronoun.

I was on the point of politely declining his suggestion owing to a lack of flexibility and the principles of physics when a hand closed over my elbow and spun me around.

Shepard.

And he didn't look especially pleased with me.

"Walk." The order was paired with a not-so-gentle squeeze of his fingers on the flesh of my upper arm.

The soles of my shoes squeaked as he marched me down the empty hallway, panic setting in as my brain reeled.

If I ran, he'd catch me.

If I screamed, he'd stop me.

If I fought, he'd win.

And so, I walked.

A door opened behind me. Closed.

Together, we sank into the dark.

# Chapter Eighteen

"You see how easy it would be?" Shepard's body was punctuation, final and unyielding as he jerked me against it. His words were hot silk filling my ear—a smaller blackness within the larger one.

Our breathing synchronized without effort. In and out. Up and down. A respiratory Möbius strip.

"I could do anything to you."

The truth of his statement lived in the brutal reality of his whole, hard person. An inescapable corporeal presence. I pushed back against him, seeing without eyes.

His ribs with my shoulder blades. His abdominals with my spine. We shared his tattoos where skin met skin.

"Do you feel this?" His hand slid down my neck. My pulse leaped against his fingers.

"This is fear."

"I'm not afraid of you."

"You should be."

I smelled his anger. Blood and skin in the iron dark. His fingers pressed against my neck just enough to bring my awareness to the life throbbing through my veins. How little it would take to end it. To end *me*.

"Why? Because you're a big bad commando who could end my life with one twist of your hands?"

"Because fear is an instinct, and instincts keep you safe."

A thin laugh bubbled up my constricted throat. "Is that why you think you're doing this? To keep me safe?"

"Why else would I be doing it?"

"My guess? This is the closest you've been to a pair of tits in God knows how long, and you're confusing the urge to bone me with actual feelings. Lucky for you, you *don't* actually have feelings for me."

Shepard's breathing quickened, his chest expanding against my back. "Why is that lucky?"

"Are you kidding me? Bixby got most of his hand shot off, and all he did was follow me out of a bar. Can you imagine the havoc I would wreak in the life of an actual boyfriend?"

His grip loosened ever so slightly.

"Dating tip for future reference, though? Herding women into closets is second only to bringing them lilies in terms of almost guaranteeing that you will go unboned."

"Really?"

"Really."

"So you're not turned on right now?"

"Absolutely not." Part of me wished the knee socks were still in my bra to provide an extra layer of insurance between Shepard's arm and my nipples, which were approximately hard enough to cut glass at the present moment.

"And you don't want me?"

"Not even a little bit."

"Liar."

We stayed like that for a moment. That word coloring in the darkness between us while Shepard's heart beat hard as a racehorse's between my shoulder blades.

"Jane." A question. An answer. An accusation.

"Shepard." A word. An apology. A prayer.

His fingers curled into my hips, my head tipping sideways to yield the curve of my neck to his descending mouth.

Which was how we were when the door swung opened and the light clicked on.

Did we look guilty?

I don't know. Does the sky look blue?

A nurse stood there, staring at us. Openmouthed. Wide eyed.

A multitude of prevarications jockeyed for position, tripping over each other in the race from my brain to my tongue.

So my surprise was understandable when what came out instead was, "What? It's not like we were banging."

*Ha! Truth, bitchez.*

I counted this as progress.

Shepard, not so much.

"You'll have to excuse my girlfriend," he said, taking me by the arm. "She's been under a lot of stress lately."

"It's the dead bodies," I said. "Three in the last three days."

"Excuse me?" The nurse blinked, looking at me like she might want to speed-dial the psych ward.

"My silly little wildebeest." Shepard squeezed my upper arm a shade tighter than affection dictated. "You forget that not everyone gets your jokes."

"But I wasn't—"

"We'd better be going." He steered me past the nurse and out into the hall, turning me to face him once we were almost to the elevator. "Could you maybe pick a different time to have an attack of honesty?"

"It's your fault, the way I figure it." I shrugged and smiled, my body all watery and loose.

"And how is that?"

"I think full-body contact short-circuits my lying engines."

The elevator opened and we stepped into it, alone in the small mirrored booth.

The change in Shepard's body language was immediate. Apparently he liked enclosed spaces about as much as he did crowded public ones.

"So does that mean I'm going to need to do bad things to you anytime I want a straight answer?"

I gripped the handrail as the question liquefied my already wobbly legs. Knees. Who needed 'em?

"Now that's something my therapist never tried."

"You don't strike me as the type."

"What type?"

"The therapy type." The muscles in his jaw flexed as he flicked a glance at the glowing floor display. Six more to go.

"Oh, yes. Mom had me logging many an hour on the leather couches of various psychologists. They never were able to break me of the habit, much to her dismay. Of course, it was okay for me to lie when *she* needed me to." A small acidic kernel took root in my stomach.

"That sounds pretty fucked up."

"Which is about what the therapists said, more or less."

The elevator opened onto the hospital lobby, deserted at this late hour save for a custodian making wide arcs with a chrome floor buffer.

I followed Shepard down a hall and into a concrete stairwell smelling faintly of motor oil and exhaust. The last leg before the parking garage.

"I'm holding you to your word." His declaration sounded ominous in this echoing space.

"Which word would that be?" I did my best to sound like one of those people who didn't get winded ascending a couple of flights of stairs.

"You promised me you'd let me protect you."

"Ah, but promises made under force majeure never hold up in court." I longingly eyed the landing a couple of levels up. Just. A few. More.

"Force majeure?"

"Irresistible . . . compulsion," I puffed, forgetting to care about my deficit of cardiovascular fitness.

"You know what I think?"

"That black T-shirts represent a ubiquitous fashion—eep!" I yelped as my legs were scooped out from under me.

Shepard altered his pace not one whit despite hoisting me in his arms fairy-tale-princess-style.

Side note for the gentle male reader and/or female readers who long to be dashing: Do this. It is hot.

"I think you like to argue just for the sake of arguing."

"That's a fascinating conclusion you've reached, Captain Obvious." I tightened my thigh muscles, mostly to fool Shepard into believing I had them.

He managed to get us through the stairwell door and over to his car, only setting me down to open my door. "You really ought to work on your cardio."

"Excuse me? I was doing just fine before—"

"Seventeen minutes," he said, glancing at the car's digital display. "Good to know for next time."

"Next time?"

"Next time I corner you in a closet. I can expect at least seventeen minutes of truth afterward."

I tried not to squirm in my seat, knowing that to do so would be to yield precious ground. "There won't *be* a next time," I said.

Shepard smiled and started the car. "Now you're just lying to yourself."

# Chapter Nineteen

There *was* screaming in the bedroom later that night.

Not owing to any extracurricular effort on Shepard's part, but because I'd shrieked myself awake in the pitch dark, caught in the grips of the kind of nightmare that hadn't haunted me since I was a child.

My mother, burning. Screaming in pain. Begging me to help her.

Subject to the telescopic zoom of a horror movie, the nearer I got to her, the more she receded. She reached for me; I reached for her. One, last, desperate grasp. Her fingers crumbled to white ash in my hand.

The kiss of her smoldering hair still lingered on my face from the dream when my nightshift "babysitter"—another of Shepard's apparently endless supply of ex-army dudes—barreled through the door, weapon in hand. He'd insisted on doing a sweep of the room despite my repeated assurances that I was okay.

Sleep evaded me for the rest of the night.

So it was with no small degree of exhaustion that I tapped on Sam Shook's office door the following morning.

Even with his dark eyes rimmed by even darker circles, Sam managed to cut a charismatic figure. The kind of man who could wear a tailored purple shirt and coordinating purple tie without looking like pimp cousin to Barney the dinosaur.

"Jane. You're here early."

"So are you." I left the floor open to see whether he'd bring up Carla Malfi, whether he had any sources that might've made him aware of her untimely end.

"Yes, well." Sam took a sip of coffee from his zombie mug, not glancing up from his laptop. "Gary asked me to come in early for one of our chats."

"Oh?"

"Apparently he feels one of the medical malpractice cases I have been working on would be better reassigned to Kristin Flickner." The look of resignation on Sam's kind face made me want to relocate Gary Dawes's saggy ball sack north of his small intestine with the pointy toe of my boot.

"Perhaps you were right to insist that she be your mentor after all."

"Sam, I'm sure he doesn't—"

"He does, and it is better that you learn this now." There was cold fire in the depths of his obsidian eyes. "I should have spent less time studying law and more time studying politics."

Having never managed to master the tactful art of reassurance, I opted for its simpler and sexier cousin—distraction. "Listen," I said, forgoing the chair and perching on the edge of his desk, clutching a warm stack of papers from the copy machine against my bosom. "Are you busy?"

"Busy having a disagreement with a congregation of imbeciles on the Walking Dead Reddit feed." His elegant fingers flew over his keyboard with a pianist's grace and precision. "What was it I heard such people called?" His eyes lifted heavenward as if searching the ceiling for a memory.

"Knobheads?" I humbly suggested. "Or perhaps wankstains?"

"Neckbeards!" he said, seeming pleased at having seized upon the correct English slang. "Sooner or later, they must see the value of logic."

Oh, sweet, naive Sam. I almost felt guilty for coming to his office with such blatant machinations in mind.

"I wanted to get your take on what happened to Carla Malfi."

"Which part? Her relationship with Valentine, or her being black-mailed by your mother?" He didn't look at me when he said this, for which I was immeasurably glad.

No one needed to see my impression of an apoplectic cod. "You knew?" I managed at last.

"Of course I knew. You are a terrible liar, Jane Avery. One of the worst I have ever seen."

"Excuse me, I happen to be a *fabulous* liar."

"You *would* be a fabulous liar," he said, thumbs hitting the space bar hard enough to clang, "if you didn't have an honest heart."

"How dare you!" I gasped.

"So which is it?" he asked, nonplussed.

"Which is what?"

"Carla Malfi. Did you want my take on her relationship to Valentine? Or her relationship to your mother?"

In my ego-fueled fit, I'd almost forgotten why I had sought him out in the first place.

"Neither. She's dead, Sam."

At last his fingers froze in their ceaseless typing. "Dead? But we just spoke with her yesterday afternoon. How is this possible?"

"She was found at the construction site for Valentine's building downtown last night." Nothing like the good old passive voice to keep from complicating this matter with the useless information that I had been the one to find her. "Her body was burned. That's all I know so far."

"She was murdered at Valentine's construction site?"

"Or she was murdered elsewhere, dumped there, and burned. But it amounts to the same."

Sam's expression bore atomic bomb–level devastation. He was slowly putting together the same pieces my mind had puzzled out dur-ing the small sleepless hours of the morning.

"This is bad," Sam said, rising from his chair to pace the brief length of his office. "This is very, very bad. Forget a divorce lawyer. Valentine is going to need a criminal defense attorney."

"Carla was going to be a character witness *for* Valentine," I pointed out. "Wouldn't that create a serious conflict as far as his motive is concerned?"

"Not if you consider that anything positive she had to say about him will be offset by the revelation that she was his mistress. Adulterers don't make convincing character witnesses in my experience. Especially from beyond the grave."

"Maybe we're getting ahead of ourselves," I said. "Valentine hasn't been charged with anything."

"Yet," Sam said, peeking over my shoulder. He looked down. "What is this?"

"This?" I glanced at the thick stack of contraband copies on my lap. The fruits of my having arrived before Judy could shoo me away from the expensive office copier. "This is a report of incorporation on First Security Enterprises. I recently found out my mother's car is registered to them."

"Your mother's car is registered to First Security Enterprises?"

"Yes. Why?"

Sam went to the tall file cabinet behind his desk, withdrawing a manila folder and walking through it with dexterous fingers. "Ahh. Here it is." He lifted a stapled document and set it atop the papers in my lap.

I saw, and then I didn't see, shock making the words crawl across the crisp white paper like ants.

Valentine's list of assets.

Sam was kind enough to state the obvious since I seemed to have hemorrhaged IQ points all of a sudden.

"First Security Enterprises belongs to Delphi Holdings Limited, which belongs to Archard Everett Valentine and Associates."

"This doesn't make any sense. Why would my mother be driving a car that belongs to a company that belongs to a company that belongs to Valentine?"

"More importantly." Sam sat next to me on the edge of his desk, a surface clean and clutter-free enough to accommodate the posteriors of at least four attorneys of average size. "Why are you investigating who owns your mother's car?"

I couldn't do it.

I couldn't look into those molten-chocolate lava-cake eyes and lie . . . badly.

The tale summarized pretty handily when I left out the corpses.

Sam's dark brows gathered as concern creased his fine, smooth forehead. "Why did you not mention this to me before?"

"Because you're my mentor. And this is my job. And Melanie Fucking Beidermeyer's mother never gets kidnapped or blackmails people."

"And you were afraid that I would be just one more person who decided Miss Beidermeyer represents an easier return on investment?"

I blinked, a little dumbfounded, still not quite certain Sam Shook wasn't some kind of Jedi mind reader after all.

"I realize we have much to learn about each other still, but this is not something you need to worry about." There was that *v-w* pronunciation thing again, making him all attractive and intriguing. Also, he smelled good. Some ambrosiac mix of shampoo, freshly laundered shirts, and good coffee that had me imagining dropping him into a paper bag and huffing him till my head went swimmy.

"Like you, my upbringing was . . . unconventional. As was my career path. I understand more than you might think me capable."

I gave him a watery smile, which he failed to return.

"This connection between your mother, Valentine, and a woman who is now dead, I do not like."

If he didn't like this, he *really* wouldn't like the parts of the story I'd left out. Like my having found the dead woman and getting shot at in the process. "I've been not liking this for several days now."

"This investigator who is your mother's boyfriend—"

"P-Ripple."

"P-*dipple*?"

I'd never be able to keep a straight face at this rate. "Paul."

"Paul," he repeated. "What is he doing to ensure *your* safety?"

"That would be where Shepard comes in."

"Shepard?"

"The . . . gentleman who picked me up yesterday evening."

"Oh," Sam said. And then, "*Ohhhh.* So he was not—"

"No."

"But the kiss—"

"All for show."

Sam's hooded eyes softened, the corners of his mouth tipping up ever so slightly.

"A rather convincing show."

"What can I say? I'm committed to the cause."

"I have an idea," he said. "It just so happens that my caseload has recently become lighter. Perhaps we could spend some time at the county courthouse this morning."

"Oh. That sounds . . . informative." See: *boring as shit.* In truth, all I could think about was when and how I could get to one Archard Everett Valentine to confront him about this new discovery. I somehow doubted Shepard would be likely to endorse this idea, despite his grudging agreement to relax security while I was at the office.

Sam's smile could blind angels. "What I meant was, perhaps we could do a little digging of our own. I happen to be acquainted with a wildly permissive county clerk who can be bribed with pens."

"Pens?" I sincerely hoped he hadn't left an *i* out of that word by accident.

"Do you have any idea the dreadful pens government employees are forced to use? Terrible, scratchy plastic things with fine points and chalky ink." He shuddered, clearly scarred by a too-recent memory, as he retrieved his suit jacket. "Would you be so kind as to retrieve a box of pens from the supply closet while I gather my things? Black ink. Bold tip."

I checked the clock on my phone, resisting the obvious "he said *tip*" joke. Judy wouldn't be in for at least another ten minutes. Ample time to raid the supply closet. "You bet."

I popped a squat before the bottom row of supplies, reading the laminated labels aloud. "Padded envelopes, paper clips (organized by their size alphabetically rather than physically), pencils, ahh—pens, *comma* black."

I selected a box and shuffled the others forward to fill in the gap. I had no doubt Judy would eventually notice the theft, anal-retentive supply nazi that she was, but there was no need to make it obvious.

I was just about to flick off the light when I heard a sniffle.

This was the part of the horror movie where Judy popped out from behind something, a letter opener clutched in a bony fist overhead. No, not a letter opener. Scissors. The *s*'s were on *her* side of the bookcase.

"Hello?"

Another sniffle.

A peek around the corner revealed not Judy, but Kristin Flickner, sitting on the floor with her back against the wall and her knees pulled into her chest. She looked a little like the "before" person in NyQuil ads. Red-rimmed, puffy eyes. Pink around her delicate seed-shaped nostrils. Her skin pale beneath her golden freckles.

"Hey," I said. "Are you okay?"

"I'm a partner at Denver's most prestigious law firm, and I'm crying in a goddamn closet. I am the reason patriarchal stereotypes of women in the workplace exist."

"Don't be so hard on yourself. I'm sure lots of people are overcome by the sight of well-alphabetized office supplies."

My heart leaped like a trout when her mouth tugged to one side. Shared DNA had made Kristin and Valentine both smirkers.

"A client of mine died last night."

Here's the thing about misanthropes. Just because we usually choose not to engage in social contracts with other humans doesn't mean we're incapable of recognizing the signs when one is being offered.

With this one sentence, Kristin had extended me an invitation.

She wanted to talk.

Self-interest snuffled ahead like an eager beagle. It just so happened that there were lots of things I wanted Kristin to talk about.

"I'm so sorry to hear that. How long had you been working together?"

"Two years. We were getting so close. *So close* to bringing the case to trial." The red of tear-swollen capillaries in the whites of her eyes turned her irises a ridiculous shade of green. Fire burned behind them.

"What kind of case was it?"

"Medical malpractice. She fought so bravely." Her mouth turned downward.

"May I ask what she died of?"

Kristin's pretty face crumpled as fresh tears polished her eyes. "That's the insane part. She was . . . *burned*."

Goose bumps rose on my arms and prickled my scalp.

"You're not talking about Carla Malfi?"

"You know her?" Surprise replaced the animal misery on her face.

"I only met her yesterday. She came in to talk with Sam about a matter relating to Archard Valentine's divorce case."

"Oh." A small bitter chuckle. "That." Kristin didn't offer up any information about their familial relation, and I didn't ask. I wouldn't necessarily go around advertising that Valentine was my brother either.

"She didn't mention that she was involved in another case at the firm."

"No," Kristin said, a small sad smile softening her features. "She wouldn't. She was part of an indeterminate plaintiff group in a medical malpractice suit I've been working on for two years. Privacy is a key factor for many clients in this case. Not that it matters for Carla now." She pulled a fresh flounce of tissue out of the open box on the *T* shelf and dabbed her eyes with it.

My mind chewed on this new information.

Valentine was having an affair with his therapist, who also happened to be part of a medical lawsuit his half sister was prosecuting. My mother had known about the affair. Had she known about the lawsuit as well?

"Does this have anything to do with the medical malpractice case Sam was working on?" I asked. "He mentioned something about one of his cases getting reassigned to you this morning."

Kristin's gusty sigh displaced the wisps of copper hair from the sides of her face. "I believe Sam has my mentee, Melanie Beidermeyer, to thank for that."

The casual mention of her name had all the organs south of my belly button trying to crawl up into my chest cavity. "Oh?"

"I guess she got wind of the case and somehow managed to convince Gary Dawes it would be especially beneficial if the case were reassigned to me. Well, to us."

"Sounds like she's very . . . determined."

"That's a nice word for it." From the sly way Kristin looked at me from beneath her feathery lashes, I got the feeling that we both suspected Melanie of blowing Dawes's baloney pony.

I heard the supply closet door open, followed by the unmistakable tracheal whistle of Judy's mouth breathing. "Who's in here?"

I didn't entirely succeed in keeping the look of panic from my face.

"I am." Kristin got to her feet, casting off her vulnerability like a cloak. She snatched the pens from my hand as she passed, holding them up for Judy to see. "I needed these for a jury panel this afternoon."

Judy was in fine form today, dressed in coordinated pantsuit separates of eye-frying electric blue. She looked me over with the delight one might reserve for cold piles of cat vomit. "And why are *you* in here?"

"I asked Jane to show me which kind of folders Sam had been using for the Koontz case files, since it was reassigned to me this morning," Kristin said. "She was kind enough to oblige."

If I had been a hunting dog, my ears would have pricked to attention. *Koontz* case files? Surely not Dean David Koontz. There had to be some sort of law of the universe that limited how many times someone whose junk you'd accidentally grabbed could wander back into your sphere of influence. Didn't there?

Kristin slipped me the pens as soon as we were out in the hall.

I sent her a grateful look and brought them to Sam, who was waiting by his office door with his laptop bag in hand.

"Question," I said.

"Certainly."

"The medical malpractice case that was reassigned to Kristin Flickner this morning. Who's the plaintiff?"

"Actually, it's someone I believe you might know. David Koontz and his late wife."

# Chapter Twenty

Shepard was going to kill me.

And I don't mean that in a metaphorical way.

The next time I saw him, he would most likely wrap his hands around my throat and squeeze until my eyes bugged out and my tongue turned purple.

I really hoped I wouldn't soil myself when the time came. Somehow, this always felt like the least dignified part about dying to me. Good thing I hadn't eaten much of the dinner I'd cooked that night. Not because it tasted like burned-ass muffins, which it likely did because grilled cheese was about the only thing I could make successfully, but because I hadn't really cooked the dinner for me in the first place.

No, the unfortunate target of my gustatory machinations was Babysitter #3—whom I'd christened Dave after he refused to tell me his name but objected to my suggested call sign, Gunsablazin'. He'd been assigned the unenviable task of keeping me installed in the safe house for the evening when Shepard had taken the night off, citing urgent business that needed attending to.

I understood exactly what this meant, of course, because I had some urgent business of my own and a guy dubbed Dave standing in the way of my being able to attend to it.

The wheels had been set in motion much earlier that day when I'd received a phone call from Paul informing me that the cause of Carla

Malfi's death had been liver failure, and Sam Shook conversationally informed me that this had also been to blame in the death of Dean David Koontz's late wife. This revelation had been the straw that broke the burro's back.

I had to talk to Valentine.

If we're looking at evidence to support the conclusion that I *tried* to do things the "right" way first, I would like to point out that I texted Shepard no less than three separate times to make him aware of my discoveries, as well as to *suggest*, then *request*, then *insist* that he arrange a meeting with Valentine.

And Shepard said?

Yep, you guessed it. No. No. And *no*.

I believe my issues with this word have been well established by this point.

So it was with much provocation that I resorted to plan B. Which is what would most likely result in my untimely (at least to me) death.

But before I shuffle off this mortal coil, dig, if you will, the genius of this plan.

Picture it: Evening. The apartment filled with the scents of cooking. Spotify playing some hipster dinner party music mix. Me, barefoot in the kitchen, fetchingly attired in cutoff shorts and tank top, hair in the kind of domestically disheveled bun you earned by slaving over a hot cooking implement. Dave staring at a laptop split screen of surveillance camera feeds, back straighter than a honeymoon dick, about 10 percent of his actual ass on the loveseat. I was beginning to suspect that, despite their multitude of "other" qualifications, not a single one of Shepard's men knew how a couch worked.

I did a quick scan and located his phone, sitting faceup on the coffee table.

*Good.*

"Dinner's ready!" I called from the kitchen doorway.

Dave looked at the pan clutched in my oven-mitted hand like it might contain a pipe bomb instead of warm rolls. *Actual* rolls with motherfucking yeast.

Estate attorney's note: if I do die, I want this on my headstone.

"My dinner break is at twenty-two hundred hours."

"I'm sorry. But, whatever it is you guys eat from those pouches can't be considered dinner. I'm not even sure it can be classified as actual food."

"MREs are a safe and sustainable nutrition source."

"Ahh. *Safe.*" I glanced at the table where a large bowl of mushroom and sausage risotto whispered parmesan-scented steam into the air. "It's not poisoned, if that's what you're worried about."

Not that I hadn't thought about it, but slipping someone a Mickey isn't easy. I don't care what the stalkers say.

"See?" I spooned up a goodly chunk of rice, marveling at the glorious parmesan threads stretching from the bowl like the strings of some heavenly harp. I managed to keep the expression on my face largely delighted even when the uncooked center of the kernels went chalky between my insulted molars.

No matter.

Dave wouldn't actually be eating it anyway.

"Negative." His mouth hardened into a resolute line. "I have my orders."

"But I made it especially for you."

I'd been worried about this part. I'd never been good at fake crying despite my mother's many attempts at teaching me the finer points. Her suggestion for summoning tears? Think about your favorite pet dying. Trouble was, we'd never had any pets. So instead, I thought about having spent an entire hour of my life spooning ladlefuls of chicken stock into a pot of stubby rice only to have it turn out like parmesan-flavored chalk. I'd actually *tried* for once.

My face fell. My lower lip began to wobble tremulously. My throat contracted over a single, sucking sob.

Through the scrim of my tears, I saw a look of abject terror begin to take over Dave's face.

"Oh, no," he said. "No, no, no. Don't do that."

But it was too late. Every lady knows the chin wobble is the official floodgate opener.

The rolls slid from my outstretched tray and hit the floor more like bricks than baked goods. Estate attorney: on second thought, scratch the yeast epitaph. My shoulders began to shake as I brought the oven mitts up to cover my eyes. Given the gale-like force of my wailing, I was almost surprised that tears didn't squirt sideways from behind them. I commenced with that awful double-pump inhale common to romantic comedy heroines and slapped orphans.

"But, but, I had the groceries delivered special and—" Half of the words made it out, the other half were swept down my throat.

"Okay, okay. I'll eat with you. Jesus Christ. Just please stop doing that." Gunsablazin' Dave had risen from the couch and was standing next to me, trying to figure out where to put his hand. It landed on my shoulder, staying long enough for a couple of pats before staggering across my back like a drunken parrot and seeking refuge in the pocket of his fatigue pants. It was pleasing on some level to encounter another human as bad at this consolation shit as I was.

My crying snapped off almost as quickly as it had started. "Great! Will you grab the salad? It's in the fridge."

Instead of setting the silverware out, I followed him into the kitchen, feeling a distinctive stab of fondness for the gait common to Shepard and the men he employed. A strut I could only describe as "which piece of furniture should I break tonight?"

I was still smiling when the handcuffs clicked closed over Dave's wrist and the refrigerator door handle simultaneously.

This may be a good time to point out that I use the term *handcuffs* loosely.

Dave stared down at them in horror.

I saw what he saw. Felt what he must be feeling, albeit with a lower level of distress. Misanthropy isn't synonymous with a complete lack of empathy, after all.

The handcuffs were pink. *Furry* and pink. Furry and pink and, unfortunately for Dave, completely functional. And it was for this reason I was pretty certain Shepard would likely crush my windpipe like a cardboard flute.

"Yeah, I'm really sorry about those," I said, making sure to stay well out of arm's reach. "They were the best Rhonda could do on short notice. Of course, what can you really expect when you call a prostitute and ask if she wants to make a quick hundred bucks that doesn't involve sucking a dick?"

"But how did you—we had eyes on you all day. There's no way you could have—"

"Ah, but I could, and I did."

I knew I needed to be on my way, but couldn't resist a very small brag about my own ingenuity. No wonder James Bond villains were always going on about how they set in motion their plans for world domination.

Nefarious plotting is a seriously underappreciated art.

The difference between me and a Bond villain was that I had no intention of leaving him under the not-so-watchful eye of one inept guard. I figured the refrigerator was at least that smart.

"It happened at the courthouse. Rhonda was kind enough to leave me a pair of handcuffs in the feminine hygiene disposal box in the third stall. She's at the courthouse a lot, as it turns out."

Dave glanced down at the cuffs, something like horror creeping across his face.

"Oh, don't get your boxers in a bunch. They were in a plastic bag. Perfectly sanitary, I assure you. Well, I guess I can't speak for what bodily fluids they might have acquired *before* Rhonda dropped them off in the tampon disposal box, but since then . . ." Here I paused, clicking my cheek and pointing at him. "Totally jizz free, you have my word."

Dave jerked against the restraints, maybe trying to figure out how much pressure would be needed to break the fridge handle or cuffs or both.

"Surprisingly durable, right? I took the liberty of testing them out earlier."

"Shepard was right about you." Dave opened the fridge, then the freezer. A half-hearted attempt to see what comestibles would be available for the duration of his imprisonment.

I smashed the butterflies attempting to take wing in my stomach. "In what respect?"

"You're like a cross between a doughnut and the devil. Tasty on the outside. But on the inside, pure evil."

At this, all I could do was nod and smile.

A more perfect description, there never was.

"All right," I announced. "Time for me to bounce." I picked up my phone, studied it, and dialed.

It was answered on the third ring.

I took a deep breath and forced the sentence out of my mouth, one odious word at a time.

"Hi. It's Jane. I was wondering if you could do me a favor."

# Chapter Twenty-One

Melanie looked like her car.

Or Melanie's car looked like her. It was one of those bizarre chicken-or-the-egg things that I had neither the time nor the patience to work out.

Both were sleek, powerful, and probably worth more money than I'd see in a lifetime.

She pulled up in front of the safe house and bleated two quick honks, the prearranged signal. I walked down the sidewalk at a pace I decided to be appropriate for hurrying out to meet a friend but not necessarily fleeing from a man I'd cuffed to the fridge with furry pink handcuffs.

*Never look guilty, Janey. Guilt gets people caught.*

Once inside, I shifted uneasily in the buttery leather seat and tried to figure out what to do with my hands.

I didn't know what it was about luxury that turned me into an over-size toddler who had just discovered her extremities for the first time.

Folding them in my lap seemed to be what the car wanted, so I did it.

"So," she said, once we were safely away from the apartment. "You want to tell me what all this is about?"

"Not especially."

"Will you at least tell me why it is you need me to get you into the country club?" She slid me a sideways glance but immediately returned her eyes to the road. Her manicured hands stayed precisely at ten and two.

*Because I got a tip-off from one of the small army of people who work at Valentine's regular haunts* seemed like maybe not the best answer.

"There's someone I need to talk to there, and I'm not a member."

"Who do you need to talk to?"

"Look, details were not part of the bargain, okay? You pick me up and get me to the country club, I get you a date with Bixby. That's it, and that's all."

Her silence was politeness personified. Had it been me, I would have surely belabored the point until Melanie, or whomever else I happened to be pestering, gave up the information I wanted.

This chick had no idea how to badger.

"You really don't mind about Bixby?" Melanie's hair listed in the gentle jet stream from the air conditioning vent. It was the kind of expensive breeze one felt off the coast of Saint Barts. One that lifted your hair just so for pictures.

"Why would I mind?"

"Well, I know it must be painful for you, thinking that he might be happier with . . . someone else."

"Someone like you, you mean," I said.

"I wasn't saying that." Worry pinched the corners of her mouth white. Narrowed the upturned corners of her Disney princess eyes.

And I knew where that worry had come from.

My acknowledging the game was a direct break from our pattern of Melanie's pretending not to notice how insulting she was being and my pretending that it didn't hurt my feeling. No, that's not a typo. I'm pretty sure I only have one and most of the time I'd name it *irritation*.

"Not out loud, no. But you were ever so delicately and deftly implying it."

Now, she wasn't worried, she was panicked. "If I said something to upset you, I—"

"You may as well cut the crap, Melanie. We're the only two people in the car, and I've already caught your whole routine. Shall I save us both some time and acknowledge that you're prettier, smarter, richer, and better than I am at probably everything?"

Her color had gone all hectic, cheeks staining a blotchy red that did nothing for her complexion. If this look had a season, it would be Nuclear Summer. "But that's not true. There are lots of things you're better at than me."

"Name one," I said.

"Well you . . . that one time when you . . . I've always noticed your . . ." She sounded like a busted record playing, the needle of her logic bumping from groove to groove.

"Ever heard of quitting while you're ahead, Mels?"

"Breaking rules!" Triumph beamed from her face like sunshine. "You're better than anyone I've ever met at breaking rules."

This brought me up short. The sarcastic reply I had at the ready froze in my throat. "What?"

"Breaking rules. You're always doing whatever you want whenever the hell you want to do it, no matter what anyone else says."

"And you don't?"

She scoffed. A harsher sound than had ever issued from that delicate white throat. "Are you kidding me? I'm great at doing what other people want to me to do. My mother. My father. College professors. Dean Koontz. Gary Dawes."

"Like what kind of stuff are we talking about here? I need a solid example." And by solid example, I mostly wanted to know if she'd choked on Dawes's hog log.

"Like playing the piano. Like getting straight As. Like going to law school," Melanie said.

These mild revelations left my tongue feeling like I'd just licked a battery. "You didn't want to go to law school?"

"No. I didn't."

I blinked at her, this creature who couldn't have been more alien to me at this moment if her head split open and tentacles started waving from the crevice. "Then why did you go?"

Melanie pulled up to the stoplight, the car gently rolling to a stop like a gliding swan. The reflection of red traffic lights turned her eyes an alarming shade of violet.

"I have two older brothers, you see. One of them is a doctor. The other is a research scientist just like Mother and Father. That left one box open for me. Lawyer."

I blinked at her. Inside the safety of my mother's construction, the fields were wide and the options endless. She'd fed me freedom along with my breakfast cereal.

*You can be anything, Janey. Do anything.*

I could not comprehend what life would be like any other way.

"But it's not like they can force you."

"Can't they?"

"You're a grown-ass woman, Melanie. What can they do to you?"

"Aside from disinheriting me? Kicking me out into the street without a dime to my name. No car. No money. Nowhere to go. When you've been given everything, everything can be taken away."

This, I had never thought about. Only how much easier life would have been had I not had to scratch and fight for every goddamn thing I ever had.

"You could get a job," I said.

"Doing what?"

"Anything. Hostessing. Waitressing."

"Jane, I've never had a job. I've never so much as filled out an application."

"But you're wrong. You would have had to fill out an application to get into college, at least. And law school."

"Not if your father is best friends with the admissions board. Or golfing buddies with Dean Koontz. You see?"

I was beginning to.

And what I was beginning to see was making me all kinds of cranky.

"I'm qualified to do one thing and one thing only. Be a lawyer. This is what my parents paid for. This is what I know how to do. I've never so much as run a cash register. I've never filled out an application. I've never even done my own laundry."

I stared at her, reminding myself to blink. How could someone get to our age and be so fantastically unprepared for life's most basic tasks? All the skills I had taken for granted. All the things my mother had insisted that I learn to do for myself.

I knew how to clean a gun before most people had learned how to ride a bike. I'd learned how to ride a bike before most children knew how to read. I knew how to read before some children had been potty trained.

*The more you know how to do for yourself, the less you need anyone else, Janey. The less you need anyone else, the safer you'll be.*

"Doing your own laundry is totally overrated. As is breaking the rules, for that matter. It's a royal pain in the ass, having to talk yourself out of trouble all the damn time."

"But you know *how*, is my point. I wouldn't even know how to start."

"Easy," I said. "Next time someone tells you to do something, do the exact opposite."

"I couldn't—"

"You could."

Then Melanie's car started ringing. Not her phone, but the car, the sound of her ringtone filling the cabin through the speakers. The glowing backlit display on the dashboard flashed "Mother."

Melanie's sigh was long and deep. "I have to take this." She punched a button on the steering wheel, and the call connected. "Hello, Mother," she said evenly.

"Melanie, darling. What are you doing downtown?" Even irritated, Melanie's mother had a voice that conjured sprawling New England lawns. Cool glasses of lemonade served on wooden verandas, the blades of outdoor fans circling lazily overhead. Old money.

"I'm on my way to the country club."

"Oh? And what were you doing in the Highlands area before that?"

"I was picking up a friend."

"And who might you be collecting in *that* area of town?" Her mouth handled the word like it was a dirty diaper—pinched by the extreme edges, held as far away from her person as possible.

"Buffy Von Lumpling," I said. "Pleased to make your acquaintance, Mrs. Beidermeyer." I affected a southern accent far more stereotypical than the one Melanie and her mother favored, knowing by instinct how it would horrify them both.

A distinct chill came over the line.

"My apologies, Miss Von Lumpling. I wasn't aware my daughter wasn't alone in the vehicle." Her diction was at once stiff, cold, and perfectly polite.

"Well, I'm mighty grateful to your daughter for being willing to give me a ride to the country club. My Festiva broke down earlier today, and I'd hate to miss my interview." I'd offered her a choice in this sentence. Two very problematic words, and she could only pick one of them to chew on. I had a pretty good idea which one she'd choose.

"Interview?"

"Yeah. I'm trying to land me a job as napkin girl in the dining room. I've been practicing folding napkin swans all damn day."

The teeniest, tiniest shadow flickered at the corner of Melanie's mouth. The mere forethought of a smile.

"I wasn't aware my daughter had friends with those kinds of qualifications."

"Oh, I don't know that I'd call us friends." I winked at Melanie. "More like acquaintances."

Relief smoothed some of the ire out of the Beidermeyer matriarch's voice. "That makes more sense, I suppose."

"It's my brother she's closest to. What with their having made out in the closet at the last Beta Theta Pi mixer."

Melanie's eyes went as wide as duck eggs as her mother made a gurgling sound through the car's speakers. I imagined top-shelf vodka fumes puffing out of Mrs. Beidermeyer's nose as she choked on her evening cocktail.

"Speaking of acquaintances, you think you could put in a good word for me, Mrs. B? I'd bet those folks at the country club would be willing to overlook my record if I had someone like you vouching for me."

"Record?"

"Oh, it's nothing major. A few misdemeanors here, an aggravated assault there. We've all gotten up to the dickens now and then, am I right, Mrs. B?"

The Mrs. Beidermeyer in my mind steadied herself on a Hepplewhite secretaire. "Melanie, please disengage me from the speaker phone this minute. I need to speak with you privately."

"There's no need to do that," I insisted. "I'll just stick my fingers in my ears while y'all talk."

*"Melanie."*

"I can hum too, if that'd help. Here goes nothing." I warbled out the first few bars of "I Wish I Was in Dixie" as shrilly and emphatically as I could.

"Melanie Leigh Beidermeyer—"

"Oh, all right, all right. We'll take you off speaker. Is that what this button here does?" I pushed the "End Call" button, and the car's interior went silent.

Melanie blinked at me, her face pale with shock.

"You just hung up on my mother." The wonder and alarm in her voice would have been just as appropriate to an announcement that the sun had imploded or something similar.

"Well, shoot," I said, not entirely out of the dialect. "Is that what I did?"

"You just hung up on my mother."

The car began ringing once again. Melanie answered it with the punch of a button. "I'm so sorry, Mother. Buffy must have pushed the wrong button."

"A thousand pardons, Mrs. B. I ain't used to all this fancy gadgetry your daughter has up in here."

"Perhaps it might be best if you acquired transportation more akin to your level of comfort next time, then." The acid in her tone could have eaten through a whole pallet of steel rebar.

"If I didn't know better, I'd think you were trying to imply your daughter shouldn't ought to have offered me a ride, Mrs. B."

"You're more astute than I would have guessed, Miss Von Lumpling."

"Why thank you, Mrs. B. And for what it's worth, I think your twat's probably warmer than the icicle you have lodged up your keister."

Melanie and Mrs. Beidermeyer favored me with identical gasps.

"Melanie, you will drop her off and come home at once."

"How about nope." I disconnected the call.

"I can't believe you did that. I could never hang up on my mother like that."

"Sure you could. Watch this." So I hit the "Redial" button and waited to hear Mrs. Beidermeyer's terse greeting on the other end of the phone before hanging up on her a third time, just for good measure "See? Easy."

"She's going to be livid."

"She's already livid. And guess what? You're okay. See how the sidewalk isn't littered with birds that fell out of the sky? See how the laws of gravity didn't come unraveled and the earth didn't cease to spin on its axis?"

"You don't understand how Mother can be. When she gets into one of her rages . . ." Melanie trailed off, her eyes wide with worry.

"How the hell did she know where you were, anyway?" I asked.

"The car's GPS sends my parents a text whenever I stray from the boundaries of my prescribed area."

What she said was shocking enough, but it was the *way* she said it. Like this was a completely natural thing for any parent to do. Track your every move via GPS and call to check should you stray out of the prescribed area. Melanie Beidermeyer was a beautiful bird that had long since stopped pecking at the bars of her gilded cage.

But. *But.*

"There may be hope for you yet," I said

She brightened incrementally. "You really think so?"

"I do. I highly doubt your parents would approve of matching you with Bixby, and yet you asked me to set you up. You probably knew you'd get tagged for coming downtown to get me, and you did it anyway. We may find a rebel in you yet."

She sat up straighter in her seat, apparently encouraged by having these small signs pointed out to her.

We pulled up through the semicircular drive in front of the country club, a sprawling building with glowing windows, immaculately clipped hedges, and the wood-shingled exterior of an unassumingly expensive Hamptons vacation home. White columns and crisp trim lent it the air of old southern money. The kind of place where the sound of golf cleats crunching on the imported gravel and the shadows of wide-brimmed garden hats would be ubiquitous in summer.

Almost immediately, two men clad in khakis and golf shirts came jogging out to the car and opened each of our doors.

Melanie handed a neatly folded stack of bills to one of them and gracefully levered herself out of the car. I followed suit with considerably more skirt adjusting and throat clearing.

Two more men opened the double doors for us as we approached, their timing impeccably attuned to our very gait, it seemed.

I had expected a broad oak entrance desk of the kind you'd expect to find at a courthouse or somewhere else where entry is carefully monitored and strictly enforced. Instead, there was only a small but immaculately neat concierge desk to the left of the entrance, outfitted with a spray of fresh flowers and a tall glass dispenser of water studded with cucumber slices and mint leaves. The slim monitor next to it was manned by a just as slim man.

His face opened like a flower at dawn when he spotted Melanie.

"Melanie! How lovely to see you. And have you brought us a friend?"

I couldn't make out a single trace of buried irony or disapproval, and believe me, I looked.

"Yes, Hillard. This is my good friend—"

"Buffy Von Lumpling," I finished for her, offering my hand.

He shook it, ending with a warm and welcoming squeeze. "What a spectacular name. I'll bet your parents just have the most fabulous sense of humor."

"They're dead." I tried on a sepulchral tone, waiting for the thin mask of kindness to shatter.

It didn't.

Hillard moved from delight to perfectly calibrated dismay in a nanosecond. Oh, this dude was good, all right. But I'd figure out his game soon enough.

"I'm so sorry," he said.

"I barely knew them. Vehicular accident was what went on the police reports, but personally, I thought it was a mob hit."

Melanie side-hoofed my ankle, apparently not a fan of the mob-hit angle.

"Hillard, Buffy is visiting from out of town for a few days, and I thought it might be nice to show her some local hospitality. Would you mind setting up a temporary membership for her?" Dark lashes feathered against her high cheekbones. This artful combination of lilting accent and demure southern femininity had felled men for as long as men could be felled. She was Zelda Fitzgerald. Scarlett O'Hara.

"How lovely. Of course I will. We'd be delighted to have you. How long will you be staying?"

"Just until the rash clears up," I said. "My dermatologist thought the mountain air would do me good."

Another horrified sideways glance from Melanie.

"Well, we'll be happy to take care of you for as long as you're here." He dipped into a desk drawer and extracted a key card, which he slid into some kind of scanner and slipped across the desk. "Here you are. Melanie, will you be showing her around, or should I arrange a tour?"

"I'll show her around."

I took the card from the desk. "Isn't there any paperwork I need to sign?"

Hillard's laugh was warm and gentle. "Not at all. Any friend of Melanie's is a friend of ours. We're delighted to have you."

I felt the protective layers of *Fuck you, fuckball* I'd girded my metaphorical loins with beginning to melt like candle wax under the radiant heat of all this unexpected kindness.

Melanie threaded her arm through mine and steered me toward a set of double doors. "Come on, Buffy. Let's go take a look at the spa facilities. I can't wait to introduce you to Vivian, my masseuse."

As soon as the swinging door closed behind us, Melanie tugged me behind a bank of oak-paneled lockers and turned to face me, hands on narrow hips.

"A mob hit? A rash? Really, Jane?"

"It's Buffy to you, and yes. It's my intrepid orphan's spirit that enables me to persist in the face of such a dermatological tragedy."

She folded her arms tightly across perky, couture-clad bosoms. "Well, little orphan Annie Shingles, what now?"

"Now, you get gone and I get to business."

"But I thought—"

"Look, Melanie. It's nothing personal. I mean, it's kind of personal because I don't like your face and being exposed to your presence for extended periods makes me want to stab puppies, but in this case, my desire not to have you around is purely practical."

The one time in our years of association that I hadn't bothered to soften the truth, and Melanie had the nerve to *grin* at me. Standing tears magnified her eyes. Frankly I was a little surprised she had them. Tear ducts, that is. I had always kind of assumed that if I poked a finger up Melanie's nose, I'd get about a quarter inch before I struck a core made of solid gold and fairy dust. Essence of unicorn, maybe.

"Oh, Jane. I know what you're about now." Then she did something so hideous, so unexpected, that I nearly fell backward into an artful wicker towel hamper.

"Whoa, whoa, whoa," I said. "What the hell do you think you're doing?"

"Hugging you." She squeezed for emphasis, releasing a series of pops down the length of my spine. Melanie might drink like a lady, but she hugged like a goddamn bear. "You may act all unpleasant and insist that you don't need anyone, but beneath that tough, unpleasant exterior—"

"Is an even tougher and more unpleasant interior, believe me." I peeled her arms away by their slender wrists and fastened them at her sides. "Get your shit together, will you, woman? Just because we have one nonantagonistic conversation doesn't mean we're friends. I hate you. You hate me. Remember how this works?"

"But I don't," she insisted. "I never did. It's just that I find your presence unbearable for the most part."

"And this is different than hating me *how*?"

"Because it's not so much how I feel about *you*. It's how you make me feel about *me*."

"How is that exactly?" I asked, maybe hoping just the tiniest bit that words like *insanely jealous* or *completely consumed by envy* might be mentioned.

"Ridiculous, for the most part."

Bummer.

"Ridiculous? What the fuck are you talking about? You're annoyingly, maddeningly, orphan-kickingly perfect."

"I know!" she wailed. "That's the problem. I'm too perfect to be taken seriously. Here I am all beautiful and rich and brilliant, and *you* roll into class all disheveled and surly and *still* make me look like an idiot with one well-placed comment. I wish I could be like you and just not care what people thought of me."

"You know, I was with you right up until the surly and disheveled bit."

Melanie didn't seem to hear me. She'd built up a head of steam now and was ranting and pacing like the world's prettiest bag lady. "You show up late to class wearing torn jeans and wrinkled T-shirts. And those *shoes*—"

"What's wrong with my shoes?" I glanced downward at my trusty Chuck Taylors, well worn and well loved and maybe spattered with the blood of assorted bad guys.

*I probably ought to do something about that.*

"What I'm trying to say is that no one accuses you of having got by on your looks. They take one look at you and they *know* that anything you have, you earned."

"It's like you *want* me to beat you like a drum and stuff you into one of these lockers."

"And that's another thing. You're always making these creative threats of violence, and people actually believe you. If *I* tried that, they'd laugh me right out of town."

"That's because you know jack shit about physical combat."

"But that's not true at all. Father always made sure I had the best self-defense teachers growing up. I can drop a man in two seconds flat."

"Oh, yeah?" In two quick moves I had her arm pinned behind her back and her face smooshed up against a locker door.

And Sam thought *I* was a terrible liar.

"You want people to start taking you seriously? Well, here's a start. Stop calling your parents Mother and Father. It's just damn creepy." I released her as quickly as I had nabbed her.

She sniffed and regained her pageant posture, haughty as freshly fallen cat. "It's a southern thing."

"Look, Melanie, it's not like I don't appreciate your giving me a ride and getting me a visitor's pass, but could we possibly unpack the various elements of our mutual dislike another time? I have work to do."

"What kind of work?" She brightened, going all keen like a terrier. "Maybe I could help."

"You can't." I elbowed her out of the way and started toward the door.

"How do you know if you don't tell me what you're trying to do?" Melanie quickly insinuated herself between me and the exit.

"Because I know." I had brushed past her a second time when she froze me in my tracks with the most sincere sentence I had ever heard her speak.

"Teach me to be like you."

For a moment, I thought I might have strayed into one of those alternate universes you see on reruns of *The Twilight Zone* where up is down and hot is cold and Melanie Beidermeyer wasn't a first-class twunt. (It's a contraction. Draw your own conclusions.)

"Excuse me?"

"I want to learn how to be like you," she said. "To wear what I want. To hang up on people when I want. To get jobs by myself instead of having my father buy them for me."

I sighed, mysteriously unable to come up with a crushing verbal blow to send her sobbing to a bathroom stall. "Okay. But another time, all right? I've got some shit to sort out just now."

"You mean you'll do it?" She looked at me with her hands clasped to her chest, her big blue eyes all enthusiasm and hope.

"If you promise to leave me the hell alone for the next hour, then yes. I'll think about it."

She clapped her hands and jumped and did some sort of cheerleader shuffle.

"Lesson one," I said. "Whatever that was? Never do it again."

"But we're finally bonding!" She grabbed both my hands and squeezed. "After all these years of secretly sabotaging each other and wishing each other dead, we're finally getting along."

"We're *not* getting along, and if you dare imply that to the general populace, I will sneak into your family estate and personally break the heels from each and every one of your Jimmy Choos."

She mimed zipping her lips, a gesture both guileless and endearing. I reminded myself that it was probably an expensive zipper made by sweatshop orphans who had gone blind from years of hand carving the teeth from blood diamonds.

"See you at work tomorrow?" she asked.

"Most likely."

She was almost out the door when a question that had been buzzing around my brain like an addled bee finally found its way to my lips.

"There's something I want to ask you before you go."

Melanie turned on her heel and looked at me, her head cocked at a quizzical angle. "What's that, sugar?"

"Kristin Flickner mentioned that you'd had the Koontzes' medical malpractice case reassigned to her. Why?"

Her expression was equal parts pleased and rueful. "Same reason I do everything. My parents told me to."

I stood there in the spa's antechamber after she left, trying and failing to think. I thought it must have had something to do with the brain-blunting effect of the luxury surrounding me. Top-of-the-line hair dryers. Creams and lotions imported from jolly old Paris. Gold-plated tampons for the wealthy cooze. All telling me there was no reason to think too hard. To try too hard.

But that wasn't how I'd been raised.

Needing a moment to collect myself before I faced down Valentine, I took a deep breath and sat on a padded leather bench.

Names floated in my head like pieces of a puzzle that refused to assemble themselves into an image.

The Beidermeyers. Dean David Koontz. Valentine. Carla Malfi. Kristin Flickner. If I squinted my mind's eye, I could almost see the tenuous and tangled threads of spider silk connecting them. I could feel the danger in them.

And then, I knew.

My mother *knew*.

My mother had found out exactly how they were connected, and that's why she was gone.

I felt it in my bones.

I felt *her* in my bones.

Together we stood and walked out to find Valentine.

# Chapter Twenty-Two

Finding Valentine turned out to be even easier than I had thought.

After just a couple of minutes of wandering around the spacious country club atrium trying to look like I knew what the hell I was doing and where the hell I was going, I caved. I gave in to the temptation of asking my question of one of the small army of uniformed employees approaching me at ten-second intervals to offer their assistance.

"I'm here to meet with Archard Everett Valentine. Would you happen to know where I might find him?"

"Ahh," my would-be assistant said with a knowing look. "You can probably find him in the bar. He usually likes the table overlooking the golf course."

"Thank you," I said, wondering if this was the sort of thing you tipped for at a country club.

Mere minutes later, I stood behind yet another tall plant by yet another maître d' station, acknowledging to myself that, when you thought about it, life really was all about patterns.

Stalking Valentine in bars. Handcuffing ex-army security types to household fixtures. Trying to wheedle an answer or two before some security guard or other tossed you out into the street with a pocketful of steak fries and regret.

I took a deep breath and plunged once again into the void.

Only, the Japanese screen partitioning off the back of the restaurant had obscured one very important detail.

Valentine wasn't alone.

Sitting across the table from him, close-cropped head flamed by a corona of sun expensively dying behind the ninth hole, was none other than my self-appointed bodyguard.

Shepard.

Shock can stretch time like taffy or burn up whole huge portions of it in an instant. It can relieve you of muscle memory or deliver owner-ship of your body to some strange and mysterious source. It can make you sob with joy or laugh with grief.

And sometimes it does all of those things at once.

I don't remember sprinting toward them at a gallop. Nor do I recall launching myself across the table. What I do remember is how the world went muffled then. I remember how the rushing of my own pulse superseded all else. I remember the skin of my face coming alive with the prickling of a thousand needles.

I remember snapping back to consciousness with about five sets of hands on my body and a steady stream of creative profanity spewing from my lips in between hysterical giggles.

A note about the creative profanity, should you find yourself in a similar situation. Just combine an animal you don't like with a sexual act you do. For example: snake-licking, toad-sucking, shark-wanking, chicken fucker.

What? Don't tell me I'm the only one creeped out by chickens. With their scratchy little talons and their dead eyes and their pecky little beaks.

But I digress. Point being, any and all of the aforementioned invec-tives could have been included in the torrent of verbal filth issuing from my gullet.

So there I was, arms outstretched like Superman, table linens slid-ing beneath me like a luxurious conveyer belt, assorted water glasses and wine goblets making crystalline explosions as they hit the polished parquet floor, when an impeccably outfitted detail of Valentine's own security abruptly arrested my progress and planted me back on the floor.

Several members of the restaurant staff poked their heads past the screen. "Would you like us to call—" One of the staff paused midsentence, seeing the full complement of goons flanking me. "Anyone?"

Valentine took a thorough accounting of me with his slow, cold, green-eyed gaze. "That won't be necessary. I believe my own employees are more than equipped to handle the situation."

The server took one look at the beefcake squad restraining me and nodded. "Of course, sir."

When they were gone, Valentine nodded to the empty chair at the table. "Please help Miss Avery to her seat."

And help they did. Roughly acquainting my ass with the padded chair in a most unceremonious fashion.

"So," I said, turning to Shepard. "Want to tell me what the actual fuck you're doing here?"

"Does he need to?" Valentine lifted a tumbler of amber liquid to his lips and sipped. "Or have you figured it out?"

"I want to hear him say it."

*Lie.*

I didn't *want* to hear him say it. I would have much preferred never to have to give ear to the words I knew were coming. The truth was, I *needed* to hear him say it. I needed it to justify the sick churning in my gut. To give causal form to my body's visceral reaction.

Those damnably beautiful forearms with their network of veins and tattoos rested on the white linen tablecloth, his broad palms flat against the table, long fingers splayed. I remembered what they felt like on my neck in the closet's close darkness.

"I work for Valentine." He stated this sentence with no more affectation than he might announce the current weather. A simple fact.

My reaction was somewhat less tranquil.

I hadn't exactly planned on picking up the fork and trying stab the eye out of the tiger twisting up Shepard's forearm, but it happened nonetheless. I didn't succeed, of course. Shepard caught hold of my wrist and pinned my arm to the table before the tines could find their target.

Which was a mistake.

Anger had been the impetus for our closet collision. It flared back to life now, threatening to incinerate the table and everyone at it. Everyone that wasn't him. Wasn't me. Wasn't *us*.

The animal I'd met in the dark sprang to the surface. The feral hunger waking behind his eyes. Desire mixed with fury. A tangle of wants.

"Don't tell me you've fucked her." Valentine's face had gone cold despite the alcohol warming the blood in his body. His smile wasn't a smile but a dark, sarcastic slash. The measured tightness of it belied the careless slouch of his long, lean body. "This tendency of yours to become involved with our targets is becoming a real liability, Shepard."

Valentine had said this for my benefit. To make sure I knew I wasn't the first. Wouldn't be the last.

I marshaled every ounce of the betrayal I felt, turning it into the acid words I spit directly into Shepard's face. "So you didn't run back and tell Daddy what happened in the closet?"

Shepard released my wrist as if it had burned him.

"What closet? What is she talking about, Shepard?" Whoever had originally labeled envy "the green-eyed monster" must have channeled Valentine's face at this precise moment.

Shepard said nothing, his eyes warning me to do the same.

A warning I had no intention of heeding.

"Oh," I said with exaggerated wonder. "You mean dragging me into a closet and putting your hands on me wasn't part of your *orders*?"

"Jane." Times like this, I really wished my mother hadn't saddled me with a name one could pronounce so perfectly through gritted teeth.

"Still. I have to give you credit," I said. "You almost had me believing that you gave a shit about what happened to me. And the way you carried me to your car afterward? Fucking clever."

Shepard's fist came down on the table with enough force to make the plates jump.

"Enough!"

In the strained silence following the outburst, Valentine reached out and coolly took a sip of his drink. Even in his rumpled dress shirt, sleeves cuffed to the elbows, it was easy to see the manner that had made him famous in boardrooms and bedrooms alike. Unquestionable command. Unarguable power.

"We have much to discuss, and I would prefer we conducted this conversation like civilized adults. Do you think that's possible?"

"Well, *I* can," I said. "I can't speak for the honorless spoodge-sack of deception to my left."

Shepard didn't take the bait as he might have had Valentine not been in spitting distance. Not that I'd spat at him yet, but I wasn't ruling it out.

"Fine," Shepard said. "But only if she drops the fork."

Until that moment, I hadn't realized it was still gripped in my clenched fist. I set it aside, and one of the minions took it from me and set it next to Valentine. Which didn't seem fair in the least as he already had all the good weapons. What with the steak knife and the brass napkin ring and everything.

"How long have you been working for Valentine?" I asked.

Shepard's eyes had gone flat. Distant. Like the man I thought I knew had wandered somewhere else inside the complicated channels of his head. "Since always."

Memories slammed into each other, backing up in my head like a massive pileup. The clues I'd seen, ignored, or flat out missed. How he'd seen me kidnap Valentine that first day. How he'd known where to find me each and every time since then when I'd tracked Valentine down.

"And Paul?"

Shepard turned his dead eyes to Valentine, who nodded. "Paul too."

With my aim and Shepard's reflexes, the floral centerpiece ended up hitting the Japanese screen and shattering on the floor in a wash of broken glass and petals. I was about as shocked as they were, as I'd never been much of a thing thrower before this particular evening.

This amused Valentine as much as it failed to amuse Shepard. "Perhaps we should remove *all* potential projectiles from Miss Avery's immediate vicinity."

His minions shuffled to obey, stripping the area around me of everything but the tablecloth. Which I might have already been considering whipping out from beneath the flatware like Houdini and using as a garrote.

"So Paul and my mother. Were they ever in a relationship, or was that a big fat lie as well?"

It was Valentine, not Shepard, who answered.

"That particular story was his idea. I only asked him to go by your mother's house. When you turned up there, I expect he thought an existing relationship might make his presence there seem less problematic."

Right about now, I was wishing they hadn't moved all the throwables out of my reach. "But it isn't even my mother's house, is it?"

Surprise stole about ten years from Valentine's face, and for a brief second, I could see what he must have looked like as a boy. All large gray-green eyes and tousled dark hair. No lines etching his forehead or bracketing his mouth. He didn't like being surprised, judging by how quickly he evicted this expression in favor of his usual bored stoicism.

Valentine motioned to the waiter, who flew over as if pulled on a drawstring. "Bring Miss Avery a drink. I suspect we'll be here a while."

The waiter angled his horsey face to me in a manner far too solicitous for what he'd seen unfold that evening. "What will you have, miss?"

"Just the water." However tempting oblivion might be, however lovely it looked when Valentine courted it, I needed my head clear for this conversation.

"Still or sparkling?"

"Wet," I said. "Beyond that, I don't give a shit."

"Should you like a lime or lemon with that?"

"I *would* not. And just so you know, there's nothing fancy about incorrect grammar."

That pea-size shadow returned to the corner of Valentine's mouth. Barest evidence of a smirk.

"Very good."

"So, you know about your mother's residence," Valentine said when the waiter had gone. His tone told me in no uncertain terms that this was something he hadn't wanted me to know. Something he'd hoped I'd never find out.

"I know that my mother's house and my mother's car belong to companies that all somehow belong to you. I came here tonight hoping you might be able to shed a little light on that in addition to a couple of other things."

"What is it you want to know?" he asked.

Oh, he was careful.

I hadn't realized exactly *how* careful until I reached for my pocket and every man standing around the table went for a firearm.

"Relax, guys." I waved the yellow sticky note I'd retrieved like a surrender flag. "It's just a list."

Valentine looked both pleased and irritated, an exceedingly strange combination for someone who rarely managed more than casual disinterest.

"You brought a list?" he asked.

I raised an eyebrow at him. "Is that a problem?"

"Not at all." That amused smile was back. The one that never quite made it all the way to his eyes. "I just wouldn't have pegged you for the list-making type."

"Well, you pegged me wrong."

*Lie.*

My mother had always been the list maker, but showing up with the assorted napkins, scraps of paper, and bits of fast-food wrappers I'd jotted all my thoughts down on over the last couple of days seemed like it might hurt my credibility somehow.

The waiter returned with my water and set it down on the table.

When he was gone, Valentine turned to Shepard. "I think it's best if Miss Avery and I speak privately."

"I'll wait outside," Shepard said, rising. "I'll take her home when you're done."

"That won't be necessary." Valentine didn't look at Shepard but at the various implements on the table, which he'd begun sliding into a more comfortable spatial arrangement.

"What are my orders?"

"Your *orders* were to keep her at the safe house, and you failed. Three times she's gotten away from you now. There won't be a fourth."

"But—"

"You may go."

*You* may *go.* Our equine-visaged waiter could've learned a thing or two from Valentine about grammatical warfare.

Shepard stood still, staring at Valentine.

Valentine stared right back.

I could have toasted marshmallows on the heat of the masculine energy clashing and crackling between them.

If only I'd had a bucket of popcorn.

Shepard jerked the chair out from behind him and turned to go. Every female eye followed as he passed, just as every male body gave him a wide berth. I doubted if this was a conscious gesture on either side.

And then Valentine and I were alone behind the Japanese screen.

"How shall we do this?" was what he asked, but what it sounded like was *How do you want it?* The correct answer being something like

*Rough* or *From behind.* "Would you like me to spin this tale from the beginning, or do you want to ask me your questions and put the pieces together yourself?"

I assessed him for the space of a breath. Long inhale. Long exhale. Eyes a shade too shiny. High cheekbones pinked from the improved circulation lent him by the scotch. He was just lubed enough to slip up and tell me something useful. I took a sip of my water, hoping he hadn't noticed the slight tremor in my hand. "Tell me," I said. "From the beginning."

"Story time, then. Are we comfy? Cozy?"

Cozy, yes. Comfy, no. The lighting was all wrong, for one thing. Romantically dim and ambient. Much better suited to the kind of underneath-the-table shenanigans that left movie characters shouting for the check rather than learning potentially damning secrets. Also, it made Valentine's cheekbones and jaw look especially rough and masculine, which helped me focus on the task at hand not at all.

"Once upon a time there was a man named Valentine."

"He sounds like a dick."

"He was," Valentine said, his expression grave. "Like his father before him. And when Valentine was still not much more than a boy, his dick father liked to spend his days not going to work and his nights drinking and cheating on his wife."

"Wait, are you sure we're not talking about Valentine himself? Because these guys sound eerily similar."

"I'm positive," he said, giving me the full smolder of his hooded eyes. "Valentine is much, much worse."

"I see."

"Now Valentine's father, let's call him Archie, for sake of clarity—"

"Wait a minute. Your father's name was *also* Archard Everett Valentine? Are you a junior?"

"Technically, I'm a third."

"Just when I thought you couldn't get any more insufferable . . ."

"Insufferable is interrupting a story *you* asked to hear." He slid an ice cube out of his drink and collected it with an unnatural twist of his tongue. "Where were we?"

"Archie."

"Yes. Archie. Archie liked to gamble when he wasn't drinking and whoring, so there were all kinds of bookies and loan sharks dropping by the house. Well, young Valentine got to be pretty good friends with some of them, and they told him how he could make some money running errands for an associate of theirs. Valentine knew how hard his mother worked and thought maybe if he could bring in some money of his own, she wouldn't have to. So he agreed to meet with one of these associates."

Here, he paused to slurp down the last of his liquid courage. No sooner had the bottom of the glass hit the table than the server came by to replace it with a fresh one. No wonder everyone around here was so goddamned nice. They were probably all loaded to the neck.

If he kept going at this rate, I was going to have to get both of us home.

"Well, young Valentine did such a good job for the first associate that he got introduced to another associate, and another, until by the time he was ready to graduate from high school, he had enough money to help his mother leave his father for good."

"Touching," I said. "When do we get to the part about Valentine owning my mother's house?" Jesus. Now he had *me* talking about him in the third person.

"So impatient." The booze began to work on his smile, loosening it like a tie. "I wonder if you're this eager in all your endeavors."

"You mean you're wondering if I'm as eager for cock as I am for answers? Or is this just that vague sexual hinting thing you do when you're trying to distract people?"

"Yes," he said. One answer for two questions.

"Keep wondering. Can we move this story along, Aesop?"

Valentine picked up his drink and swirled it, ice clinking against the sides of his glass. "By the time Valentine graduated from high school, certain people had gotten used to him running their errands and weren't all that eager to let him stop, so they offered him even more money to do even more things."

"Like break into houses and steal shit?"

His forehead creased as his dark brows pushed together. "Have you heard this story before?"

If pressed, I might have had to admit that drunk Valentine was just the tiniest bit adorable. Luckily, no one was pressing. "No, but I talked to your buddy Jeremy yesterday. He acquainted Sam and me with some of the finer points of your career as a petty criminal."

"Sam?"

"Sam Shook. Of Dawes, Flickner, and Shook."

"Ohhh. That Sam. Good guy. He's my divorce lawyer."

"I know that. You made sure he got assigned as my mentor, remember?"

"I did?" He was squinting now, maybe to try and press the two or three of me he had to be seeing into one solid image.

"Jesus, Valentine. Are you going to be able to hold it together to finish this story or what?"

"I'm good," he said, reaching for and missing his drink, which I'd quietly slid away from him. "What was I saying?"

"You were talking about your enterprising career as an up-and-coming *b*-and-*e* artist?"

"Right. It started with the houses. Figuring out ways to get in without anyone knowing we'd gotten in. Small ones. Then bigger ones. Then it was the businesses. Mom-and-pop shops. Then the ones with security systems. Before long, Valentine earned a reputation as a guy who could figure out how to get into all kinds of places just by looking at the building schematics."

"Your interest in architecture is suddenly making more sense." I took a sip of his scotch instead of my water, the amber liquid seeming a hell of a lot more interesting at the moment.

"Soon, Valentine's reputation caught the attention of one very powerful man with a reputation of his own."

"Better than magically getting himself into buildings?"

"Much. This man had a reputation for making people he didn't like disappear."

An inexplicable chill traveled up my arms despite Valentine's miming a *poof* with his fingers.

"And what did he want?"

"Same thing they all wanted. For Valentine to get him into a place he wasn't supposed to be to get something he wasn't supposed to have."

"And you did it?"

Valentine's face screwed itself up in a look of boyish exasperation. "You did hear the part where I said this man had a reputation for making people disappear, right?"

"So, you got the man into the place . . . ," I said, not wanting him to lose track of his story once again.

"Have you ever heard the saying 'be careful what you're willing to do well, because then people will want you to do it all the time'?"

"I have." In truth, this very saying had contributed in no small way to my dire commitment to being an underachiever when it came to skills useful to other humans.

"Well, this man wanted Valentine to recreate his little trick again and again. And each time, for a bigger score. He wasn't happy with just middle-range businesses anymore. He wanted Valentine to get him into banks. Into government buildings. But see, the feds didn't like how this man was getting into banks and government buildings."

*Feds.*

If *cops* had been a dirty word in our home growing up, *feds* had been the equivalent of an unforgivable curse. The kind of thing you'd say before you spit through forked fingers.

"But as much as they didn't like this man getting into banks and government buildings, they liked the man's ability to make people disappear even less."

"Understandable."

"The trouble with building a case against a man who can make people disappear is—"

"That no one is willing to testify against him." Three years of memorizing precedence cases and reviewing the outcome of complicated criminal defense strategies had helped me foresee this particular twist. "They offered immunity?"

"They offered immunity," he confirmed. "But the people closest to the man knew what he liked to do to people who displeased him. So even with the offer of immunity, only one person was willing to turn state's evidence and testify against him."

"And young Valentine was that person?" A guess, but a decent one, I thought.

"Yes." Valentine, who had been swimming in the depths of memory, surfaced to pin me with the intensity of that green-eyed gaze. "So I testified. My criminal record was expunged. But the one thing I had really wanted, the feds were unable to deliver."

"An endless supply of hookers and coke?" My ill-timed joke failed to draw his usual smirk.

"Safety," he said. "Safety from the network of associates I betrayed when I testified."

"But what about the witness protection program? Couldn't they—"

"They found me anyway. Every. Single. Time. A new place. A new name. A new start. It didn't matter." He stared at the candle's refracted flame in his cut-crystal glass, making it dance around the rim as he swirled the contents.

Signs I had attributed to a life lived in excess screamed at me anew. His red-rimmed eyes. The hollows beneath them. In the same face I had seen so many times now, I read new volumes of pain. The aftermath of too many years lived hand in hand with fear.

"I got tired of running," he said. "Tired of hiding. So I got creative. I started researching *different* ways to protect myself. Word got out after a while. And soon, different people started to seek me out."

"What kind of people?"

"People whom the system had failed, generally. People whom the witness protection program couldn't protect. People like your mother."

# Chapter Twenty-Three

Mom and I used to do puzzles.

When the nightmares were the worst, she'd let me crawl into bed with her. After I was good and snuggled in, she'd drag the biggest cookie sheet from the kitchen and set it on the bedspread between us. Together we'd pick pieces from the upended puzzle carton until daylight bled through the blinds and I could finally sleep.

Me? I'd always gone straight for the pieces in the center. Those with the brightest colors or most recognizable shapes.

Not Mom.

Mom patiently sorted through the box until she located each and every piece with a straight edge. Then, meticulously, she assembled the border around whichever random section I happened to be laboring over.

*You have to see the big picture before you can understand its parts, Janey.*

The big picture.

Valentine had sketched the border for me, and now the pieces began falling faster, clicking into place.

The frenetic energy that had driven us state to state. House to house. The reason why my mother would have done her best to erase all evidence of her existence. In order to protect mine. The nightmares.

The memory of my mother's screams. Her insistence that I know how to defend myself. How to shoot a gun. How to disappear. How to hide.

My entire life. Every word she had ever said.

All to protect me. Not from *every*one, but from *some*one.

I forgot how to breathe.

How to speak.

So many words I'd learned in the course of a lifetime. Plenty to form the million questions battering my brain. And yet, I sat there saying nothing. My face going numb and my fingers turning cold and my stomach tightening into a little ball directly below my heart.

And my heart.

My stupid, foolish heart began bleeding out wishes.

*I wish I were at home, with my head in my mother's lap, her fingers sliding through my hair. I wish the goose bumps on my scalp had been put there by her.*

*I wish Carla Malfi's face didn't appear on the backs of my eyelids every time I blink.*

*I wish.*

"Who?" I asked. "Who was my mother running from?"

Some steel doors slid shut behind Valentine's eyes. "That's a question you'll have to ask her. It's not my place to say."

The pain in my chest flamed into anger, settling low in my belly. "And how am I supposed to do that? She's gone! Or have you been too busy swilling booze and boffing whores that you hadn't noticed?"

"Yes." Valentine smoothed the crease in his linen napkin, bringing it to a precise 90-degree angle with the silver-embossed placemat. "She's gone. And the way I see it, she's gone for one of two reasons. Because of her own secrets, or because of someone else's. We won't find out which until we know what she knew. Since I obviously can't prevent you from trying to find out what that was . . ." He paused, glancing at the chair formerly occupied by Shepard. "I will tell you what *I* know, and we'll go from there. Fair?"

"Fair," I said.

"Your mother reached out to me a few years ago—"

"Years?" My chair scraped the parquet floor as I leaned across the table. "You've been protecting my mother for *years*?"

"This will go a lot faster if you don't persist in interrupting me. Do you think we could try that?"

"Maybe." I sat back in my chair and tucked my hands beneath my thighs. "I make no promises."

Valentine took a deep breath and began again. "*Protecting* is the wrong word."

"It was *your* word," I pointed out.

A muscle tightened in Valentine's jaw.

"Sorry," I said. "Go on."

"*Protecting* makes me sound like some noble, steed-riding knight. I am not."

"I'll say," I snorted. When his eyebrow ascended his forehead, I bit my lower lip. "My apologies. I thought I said that in my head."

"As I've mentioned before, I'm a businessman. Anyone who comes to me needing my services must provide value in return. Sometimes that value is a simple cash transaction. Sometimes not. Your mother was a *not*."

I nodded my silent encouragement for him to continue.

"When you decided to come here for law school, she knew you couldn't afford to pick up and move again halfway through. As your mother most likely taught you, there are lots of ways to track people down, and most of them begin with where you call home. Creature comforts. Cell phones. Car registration. Utilities. She needed these, but needed them not traceable back to her."

I raised my hand and waited.

The ghost of a smile haunted one corner of Valentine's mouth. "Yes, Jane."

"Explain something to me?"

"If I can."

"Why is it that you help other people disappear, but you yourself are on every damn tabloid from here to Vegas? I mean, even with the security detail, wouldn't it be harder for the people who want you dead to find you if you weren't a gajillionaire architect who's constantly in the public eye? You're not exactly making yourself a difficult target."

"The way I see it, there are two ways to keep yourself from getting killed." He held up two fingers bunny-ear style by way of a visual aid. "Make sure no one knows where you are, or make sure everyone does. Your mother chose the former. I chose the latter."

"Let me get this straight. You made sure to keep yourself in the public eye *on purpose?*"

"Sound strange? Let it settle in for a moment. I have the eyes of the paparazzi on me all the time. They track my movements. They keep a running record of every single person in my world. Anyone they don't know so much as breathes in my direction, and they start snapping photos. As an early-warning system, its unbeatable."

I sat back in my chair, grasping at the questions swarming my head like a cloud of flies. "So the scandals, the prostitutes who blabbed to the papers. You never . . ." *Paid extra for butt stuff,* I thought, but couldn't bring myself to say.

"Each and every woman I have ever been photographed with was paid for her services. It just so happens that those services did not include sex."

I blinked. I swallowed. I raised my finger and tapped my forehead like a microphone. *Is this thing on?*

"And it worked," he said. "It always worked. Until Carla. For her, I broke one of my own cardinal rules. And she paid the price."

"Which rule is that?" I asked.

"Never protect someone you're involved with. And never become involved with someone you protect."

My mother had often advised something similar, though hers sounded more like *Don't shit where you eat, Janey.*

"Carla was sick," Valentine continued. "She hid it from me for longer than she should have been able to." He raked a hand through his hair, harrowing wild furrows among the espresso-colored waves. "When I finally dragged the truth out of her, she told me she'd been involved in a medical trial for some new miracle drug and was somehow worse off than ever. Arrogant fool that I am, I thought, I have more money than God. I have a half sister who's a medical malpractice lawyer. Slam dunk. Right?" His laugh was as bitter as bile. "Wrong."

"Wrong how?" I asked.

"It wasn't long after Kristin and I started working together on Carla's case that some of the more damning accusations hit the press. As I've told you, I always maintain somewhat of a reputation, but this was something different. Someone was doing their sabotage of my businesses and investments by convincing everyone I'm a lying, cheating scoundrel of the first order."

"Have you ever considered that your soon-to-be ex-wife might have had something to do with it? She can't have been thrilled with the idea of you leveraging said money for a woman you'd been cheating on her with."

"*Her.*" Valentine's expression changed yet again, and I wasn't sure exactly what it was I saw there this time. Bitterness. Regret. Exhaustion. Maybe all of those things. "I doubt my dalliance with Carla bothered Miranda all that much. My soon-to-be ex-wife has been screwing around since the day we were married. Before that, actually, as your mother discovered."

"Discovering things is what she does best," I said.

*Revealing* them, not so much.

"Anyway, she followed the trail of information from the press all the way back to where it started."

"And where was that?"

"Dawes, Shook, and Flickner."

A bolt of energy shot up my spine, my fingers beginning to tingle and sweat. I shook like a terrier as a lightning clap of realization split my brain.

"Your divorce proceedings. Someone was leaking information gathered in your divorce proceedings to skewer you in the press. That's why you paid Rhonda and the others to come in and give a bunch of phony testimony. To see what would get leaked, and when."

"You're getting warmer," Valentine encouraged.

"And that's why Carla came in and said that my mother had been blackmailing you both. Because you didn't want anyone at the law firm to know that you'd been working together on Carla's case."

"You're on fire." Valentine fanned himself with a lazy hand.

"So that's what my mother was investigating before she disappeared? Finding out who had been working so hard to discredit you?"

"She had a promising theory."

"Which was?"

"That whoever was leaking damning information from my divorce proceedings to the media wanted to sabotage my businesses so I'd have to stop funding Carla Malfi's lawsuit, and—"

"And if they were to successfully pin her murder on you, you'd take the blame, you'd take the fall, the lawsuit falls apart, and they're off the hook."

Valentine reached up and tapped the end of his nose with an index finger. After all the booze he'd guzzled, I was mildly impressed he could still find it.

"Why take the risk?" I leaned forward, resting my chin on my palms, my head buzzing like a beehive between my hands.

"Pardon?" Valentine traced the rim of his empty glass with the tip of his index finger.

"All this time, you've been damn near untouchable. Then Carla comes along and you jeopardize the safety of the entire world you've built to help her. Why?"

"The same reason most people do stupid things."

"Shitty judgment?"

"Love." He raised his empty glass in a boozy, ironic toast.

"Love," I scoffed. And believe me, scoffing is definitely the word for what I did.

"Have you ever been in love, Jane Avery?" He examined my face as if trying to find the answer to his own question hidden somewhere in the crease of my eyelids or the curve of my lips. "No," he said. "No, I don't think you have."

"How would you know?"

"That kind of obsession marks you. Changes you."

The tips of Valentine's fingers, these hands that bid buildings to rise, now mapped the transition from my cheekbone to jaw. His eyes following the places he had touched.

And Valentine had touched me before. Dragged his thumb across my lower lip to smear my lipstick. Grazed my hand beneath the table when he'd collected my panties.

This time was different. This time, he didn't seem to know he was doing it.

I couldn't move, couldn't breathe for fear he would realize it and stop.

"When you've known what it's like to need another person more than you need air. When a few stolen moments, a kiss, a touch, is the only respite from the bone-deep ache of craving it. When a part of your soul has been sheared off and grafted into a heart that's not your own. That kind of love . . . it lives in your skin."

At least a dozen sarcastic comments suggested themselves. Things I could say—*should* say—to reduce this moment to rubble.

But I couldn't.

Not when Valentine's face was so close to mine. So close I could see the flecks of bronze like metal shavings scattered in the threads of his irises. Close enough for the air he exhaled to perfume my indrawn breath with the smoky scent of whiskey.

And then there was a pause.

No. Not just *a* pause.

*The* pause.

I could have stopped it then, but I didn't. The reasons were as complex and simple as this: right that second, I wanted to be whatever version of myself Valentine thought he saw.

I let my eyes fall closed, readying myself for the kind of mouth-on-mouth smash that had gone out of style with Bogie and Bacall, for I knew in some primal way that this was how Archard Everett Valentine would kiss.

Without preamble. Without apology.

Countless seconds went by during which I couldn't figure out if this was really happening. If these were really Archard Everett Valentine's lips hovering over mine, the heat from them making the few air molecules between us dance.

And then some titanic cock-goblin had to go and clear his throat.

Valentine jerked backward like a dog that had just run out of leash, leaving me pre-lip-lock tilting in the open air. The desperate-chick version of the Leaning Tower of Pisa.

The cock-blocking newcomer, whom I recognized as one of Valentine's own men, did everything short of holding up a hand to erase me from his vision while mumbling apologies to his employer.

"I'm sorry to interrupt, sir. But you've had a lot to drink, and you said if you . . . that is, if it seemed like you were trying to—"

Valentine looked at me, realization doing its best to form surprise with his uncooperative features.

"Jesus Christ," he said. "Were we about to—"

"Of course not," I said. "We were just having a conversation, and then you paused, and I thought maybe you—"

"She was leaning in, sir. And her eyes were closed."

I cast a withering look in the direction of Valentine's paid stooge.

"I was not. I was just stretching." *Lie.* I shifted in my seat demonstratively and rubbed at my lower back. "I don't know what kind of establishment you're running here, but these chairs are shit."

"But you—"

"What's your name?" The interruption was just enough to throw the lackey off his game.

"Jones," he said.

"Jones, if one more word comes out of your piehole with regard to what I may or may not have been doing, Valentine is going to need to find himself a new ass watcher."

"You can't fire me."

"Who said anything about firing you? Valentine will have to find your body first. Do we understand each other?"

Jones's Adam's apple bobbed over a swallow. "Yes, ma'am."

"Yes, *Jane.* Ma'am makes me feel oogy."

"Yes, *Jane,*" he repeated.

"We should go," Valentine announced. "Jones, we need to arrange safe transport home for Jane."

"I'm not going back to the safe house," I said.

"I didn't say you were. You're coming with me."

"Forget it. I'm done with babysitters. Give me a decent weapon and I'll take my chances."

Valentine gave me a look that was far more assessing than I would have figured he could manage at this point. "I'm afraid I can't do that. I made a promise to your mother."

"Come the fuck again?"

"Your mother made me promise that if anything happened to her, I would make sure you were safe. It's the whole reason I assigned Paul and Shepard to you in the first place."

I shook my head, trying to understand what he'd just said. This whole Valentine and my mother as bosom buddies thing was officially creeping me the fuck out.

"Fine. I'll go to your place. But only because I'm exhausted and my apartment probably still has dead-guy cooties in it."

"Good. It's settled."

Valentine tried to stand but stumbled against the table.

I steadied him by the hips. Feeling their particular unyielding shape against my palms was strangely intimate. He was a man it didn't feel normal to know.

"I'm drunk," he said.

"I gathered."

Jones poked his head around the screen and nodded to a couple of his comrades. Together they propped Valentine up like a scarecrow and commenced to march him out of the restaurant.

The other diners kept right on chewing their prime rib and acting like a billionaire stumbling his way out on the arms of three CIA types was the most natural thing in the world. And for them, maybe it was.

The Phantom was waiting at the curb.

Valentine's men poured him into the back, and I stepped in after him, seating myself across from his bench. They closed the doors behind us and signaled to the driver, who didn't look any happier to see me than the last time I'd bid him adieu.

We'd barely pulled away from the curb when Valentine reached for that same decanter he'd availed himself of the first time we had spoken.

"No cock blocker?" I asked. "Who's going to stop you if you try anything this time?"

"I suppose you'll have to."

"I don't think that's such a good idea," I said.

"Why?" He upended the decanter. Some of the scotch even made it into the cut-crystal glass. "Don't think you can resist me?"

"More booze, I mean. If I didn't know better, I'd guess you were a raging alcoholic."

"*High-functioning* alcoholic," Valentine said. "With anger issues and OCD. But who's counting?"

Carla had been, and now she was dead. This was a sobering thought. If only Valentine had been the one to have it.

Valentine took a sip, closed his eyes, and let his head fall back on the buttery leather headrest. "You need to be more careful around me, Jane."

"Why is that?"

"Because I'd like to fuck you."

It was a damned good thing I was already sitting down, because right about then my body turned to liquid from hips to knees. Meanwhile, my stomach did some kind of flip that should have been scored by a panel of Olympic judges.

"Wouldn't that be breaking your own cardinal rule again? Becoming involved with someone you're protecting?"

"Technically, *Shepard* was protecting you." Valentine's eyelids were closed, the fringe of dark lashes fanning against his high cheekbones.

"Technically you fired him." A pang of something like guilt spilled cold liquid through my middle.

"Oh, I agree there are plenty of reasons you shouldn't let me," he added. "Fuck you, that is. I'm just saying that I'd like you to."

As if I needed clarification.

"Not that I would ever even consider it"—*(lie)*—"because I wouldn't"—*(also lie)*—"but why is it I shouldn't let you, exactly?"

He rolled the tumbler between his hands, the liquid within a small, boiling sea of oblivion inside wickedly refracting angles.

"Because any woman I fuck literally ends up getting fucked figuratively. There's a long, long list of Women Archard Everett Valentine Has Literally or Figuratively Fucked, and you don't want to be on it."

"Good to know."

"But." He poked his index finger into the air like a Kennedy. "*But* there plenty of reasons why you *should* let me fuck you."

It would have been just plain rude of me to stop him then. Blotto as he was. And okay, maybe I was the tiniest bit curious.

"You may approach the bench. Figuratively," I said, borrowing his word.

"I'm good." He looked at me from beneath the fringe of those dark lashes. One corner of his mouth curving up like the sickle moon. Mischief. "I'm very, very good."

"You and every other man," I muttered.

"You misunderstand me." He set the tumbler aside and rested his elbows on his knees. Though this small posture erased only about two inches of the space between us, I would have sworn under oath that I could feel each and every last micron.

"Some men can blunder their way into learning a trick or two. But like anything that interests me, I've made a study of fucking. With them, It's a hobby. With me, it's an art."

"Are we talking modeling clay and gum erasers?"

I regretted the joke as soon as I'd made it, in no small part because Valentine looked like he was actually considering ways that these particular implements could be incorporated into some seriously dirty sexy times.

"You shouldn't say those things." Valentine's hand stirred on the long, lean mound of muscle so perfectly revealed by his tailored slacks. His artist's fingers flexing, looking for one terrible moment like they might slide upward to stroke his crotch.

And what would I do if he did?

Avert my eyes and watch the city lights slide off the windows? Zip across the seat and slap his hand?

Watch him?

The last thought made my stomach feel heavy. I had begun to sweat in strange places. The creases at the backs of my knees. The insides of my thighs. Even behind my ears, for God's sake. And from the unblinking, feral way Valentine looked at me and the timely flare of his nostrils, I could almost believe he could smell my longing.

Like a wolf.

I cleared my throat and crossed my legs in the most businesslike way possible. "So you're a dynamo in the sack and would most likely ruin me for all other men, if you didn't ruin my life first. Is that about the point you were trying to make here?"

"Sounds tidy enough."

I heaved an inward sigh of relief when he leaned back and retrieved his tumbler. The more of that stuff he sucked down, the easier he would be for me to manage, should he decide to get handsy. A drunk Valentine would be easier to subdue, physically speaking.

"Point well noted." Time to shift the subject back to less dangerous things, like betrayal and murder. "There was something else I wanted to ask you about."

He lifted his hand in a grand, magnanimous sweep. "Ask away. I've told you everything else you're not supposed to know."

This dug barbs into my guts, even now. The idea that a man like Valentine could know more about my life than I did galled me somehow.

"Earlier today, I learned that David Koontz's wife also died of liver failure and that he and his wife had also been involved in a medical malpractice case. This morning, that case was reassigned from Sam Shook to Kristin Flickner at Melanie Beidermeyer's request. Were their deaths related?"

"Dean David Koontz." Valentine pronounced the name with the nostalgia some men reserve for their alma mater. "And I thought *I* was good at eating ass."

My stomach did another one of those alligator death-roll things. "What's that supposed to mean?"

"It means that Koontz is so far up the Beidermeyers' collective backside, he could probably tell you what they ate for dinner a week running. I'm not the least bit surprised he'd want Melanie involved in his wife's wrongful death suit."

"Why? What does he want from them?"

"Money. Expert testimony. Who the hell knows? The Beidermeyers are in the pharmaceutical industry too, if you'll remember. If there was one thing I learned when backing Carla's fight, it's that these cases are brutal. Having an ally like the Beidermeyers in your corner can make or break you in the long run. And whatever he's doing to ingratiate himself, it must be working."

"Why do you say that?"

"They've given him an honorary position on the board of their charity. In fact, I'll have the unique displeasure of listening to him drone on at their annual Chow for the Children luncheon tomorrow at the Beidermeyer estate."

"Oh?"

"Yeah. Three hundred bucks for a plate of truffled macaroni and cheese and *Wagyu* beef hotdogs. Château d'Yquem snow cones and bumper cars made by Maserati. A bunch of rich adults who can pay to be treated like spoiled kids for an afternoon. All in the name of charity, of course." Valentine's eye roll went a little sideways.

"Strange to have that kind of thing smack in the middle of the work week."

"Most of the attendees aren't the kind of people who actually have to work, strictly speaking. Why the sudden interest in our good dean, if I may ask?"

"His wife's cause of death being so similar to Carla's, then Melanie requesting Kristin take on their case. There's just something . . . off."

I would have thought nothing short of a crowbar could have pried Valentine's hand from his drink. But there he was, voluntarily setting it aside. His features recovering a measure of their abstemious sharpness. "Why didn't you mention this before?"

"Because this is the first opportunity I've had to talk to you since I learned about her case this morning."

*Stricken* was the only word I could think of to describe Valentine's face. His skin had gone a bloodless, waxy white. His lips blanched and tight. His eyes were the most disturbing of all. What looked out from behind them was raw, untrammeled dread.

"What?" I asked. "What is it?"

He wasn't looking at me when he answered. Wasn't looking at anything, really. "I know who the mole is."

# Chapter Twenty-Four

But, to my consternation, Valentine refused to tell me who, insisting he needed to "make some calls" in order to prevent any "catastrophic and undeserved consequences."

Bullshit, am I right?

The only call *I* was going to make was on the telephone conveniently located in the bathroom I'd have access to for the evening. Between this device and the bathtub located directly across from it, I may have stood for a full minute with my chops dangling somewhere near my bellybutton.

Valentine called it a soaking tub.

I insisted it was a wading pool.

Either way, it belonged to the suite located on the penthouse level of Valentine's downtown skyscraper, and I immediately decided my ass was going into it as soon as humanly possible.

Valentine had insisted on parading me through the space in its entirety, pointing out the various features and amenities.

I did a lot of nodding and not quite as much smiling, mostly managing to keep my composure . . . until we got to the bed.

I had paused at the end of it wondering how recently Carla Malfi had slept beneath its canopy.

"We weren't sleeping together," Valentine said.

I gaped at him, wondering if he had picked my thought right out of the air.

"Hadn't been for a while. Not since she got sick, anyway." He gripped one of the wooden bedposts, sagging from the kind of tired you get when a long drunk starts to wear off.

"It's none of my business," I said.

"No," he agreed. "It's not. But that never stopped you before, did it?"

"What kind of sick was she?"

"Autoimmune hepatitis. She would stay here on the worst nights." He stared at the fluffy white comforter, seeing something I couldn't. "Kind of strange to sit there feeding someone soup in the bed you'd tied them to once upon a time." It was the most romantic terminal illness/ bondage–related thing I had ever heard.

"It was very kind of you to take care of her like that. She was lucky to have you."

Now it was his turn to scoff. "Lucky is one thing the women in my life are not." His fingers tightened on the bedpost, knuckles whitening before he released it for good. "Sleep well, Jane."

He shuffled off then, closing the door behind him.

I stood alone in the empty, foreign space, wondering how many women had occupied it before me.

My mother had methods for answering such questions.

When occasion dictated that we stay in hotels, after she'd duct-taped the windows closed, propped chairs beneath all the door handles, and set an elaborate series of booby traps, my mother had whipped out a portable black light to search for bodily fluids. A practice that saved us from bedding down in more than one fluorescence-spattered comforter.

Black lights were a bit of a luxury when I didn't even have a pair of panties to speak of, everything I owned still being located in my abandoned apartment or the safe house I'd fled. Valentine had promised the premises were stocked with everything I might need, but truthfully, the fact that he might actually keep a collection of panties in every size directly contributed to my reticence to go looking.

I turned a single circle and floated over to the large picture window, grateful for the view after so many nights spent buttoned down behind blackout blinds.

Beyond the glass, the skyscrapers of downtown Denver stabbed jagged teeth into the night sky. Some of the tallest put there by Valentine, a man who had changed the very shape of the horizon. Standing in the physical confines of his kingdom, I felt his pull on the world around him and the accompanying relief of allowing myself to sink into his orbit.

His was a force just as big as the fear threatening to swallow my heart.

Just as that bathtub would swallow my body.

First I supposed I'd have to find something clean to change into.

I kicked out of my shoes and plopped down on the bed, deciding the nightstand was as good a place as any to begin my search. I pulled open the drawer, half expecting to find an assortment of vibrators and dildos.

What I found instead dumped what little adrenaline I had left directly into my veins.

A gun.

Not just any gun.

*My* gun.

My gun, in Valentine's mistress's apartment.

I lifted it from the drawer, its weight familiar and welcome in my hand. And that's when I saw what had been tucked beneath it.

A creamy linen envelope with *Janey* crawling across its face in my mom's distinctive looping script.

I stared at the letter, wanting and not wanting to touch it. Feeling that the words within it were somehow more dangerous than the firearm in my hand.

Face-Gravy sank into the cosseting down comforter as I set it aside and reached for the envelope.

With my heart in my throat, I unfolded the sheaf of papers and read.

*Janey,*

*If you're reading this note, one of two things is true. Either you've become Valentine's mistress (in which case, you are totally grounded for the rest of your life), or I'm gone, and you've somehow managed to piece together at least some of what happened. All roads lead to Valentine. I think that's in the Bible. Somewhere near the back.*

*Since I've dragged the V-word into the conversation, let's go ahead and have at it.*

*The reasons I didn't want you to know I've been working with him are as complicated and problematic as he is. And believe me, Janey, he is.*

*Okay, I literally just felt you get more interested in him.*

*What is it about dangerous men, anyway? Oh well. Like mother, like daughter, I suppose.*

*A couple of things to remember about Valentine. First, you can always trust him to act in his own best interest, and as long as your staying alive is in his best interest, he'll probably help that happen. Second, vice is weakness, and Valentine has many. Know them. They will always be a liability in his capacity to protect you.*

*Now, about you and me.*

*About us.*

*I knew there was a possibility when I started down this road that this is where it would end. That one day, either by choice or by consequence, our time together would come to an end despite my best efforts. Since that day has come, I need you to know something.*

*Having you, keeping you, was both the best and most selfish thing I ever did. But in choosing to keep you, I chose a difficult life for us both, and I kept on choosing it. Probably longer than I had any right. And that's the final irony, I guess. I tried to keep anyone from hurting you, but in the end, I hurt you most of all. And for that, I am sorrier than I'll ever be able to say.*

*I won't ask for your forgiveness, because I'd do what I did again. I would do it again every day until the end of time just for the chance to see you in that badger costume. To be the one who got to hold you when you woke up scared.*

*But my choice had its price, and you're still paying it every time you lie.*

*But here's the thing about that.*

*I don't care what you tell anyone else. I never have. You can make up any damn story you want and tell it to anyone who will listen. You can lie to the entire damn world for all I care. I only care what you tell yourself.*

*You'll be okay, Janey.*

*Your whole life, I've been preparing you to have me not in it. The things I taught you. The way you were raised. Unconventional, I'll grant you, but geared toward your survival. You are stronger and smarter than I ever was. You have everything you need.*

*You know who you are.*

*You are my daughter.*

*I love you.*

*—Mom*

*PS. Okay, you have to level with me about the Valentine thing. If you're his mistress, just put an ad in the personals section of the Grapevine on the first Saturday of any month with the words: Intelligent brunette seeks double-jointed billionaire with an oral fetish. I'll get the point.*

The letter fluttered from my numb fingers to the plush carpet at my feet.

My body couldn't decide how to laugh and cry at the same time, so it settled for braying like a donkey through great hiccuping sobs. My chest felt hollow. Scooped out. The emotions within crashing into each other like rocks in a tumbler. Grief. Anger. Sorrow. Love.

The sum total of all was one immutable fact.

My mother wasn't coming back.

No matter what I did, how hard I tried, or how much I hoped, or bled, or cried, she wasn't coming back.

I took the gun to the bathroom but left the letter on the bed. Before stripping, I flicked off the bathroom light, guessing the whole damn place was probably crawling with security cameras. I had no intention of giving Valentine a peep show.

In the dark, I finished my introduction to the palatial bathroom, feeling my way by sound, scent, and touch.

Sound: water sluicing from a silver tap. Scent: lavender bathwater. Touch: warm, silky marble.

I sank down into the fragrant water, anchoring myself with arms on either side of the bath. With my neck pressed against the sloping headrest, my feet didn't reach the opposite end. It had been built to the proportions of a taller woman. The sort of woman Valentine seemed to prefer.

Which didn't even matter a tiny bit, because I was not now, nor would I ever be, placing an ad in the *Grapevine*. I would not be Valentine's mistress.

Reaching into the basket next to the tub, I withdrew a downy wash-cloth and soaked it in the water, dragging it over my face. Breathed its perfumed steam into my lungs.

And so, floating in the dark, I made my decision. Mother or no mother, I would see this through to the end.

Dean Koontz. Valentine. Kristin Flickner. The Beidermeyers.

Tomorrow, all the players would be in one place.

And so would I.

# Chapter Twenty-Five

Like only the truly wealthy can, the Beidermeyers had procured for themselves a sprawling twelve-acre estate in the center of Denver. Downtown proper may have been only a couple of miles away geographically, but the grounds had definite plans to make you forget it: the white picket fences, immaculate hedges, sprawling green lawns, and tree-lined drive leading up to a circular drive. And at the apex of it, a veritable château looking like it had somehow gotten confused and wandered away from the south of France and straight into Colorado.

And into this province of pleasant dreams stepped a panda.

Okay, *not* a panda.

A person, in a panda suit.

Me.

Valentine and I might've had conflicting opinions on the particulars, but this part of my plan we both agreed on: *I* wouldn't be in danger if no one knew *I* was at the party. And no one would know *I* was at the party because *I* was in a panda costume.

Simple, right?

The red-suited attendant, little more than a boy, almost fell backward when my fuzzy black panda foot popped out of the Uber—a vehicle I was grateful for. By the way Valentine had said he'd arrange "transportation" for me after refusing me entry into his limo, I was a little afraid he might have a human-size kennel in mind.

"Uh . . . ," the valet boy stammered.

I handed him a fiver and walked—fine, *waddled*—over to the security podium, where a man dressed like a haute couture carnival barker consulted a clipboard of names at my approach.

His nose looked like it wanted to crawl up his forehead so he could look down it at me from as high as possible.

"Name, please."

I didn't answer.

I had decided that for once in my life, a *not*-talking shtick might just be in my best interest. I did, however, produce the gilt-edged card Valentine had given me before we parted ways.

In the little space for the name that preceded *Guest of Archard Everett Valentine*, I had simply written in *Panda*.

He took it from my oven mitt–shaped paw and held the invitation by the corner like it might piss on him.

"Are you part of the entertainment, then?" he asked.

I nodded my oversize globe of a head.

Through the filtered screens over my eyes, I watched him decide whether he wanted to call a power higher than himself to weigh in. I put my paws on my rounded hips and tapped my oversize foot, miming impatience.

He sighed and handed over what looked like an amusement park map. "Hired employees must check in at the entertainers' tent." He pointed one tapered fingertip at the illustration of a smaller tent next to the large striped circus tent at the center of the property.

I aimed my furry thumb skyward and took the map from him, setting off in the direction he'd pointed out. Carnival music floated over to me on breezes scented by popcorn and the burned-sugar smell of cotton candy. I swear to God, it wasn't just *my* stomach but the whole rounded, protuberant bear belly that growled.

I really hoped that what had started as a very simple plan (i.e., dress up as a giant panda so I could sneak into the Beidermeyers' charity carnival and spy on Dean Koontz) didn't end with some sort of horror movie twist, like me actually becoming one with the suit.

From the vantage point of a set of stairs attached to the side of the Beidermeyer manse, I scanned the perimeter, trying—and failing—to spot Dean Koontz's polished bald pate. Lacking direct visual confirmation, I determined that the best place to wait him out would be at the complex network of buffet tables—the apparent heart of the action.

Only, on the way there, unaccustomed to my new and somewhat less sleek proportions, I somehow managed to knock the trays from at least two hors d'oeuvres-bearing waiters' hands.

I did my best to portray remorse, which looked something like covering my little bear mouth with both paws and shaking my giant head regretfully, but not so regretful as to arrest my progress to the food tables.

Once there, I made my way down the line, lifting the costume's nose to shove various comestibles through the little hatch beneath it. Meatballs. Mini funnel cakes. Bites of deep-fried potato and smoked turkey leg.

After about five failed attempts to angle the contents of a champagne flute into my furry chops, someone handed me a red-and-white-striped straw.

"Found him yet?"

Valentine.

He'd been at the bar already. Even without the glass of scotch in his hand, I would have known by the sultry look in his hooded eyes, the almost sexual flush in his cheeks.

I shook my head no.

"You should have just come as my date, like I suggested. Not only would we have given the gossip rags something to write about for the next ten centuries, but I could have gotten you right into his lap. I go wherever the fuck I want."

I made a fist with my paw and jerked in the general direction of my crotch. The panda equivalent of *Good for you, fuckstick.*

The gesture seemed to draw Valentine's attention in a strange and alarming new way.

"I've never fucked a panda before," he said.

*And the ASPCA heaves a collective sigh of relief.*

"Want to step behind a tent and mate?" He was only half kidding. Maybe even just a quarter kidding.

I would have flipped him off, but at the moment, I found myself curiously devoid of fingers. So instead, I put both paws over my belly and pretended to retch.

"Suit yourself." He shrugged. "Oh, wait. You already have." I wondered exactly how soused he'd have to be to snicker at his own joke, and a terrible one at that.

I had always believed that drunk punning should be an offense right up there with drunk driving. A theory that Valentine did more to confirm than dispel.

"If you change your mind." He squeezed the costume's cushioned butt before wandering off. Luckily my own cheeks lived at an altitude a good deal higher, so he mostly got fluff.

I had just convinced myself that I might have caught sight of Dean Koontz next to the custom deep-fried macaroni and cheese station when my momentum was arrested by a new and horrifying development.

A child.

The kind of pale, bored, sneering little shit who's used to getting whatever the fuck he wants whenever the fuck he wants it. He stood there staring at me with cotton candy in one fist and a better cell phone than mine in the other.

"What are you supposed to be?" he asked.

I gestured from my ears all the way to my round white belly. Which was panda for *What the hell does it look like, kid?*

He aimed the cell phone at me and pressed a button. "Do something funny," he ordered.

It was as I glared down at him, deciding exactly how I was going to extricate myself from this situation, when I really *did* spot Dean Koontz making his way toward an opening in the *Shining*-style maze with a curvy little blonde.

*Bingo.*

I sidestepped the spoiled squirt, shuffling as fast as I could in my oversize panda feet, when I felt myself jerked backward.

The little shit had grabbed my little nub of tail.

And so, with a gentle but judicious nudge of my cushioned hind paw, I sent him flying into the hedge. His surprised yelp was just a hair more satisfying than it should have been.

Slowly, mindfully, I crept into the maze, listening as I inched along the shrubbery.

I recognized the sound by degrees.

The same voice that had so often criticized and cajoled me in an office crowded by books and leather furniture. The space where Dean Koontz, blocked by the wooden moat of his desk, tried to convince me with words larger than necessary not to do whatever it was I was doing.

But that's not at all what he was saying to the fresh young thing trapped between him and six feet of perfectly clipped hedge.

Nope.

Dean Koontz was trying to score himself a blow job.

In exchange for grades.

Bits of conversation filtered through the shrubbery like lawn clippings on the breeze. Things like "underwhelming performance" and "oral examination," and "library in ten minutes" and "special study session."

Sweat poured down my face. And not just because my head was currently encapsulated in a personal sauna of fur and foam.

How come *I* had never been offered this option?

I mean, not that I would have taken it, because *eww*, but still. I was a little insulted.

The girl, apparently, was not. She stood there tremulous in the wake of his departure.

I was on the point of whispering to her through the hedge like Jiminy Cricket when a voice on the opposite side of the leafy pathway hijacked my attention. Even harsh and quaking with rage, it was a voice I placed immediately.

Mrs. Beidermeyer.

I crossed to the opposite wall of the maze, boring a hole in the small branches with my paws.

Mr. Beidermeyer stood opposite his wife, looking like a *Great Gatsby* party guest in his 1920s straw boater hat, bow tie, and deck shoes. A sad attempt at classy carny chic.

The snatches of conversation I heard were enough to send the meatballs racing up my throat. I swallowed hard, lest I vomit inside my own costume head.

*Library. Body. Rid of it.*

And then I could hear nothing over the hammering of my heart.

I needed to get to the library and fast.

I shuffled back the way I'd come and had barely escaped the maze when I was forced to duck behind a midway game booth. The kid I had nudged into the hedge was clutching the sleeve of a red-faced woman, who was in the process of haranguing some poor security guard.

"What do you mean, you can't *find* it?" she shrieked. "How hard can it be to track down a giant panda?"

The guard mumbled something about security perimeters and assignments.

"But the panda assaulted my child," the woman insisted.

"He doesn't look assaulted."

I could have told the guard this was the wrong answer even before the woman's face went white with rage. Not that I would have, because the woman taking a swing at him happened to be the perfect distraction. By the time he had her subdued, I had already slid out of my hiding place and was hauling ass across the lawn toward the house.

———

"Staff restrooms are outside." The Beidermeyer butler stood in the grand foyer, blocking my progress purely with the authority of his fussy, tuxedoed presence. "If you go back outside, you'll find that several porta-potties have been set up on the west lawn."

Now, violence wouldn't have been my first choice.

But as time was of the essence, and there was no way in hell I could figure out how to communicate with gesticulation of paw that my purpose was to stop some hapless coed from gargling Koontz's noodle, I tased him a little.

Just a quick thirty thousand volts to relieve him of his knees.

Which is about when I remembered that I had absolutely no goddamn clue where the library actually was and probably should have asked the butler before dropping him. I briefly considered calling Melanie, whom I'd yet to encounter among the carnival's attendees, when I passed a double-door entryway to a room sporting plentiful rows of books.

Promising enough.

Suffocation imminent, I stripped off my costume and dropped the mound of sweaty fur outside the door.

I crept around the corner and froze.

Dean Koontz loved a desk, all right. So much so, he'd decided to park his ass on the edge of one while a blonde head bobbed over his crotch.

"Small . . . price to pay for . . . three-tenths . . . of a point," he puffed in time with her bobs. His eyes closed tight, sweat oiling his brow. "I have to say, I'm not looking forward to the end of our install-ment plan."

Three-tenths of a point.

It hit me with the force of a Mack truck.

This wasn't the blonde from the maze at all.

"Melanie?"

"Jesus Christ!" Koontz's eyes flew open. He scrambled off the edge of the desk and yanked his pants up, but not before I discovered a schlong far more sizeable than the one I'd accidentally palmed on graduation day.

I gasped, my hands flying to my mouth.

"I know," Koontz said, oozing confidence. "I'm a grower, not a shower. Come to take a turn?"

Melanie was still on her knees. Not turning around. Not looking at me.

I couldn't breathe. Couldn't force air into my lungs. "You—"

"I imagine your mother had a very similar look on her face the first time she made the connection you're making now. If she hadn't been so insistent about her daughter being the valedictorian, she might have been able to stay for the graduation. Funny old life, eh?"

My head reeled with memory.

Camera flashes.

The smell of mums.

The feel of leather on my damp palm.

The look on Dean Koontz's face.

My mother. Gone. "Where is she?" The words arrived thick with the emotion I'd battled to hold at bay since the second I'd seen the empty space in the crowd.

He shrugged. "I really don't know. *I* wasn't in charge of the arrangements."

"Arrangements—"

Voices from the hallway stopped me short. The tail end of an argument.

Mrs. and Mr. Beidermeyer cantered into the room side by side like a couple of thoroughbreds. Necks stiff. Nostrils flared. Color high.

I think Mr. Beidermeyer twigged to it first.

Dean Koontz's sweaty face. His daughter on her knees by the desk.

"Oh, Melanie, darling. *No*. We *pay* for things like that," he said.

Melanie finally got to her feet, wiping her mouth with the back of her hand as she faced her parents. "At least I earned it myself."

"Technically, *I* earned it," I pointed out. "You stole it by sucking cock." The rush of anger I expected to feel failed to materialize. Pity, yes. And something like sadness. Maybe even a little admiration.

"Yes, right. But I didn't have my parents *buy* it for me. That's what I was getting at."

Mrs. Beidermeyer, who had been looking from her daughter to Koontz with puzzlement marring her fine features, finally caught up to the rest of us.

"*David?* You . . . my daughter . . . We had a deal."

"We did," Koontz said. "But your daughter didn't know that."

With a high, thin scream, Mrs. Beidermeyer launched herself at him with the ferocity of a lioness. Her body barreled into his, the desk squeaking as the momentum of both bodies knocked it a good few inches across the parquet floor.

Which is when the hand flopped out from behind the desk.

Dean Koontz jumped away from it like it was a bomb.

Garland Beidermeyer clucked disapprovingly, regarding the upturned palm and stiff fingers like a rat that had crawled from beneath the antique credenza.

Melanie gasped and executed a perfect swoon onto a nearby chaise longue while her mother stared with a kind of cold, detached satisfaction, her ire temporarily forgotten.

I alone moved *toward* it. Drawn as if through water. Weightless and strange in my approach.

"Four-tenths of a point?" A sudden pop of joy fluttered through my chest. "I beat Melanie by four-tenths of a point?" I was on the verge of a spontaneous happy dance when I glanced around and remembered where I was and why. Dead bodies. Missing people. Big, hairy scandal.

In short, suboptimal dance conditions.

Dean Koontz cleared his throat, a sound I had come to loathe as it generally preceded an extended period of his self-important prattling.

"As a close friend of the family for some time now, I've been privy to certain information. And if Grace chose to confide in me about the ongoing saga of the medical trial and her *concerns* about her daughter's progress, what sort of friend would I be if I didn't offer to come to her assistance? In exchange for a very small favor, that is."

"I'd hardly call assisting with your wife's demise and falsifying medical records to make it look like she'd been taking part in our medical trial a *small* favor," Grace commented.

Dean Koontz held up a hand. "Small or large, it would have worked perfectly, had *someone* not gotten greedy." The dean cut his eyes to Mrs. Beidermeyer, whose narrow body had gone as tense as a suspension wire. "If you'd just let Carla burn without sending little Jane here to the site, she might never have looked into the medical trial in the first place. Nor realized that there were also records including my wife in it."

"Greedy is filing a wrongful-death suit *after* I falsified the records of your wife's involvement in the medical trial," Grace said through clenched teeth.

"You know that was just for show," Koontz said. "It would have looked more suspicious if I *hadn't*."

"Looks to me like Dean David was doing a little double-dipping," I said, wagging my finger at him. "Making a deal with Mrs. Beidermeyer, then giving poor Melanie the squeeze. Trying to sweep his wife's death under the medical trial rug, then make a buck on the lawsuit."

Mr. Beidermeyer, whose eyes had been pinballing back and forth all this time, cast an irritated look at his wife. "Do realize what you've done, Grace? If it weren't for this ridiculous valedictorian business, Alex Avery wouldn't have followed that trail straight back to *you*. To *us*. And now, instead of one dying woman, we're accountable for the deaths of his wife"—here, he cast an accusatory finger at Dean Koontz—"the Flickner woman, and Jane."

Bolstered by the revelation that my mother's name was not among this list, I raised my hand. "Technically, I'm not dead yet, so I'd really appreciate it if you don't lump me in with that crowd. But since I'm going to die anyway, I have to ask: Why kill Carla Malfi in the first place? Historically speaking, murder has the unwanted effect of bringing more, not less, attention to bear on the complainant of a lawsuit."

"She's the only one who refused to settle out of court." Flat reportage from Grace Beidermeyer, her voice as dry and dead as a tumbleweed. "She'd have fought until doomsday with Valentine's money backing her. And with Valentine bringing your mother in to nose around, it was only a matter of time before they connected everything back to us."

"If you killed Carla and framed Valentine, you'd effectively be neutralizing two threats with one blow," I said. "Do I have that right?"

"See?" Garland Beidermeyer gestured to me with an open palm. "She understands it. No wonder she's the rightful valedictorian."

At this, Melanie flinched like a kicked puppy.

"Melanie *will* be the rightful valedictorian." Mrs. Beidermeyer stared out into the middle distance, an extension of the landscape of her incomprehensible mind. "When Jane is *dead*."

"I don't want to overstep my bounds here," I said, turning to Melanie's mother, "but I get the feeling you might just be harboring a grudge against me. Which, frankly, totally hurts my feelings." *Lie.* "What have I ever done to you?"

"It's not about what you did. It's about what you knew." Mrs. Beidermeyer's dark-blue eyes shone like precious stones, her face just as hard. "The day of the graduation, when we encountered you in the parking lot, and you mentioned Melanie's *slim* victory and Dean Koontz's wife passing, I knew your mother must have told you something."

I flashed back to our conversation. The sarcasm that had dripped effortlessly from my tongue.

*Did he not get enough of a chance to heap praise on you at the graduation for your slim victory?*

*It's a good thing he has friends like your parents to lean on. I'm sure Mrs. Koontz's recent passing has been very hard on him.*

Suspicion always haunts the guilty mind.

I couldn't remember if my mother had said this or Shakespeare.

My chest deflated on an exasperated sigh. "My mother didn't tell me *shit*. I was being an asshole. It's my thing. It's what I do."

Grace's eyebrows tried, and failed, to crease the center of her obviously Botoxed forehead. "You mean you didn't know anything about Dean Koontz? Or his wife? Or the medical trial?"

"No!" I shook my head emphatically. Because emphatically felt like the only correct way to do anything when someone was describing why they had decided to kill you.

"Well, isn't that an unfortunate misunderstanding." Grace folded her arms across her chest and slouched like an elegant—if slightly unhinged—scarecrow. "And here I had assumed your mother must have gotten word to you when she realized that she was being watched at the graduation—"

"My mother was being watched at the graduation?"

"Oh, yes." An ugly smile tugged at the corners of Mrs. Beidermeyer's mouth. She wiped it away with bony, beringed fingers, smearing her own lipstick into a manic, clownish grin. "By the same two gentlemen who visited your apartment later that evening, in fact. Of course, *they* believed they were watching your mother for Valentine. Just as they believed that Valentine had sent them to kill you. Men like that don't care who they're working for as long as the cash comes on time."

The bottom dropped out of my stomach.

During the entire graduation, I had been so concerned with looking for my mother that it never had occurred to me someone else might be looking for her. Or *at* her.

Shepard was right.

I was oblivious.

"By the time we came across you in the parking lot, I'd already heard from my contacts. I knew your mother had given them the slip. So I had them follow you instead. I thought surely she'd come back for you at some point."

"But Shepard slaughtered your *contacts* at my apartment, so when you saw me at the Tilted Tiger, you decided to lure me to Valentine's building site so you could have someone pick me off with a rifle."

Grace nodded. "I would have preferred a more creative demise for you, but it was the best I could do on such short notice. But that awful Officer Bixby followed you and spoiled everything."

"Are you hearing this?" I asked, turning to Melanie, who had been watching this exchange with openmouthed dismay. "Your mother is directly responsible for relieving your intended of three fingers. I want you to consider this when you're engaged in an intimate moment and he has to switch hands."

"Bixby's not my intended." Melanie's cheeks flushed piglet pink. "He hasn't even agreed to go out with me yet."

"Oh, yes, he has." *Lie.* "He said as soon as he's out of the hospital and can dial a phone again, he's totally calling you."

"He did?" Melanie brightened, a hand floating up to fluff her hair as if the mere mention of Bixby's name would allow him power to see the room.

"Swear to God." I brought my arm up, elbow bent, palm forward, hoping it wouldn't act as a lightning rod when He/She/It finally tired of my bullshit and elected to smite the bejesus out of me.

"We will not have our daughter shacking up with some blue-collar, badge-wielding paper pusher." Garland's manicured hands tightened into fists at his sides. I highly doubted that he'd know what the hell to do if he actually had to swing one.

"I quite agree." Melanie's mother stood beside her husband in a show of solidarity, resting a gem-studded hand on his bicep. If such a meatless bone could even deserve that title.

"Why?" The anguish in Melanie's voice cut straight through to my heart. "Why are you doing this? Why couldn't you just run a legitimate business?"

"Oh, darling." Mrs. Beidermeyer flitted over to her offspring, hovering like a nervous bird. "We've become used to a certain way of life. And in order to maintain it, B-Tech needs to sell for a certain amount of money. And if the problems we've been having with the clinical trials got out, there's no way that could happen. You see?"

"The point everyone seems to be missing here is that Jane has to die." Koontz spoke up at last, having endured this whole conversation with a good deal of foot shifting and eye rolling.

"Well, fuck you hard and to the left," I said.

"No thanks." He made a show of patting his pants-weasel. "I'm no longer accepting bribes."

The infinite stretch of what happened next began with the subtlest shift of Dean Koontz's eyes. Starting with me and flicking to Garland Beidermeyer.

Then many things happened at once.

Garland made a grab for his sport coat. I reached back to the waistband of my pants. One of us would get there first.

The world went quiet.

I felt her around me.

My mother.

Some sensory memory remnant from the time we had both shared her body. When both of our hearts beat inside her. Her words blew around me like a swirl of leaves, brushing my cheeks with an almost physical presence.

*Courage, Janey.*

*Panic gets people killed.*

*Keep both eyes open.*

*Breathe slowly. Think calmly. Then decide.*

The gun came out of Garland Beidermeyer's pocket. Rising. Rising until that lidless, empty eye stared directly at the flat space between mine.

The space between life and death can be both as narrow as one breath and as slow and searing as hot tar. I was both acting and watching everything unfold from somewhere far above the fray.

I stepped into Garland Beidermeyer instead of away. Drove an elbow upward into his jaw. His head snapped backward as I rode him to the ground, my hand aiming for the wrist that aimed his gun.

Dean Koontz was a blur in my periphery. Melanie flashed into action, dropping him with some kind of complicated pirouette/karate-chop thing and somehow still managing to look graceful as she did it. I guessed she hadn't been shitting me about those self-defense lessons after all.

Somehow, Garland and I were still falling. It didn't seem right that we could still be falling when so many things with a beginning and a middle and an end had happened and were still happening. At last I felt the impact of the marble floor through his body. Felt his chest depress as the air was knocked out of him and the gun clattered from his hand.

"Garland!" Mrs. Beidermeyer shrieked as the dreadful sound of his bones meeting the marble echoed through the room. She leaped at me, clawing at my hands as I fought both to lay hold of my gun and to keep Garland from grabbing his.

And to my absolute and utter shock, Melanie launched herself *at* her mother, pulling her off me as they rolled.

Of course, if Melanie had bothered to consult me first, I could have told her that they only do that kind of thing in the movies. It may look great on camera, but in real life, it's difficult to control your momentum, and you're as likely as not to end up with a bruised ass and not a whole hell of a lot to show for it.

Which is about how it ended up this time.

Melanie and her mother lay on the ground in a tangle of long, elegant limbs and blonde hair, yanking and slapping and growling elegant little threats through their nearly identical, even teeth.

Much later, when I was analyzing exactly what it was that I felt guilty for not mentioning to Melanie, this moment would return to me.

Because not only had Melanie halved the number of assailants I had to fight off, but her swan dive from grace had also successfully hijacked her father's attention for the split second I needed to gain the upper hand.

By the time he'd fully returned it to me, I was standing over him with his own gun (a tactically inferior but showy Smith & Wesson) in my left hand, trained at the space between his silvered eyebrows, and Face Gravy in my right, aimed at his wife's sternum.

"Hands up, kids," I said.

Melanie's parents glanced at each other, their arms creaking skyward like action figures whose parts weren't designed to bend to such an undignified posture.

"At least they follow instructions," I said. "Melanie? Would you be so kind as to call the police while I keep an eye on these two?"

Melanie slowly rose to her feet.

"Melanie, wait!" Garland's Adam's apple bobbed under the smoothly barbered skin of his throat. "We were only doing what we thought was best for you. That's all we ever wanted. For you to have the things we didn't. To be respected. Successful. Admired."

And watching how his words changed Melanie's face made me realize that all this time, I'd had something she hadn't.

*Love?*

Have you learned nothing about me yet?

I'm talking about the ability to disable someone's voice box with a swift throat-stomp.

Which I did, very carefully.

"I'm so sorry, Father," Melanie said, striding toward the door. "This is for the good of the family. I hope you'll understand."

I inwardly applauded her as she sashayed out of the grand library entrance.

"We could adopt you," Garland offered when she was out of earshot. His voice was the raspy croak of a frog with throat cancer. "You could be an heiress. Our daughter."

I cocked both guns at once. "I'm Alex Avery's daughter, and you and your wife are so going to jail."

Seconds later, Melanie returned from wherever she'd gone to make the call and stood by my side.

"Thank you," she said.

"For what?"

"For everything, I guess."

I endured her awkward side-hug. Melanie's bony hip jutting into the bottom of my ribs. Her cold, slender fingers squeezing my shoulder.

Where the hell were people supposed to put their hands in a situation like this anyway?

"This doesn't mean we're friends, you know," I said.

"But why not? I incapacitated Dean Koontz and tackled my own mother for you."

"(*a*) Your mother is about as difficult to tackle as a three-legged dog, (*b*) Dean Koontz got away, so your incapacitation game needs some serious work, and (*c*) I still haven't forgotten about the whole valedictory suck-off thing."

We stood by like every fictional private detective and assistant combo in literary history as the police flooded the library.

It took everything I had not to point to her parents and utter a terse *Get them outta my sight*, or *Take them away*, or something similar.

What they did take away were my guns, apparently unconvinced that the finders keepers precedence superseded the need to secure the scene of Kristin's homicide.

A scene that was short my discarded panda suit and one pencil-necked dean. It's not like I could blame him. I mean, if I had been running from a full complement of police officers, I might have been tempted to snag the first available disguise as well. Opportunity and all that.

"There was one more," I said as they hauled the Beidermeyers to their feet, hands cuffed behind their backs. "But he shouldn't be too hard for you to find. And I have a suspicion he may be dressed as a giant panda."

The officer in charge asked me to repeat my description three separate times before reaching for the radio clipped to his belt, perhaps not especially thrilled with the idea of calling this one in.

Unfortunately for Dean Koontz, it wasn't the cops who found him. It was Shepard.

After my third interview with the cops in less than a week, I'd made my way out to the lawn, where the party equipment was mostly broken down. Flapping canvas tents and felled poles. The disassembled remains of bar tents, and the olfactory siren's song of funnel cake still heavy on the air.

But it was the man pinning a headless panda to the grass that made my mouth water.

Shepard hunkered over Koontz like a great dark cat. Deadly sleek in his uniform of tight black T-shirt and fatigue pants, he had one knee between the panda's nondescript shoulder blades and a tattooed, muscular forearm bunched beneath his neck.

The panda head sat nose down in the grass several feet away, likely knocked off in the takedown.

"What are you doing here?" I asked.

"D-Town and I were doing surveillance nearby and listening to the police scanner. When we heard a call go out for an unknown assailant in a panda suit wanted for assault and destruction of property, I had an idea you might be involved somehow. D-Town stayed on the job. I came here."

Over his shoulder, I saw Valentine emerging from the collapsing bar tent, a half-empty glass in his hand and pain legible in his alcohol-blunted eyes.

He knew about Kristin. He knew about all of it.

I had no doubt Koontz had sung like a bird while he still had air enough for singing. At the moment, his face had begun turning that particular shade of purple common to eggplants and erotic asphyxiation victims.

"I'm so sorry about—"

Valentine held up a hand to silence me. "Not here," he said. "Not now."

"But—"

"Jane, you're a decently intelligent woman. Perhaps *you* can tell me why it takes someone I've fired to successfully foil an attempt on my life."

As much as Shepard could ever be said to brighten, he brightened. Which was really just him looking slightly less like he wanted to tear someone's arm off and beat them with it. The security guards flanking Valentine from a respectful distance all glanced at their shoes.

"At first, when the panda came cozying up to me with a strangulation wire in its paws, I was hoping you'd decided to take me up on my earlier offer. So imagine my disappointment when Shepard here tackles the panda to the ground and pulls its head off, and I see it's Koontz."

I knew what Valentine was doing, of course, being somewhat of an expert in the classic psychological hand-waving techniques. When someone gets too close to anything with the power to actually hurt you, force their attention to something else.

"And what about you?" I caught Shepard's eye again. "Did you tackle the panda thinking it was me?"

"No," Shepard said. "I knew it wasn't you."

"But you couldn't see my face."

"I know how you move."

Our eyes met, and I swear to God, I felt an egg drop into the chute.

"This doesn't mean you're forgiven, you know."

"I know," he said. "But I did get my job back."

"I'm delighted to hear it," I said, with perhaps a hair less delight than the assertion called for.

"Also, I wanted to apologize." It was the first time I could remember someone offering me an apology while pinning another human to the ground.

Part of me hoped it wouldn't be the last.

"For what?" I asked.

"For a lot of things." The dean grunted as Shepard leaned onto his forearm, driving his elbow farther into Koontz's back. "For the way I acted at the hospital. For the things I said. I was out of line."

I smiled to show there were no hard feelings. Aside from the one I remembered pressed against my back. "And I'm sorry for calling you a monosyllabic meathead."

"Apology acc—wait. When did you say that?"

I waved a hand at him. "Not important. The point is, we're both sorry, and we can enjoy a very fruitful and pleasant *business* relationship."

He nodded despite his mouth tightening into a flat line.

We understood each other.

"I don't know what sickens me more." Valentine swayed over Koontz, looking for the briefest of seconds like he wanted to crush his skull with the heel of his expensive Italian leather loafer. "That Melanie's own parents probably sent her to try and suck my cock, or that she actually succeeded in sucking his."

"Say again?"

"Melanie contacted me. Said she had a particular interest in architectural design copyright law. Only, once we sat down, she seemed more interested in putting her foot in my crotch and her tongue in my ear."

An irrational stab of jealousy punctured my chest. He hadn't exactly *said* he turned her away. "So you think her parents sent her to try and seduce information from you?"

"To establish blackmail fodder, more likely. But she didn't get any of either. Which is why I made sure Kristin ended up as her mentor," he said. "To keep an eye on her."

We both glanced over toward the disassembled remains of the carousel, where Melanie was talking with a couple of uniformed officers.

"About the records she stole," I began.

Valentine slid me a sneaky side-eye. "Don't tell me Jane Avery is feeling benevolent toward Melanie Beidermeyer."

"Of course not. It's just that we all make mistakes, and once this mess with her parents hits the paper, she's going to have a shit storm of epic proportions on her manicured paws. I thought maybe—"

"I'm not going to say anything to Dawes," he said. "There's enough shit shoveling going on at that firm as it is."

"Which reminds me. I know why you made sure Melanie was assigned to Kristin. But what about Sam Shook? Why is it you made sure I was assigned to him?" The mere mention of my mentor's name conjured into existence a vision of his dark, serious eyes. The way they might look at me when I came clean about everything. Which I fully intended to do come tomorrow morning. Or maybe the next.

"He's the only one at the law firm I fully trust, outside of Krist—" His lips clamped down on her name. He shook his head as if to clear it of sorrow.

My hand floated up and landed between his shoulder blades. His spine stiffened against my palm before relaxing.

"I'm sorry for your loss. Your *losses*."

"And for yours," he said. A shadow crossed Valentine's face, darkening his green eyes.

It took me a minute to twig to the fact that he was talking about my mother.

Well, shit.

I had been hoping he wouldn't bring that up.

Mostly because I hadn't told him about the note. Half because I didn't want to ask him how my mother had gotten into his mistress's quarters, and half because I still needed his help and wasn't sure he'd give it if he knew there was a chance my mother had disappeared without telling him what I'd only recently found out the hard way.

One mystery solved, a deeper one only beginning.

"About my mother. I sort of, kind of, got the impression that neither Koontz's nor the Beidermeyers' hired goons succeeded in nabbing her."

"That's good," he said.

"Not entirely," I said. "She's not coming back." I hugged myself against a sudden chill. A cold current that had wandered my way from a distant hollow still smelling of winter's dead leaves.

"How do you know?" Valentine asked.

"I know."

"Well, there's only one thing to do." Valentine drew a deep breath and exhaled slowly. "You'll have to move in with me."

I felt like I was going to choke, but it was Koontz who made a strange gurgling sound. Probably because Shepard's arm had inexplicably tightened around Koontz's neck.

"Excuse me?" I asked.

"I promised your mother I would keep you safe in her absence. As long as she's absent, I'm on the hook."

"But there's no one to keep me safe from anymore. Dean Koontz here and the Beidermeyers are totally busted. Last time I checked, that's pretty much everyone who wants me dead."

"That remains to be seen," he said.

"That's him, Mommy!" We both glanced up just in time to see a certain annoying little shit dragging his mother toward Koontz, still pinned to the grass by Shepard.

"That's the one who pushed me into the bushes."

I couldn't decide which was more priceless. The look of confusion on Dean Koontz's face right before the little shit kicked him straight in the chops, or the fact that he was being punished for something he hadn't actually done.

But I guess justice has a way of finding us all in the end.

And that's no lie.

# Epilogue

"And then I told her, I don't care if Ida's housebound or not, no way am I coming back to that team unless they beg me."

*Beg* was pronounced like *bayg* by the woman sitting in the pedicure chair next to mine, who'd been extemporizing for the last thirty minutes on the dramatic developments of her church's bunco group.

It was a regular hotbed for scandal, apparently.

I'd been nodding off to the lullaby of nail drills and salon chatter when my regular pedicurist held up a copy of the *Mile High Grapevine*, hot off the press and still smelling of printing ink.

"Magazine?"

"Sure," I said.

I couldn't contain my grin as I read the headline screaming across the front page in seventy-two-point Railroad Gothic: *Dirty Dean David Diddles Debutante!*

The Beidermeyers' biotech company tanking had been a bigger story, of course, but unlike Dean David Koontz, they had enough juice left to keep it out of the scandal sheets, if not the traditional press.

Also, I had it on good authority that the *Grapevine* had a *very* willing if not very reliable source.

I flipped through the usual schlock about babies born with bat wings and Elvis sightings and came to the personals.

My heart squeezed involuntarily.

There, the first line of the first ad in the first column of the first page stopped me cold.

*Intelligent Brunette Seeks Rescue.*

My mother. It had to be.

*Looking for a partner in crime to share in occasional adventures and recreational flaying. If you enjoy walks on the beach and the smell of patchouli oil, you might just be the person I'm looking for. Find me before it's too late.*

*Walks on the beach and patchouli oil.* How often had we poked fun at people from the Pacific Northwest region with that specific combination of words? She was somewhere in Oregon or Washington, but wouldn't be for long.

And she wanted me to find her.

*Before it's too late.*

This last phrase sent a thousand invisible ants crawling over my cheeks and down my spine.

Just then, my phone rang on the tray attached to the pedicure chair's cushioned arm.

"Did you see it?" Archard Everett Valentine sounded younger than I had ever heard him. Terribly agitated and impatient.

And I knew exactly which *it* he was referring to. In the days since the Beidermeyers had been brought low, I'd refused several offers of "strictly platonic cohabitation" from Valentine, going so far as to quote to him the ad my mother advised that I place should he and I ever become lovers. Apparently this had been ample motivation for him to begin perusing the *Grapevine* as well.

"Yes," I said. "I saw it."

"Where are you?"

His asking was a courtesy. We both knew he'd not only been monitoring my every move, he'd also assigned a brand-spanking-new but poorly concealed security detail to ensure my safety.

Even now, the chair next to me normally occupied by my mother was currently filled by the hulking form of a nonverbal beefcake. I was pretty certain he'd never allowed a woman to touch anything more than his cock in his entire gun-toting, camo-wearing life. He was white-knuckling the chair arm as the pedicurist took a smallish cheese grater to the soles of his feet.

"At Le Vogue nail salon. Sitting right next to one of your goons." I gave the man next to me a little finger wave.

"Stay there." Valentine's voice was smoky but stone-cold sober. A tone that sent fresh chills prickling up my arms. "I'm coming for you."

# ACKNOWLEDGMENTS

I don't leave my house much. Which means I owe a huge debt of gratitude to a whole slew of people for telling me all kinds of things about what goes on outside it. This is probably a good time to mention that any mistakes made in the portrayal of any of these noble professions are purely my own, because the list of people that follows is full of ninjas and badasses who are the very best at what they do.

To Variable, for taking me on an actual stakeout and not laughing at me when I got mistaken for a prostitute . . . twice. To G-Unit, for telling me the best stories and answering my many pesky questions. To Rick, for letting me sit in on actual private investigator training classes and bringing me to eat pie with everyone afterward. Because pie.

To Heather, for putting me in the mind of a fresh-faced law grad and letting me pick her top-shelf-quality brain.

To Nathaniel, whose vivid recounting of army life changed the way I conceived of not just a character, but my world.

To Kerrigan Byrne (whose books you should totally read, by the way), for hauling me out of the trenches both literally and figuratively and to Christine, my agent lady, for believing.

Lastly—but not leastly—to my husband, Andy. I owe you all.

# ABOUT THE AUTHOR

*USA Today* bestselling author Cynthia St. Aubin wrote her first play at age eight and made her brothers perform it for the admission price of gum wrappers. A steal, considering she provided the wrappers in advance. She never quite gave up on the writing thing, even while earning a mostly useless master's degree in art history and taking her turn as a cube monkey in the corporate warren.

Because the voices in her head kept talking to her, and they discourage drinking at work, she started writing mysteries instead. When she's not standing in front of the fridge eating cheese, she's hard at work figuring out which mythological, art historical, or paranormal friends to play with next. The author of The Case Files of Dr. Matilda Schmidt, Paranormal Psychologist series, Cynthia lives in Colorado with the love of her life and three surly cats.